PUCKING SAVED

THE CHICAGO YETIS SERIES

Pucking Saved

go to www.nicolekeefer.com
for books by Nicole Keefer

Pucking Saved

Copyright © 2026 by Nicole Rae

All rights reserved.

No part of this publication may be reproduced, stored or transmitted in any form or by any means, electronic, mechanical, photocopying, recording, scanning, or otherwise without written permission from the author, except for the use of brief quotations in a book review, and except permitted by U.S. copyright law.

For permissions contact: author.nicolekeefer@gmail.com

This novel is entirely a work of fiction. The names, characters and incidents portrayed in it are the work of the author's imagination. Any resemblance to actual persons, living or dead, events or localities is entirely coincidental.

Cover Design: Kellie at KELLIES COVER DESIGNS

Character Artist: Mayhara Ferraz

Editing by: Danielle Polisseni of D.P. Editing

PUCKING SAVED

NICOLE RAE

To the Hershey Bears,
for whom my obsession with hockey and
violent contact sports started.

Introduction

Hello reader,

If you have read any of my books under the name Nicole Keefer, you know I'm a fan of torture and questionable decisions.

This book contains themes common to suspense/thriller novels, including stalking, kidnapping, strong language, sex, possessive & obsessive MCs, drugging, and captivity.

Please remember to always put your mental health first.

,
Nicole

TEAM ROSTER

Alexander (Alex) Bensen - Defenseman # 21
Gunnar Knight - Goalie # 13
Scott (Scottie) Kasper - Forward # 34 - Asst. Captain
Charlie Hawkins - Defenseman # 88 - Asst. Captain
Axel Caddel - Defenseman # 29 - Enforcer
Bjorn (Bear) Olsson - Forward # 9 - Captain
Misha Wilder - Forward # 60
Roman Hunter - Defenseman # 6
Landon Bardot - Forward # 53
Phoenix Calloway - Forward # 42
Emerson Banks - Defenseman # 20
Flynn Lawson - Forward # 87
Grant O'Reilly - Goalie # 1
Austin Mackson - Forward # 25
Brax McKenna - Forward # 10
Ryder Larkin - Defenseman # 24
Johnny Hall - Defenseman # 5
Giovanni Bradford - Forward # 18
Aquilla Martinez - Forward # 27
Miles Deacon - Forward # 11
Anton Barnes - Forward # 33
Elias Richards - Defenseman # 4
Tyler Web - Goalie # 30

STAFF

Duncan Reyes - Head Coach
Riggs Jameson - Assistant Coach
Warren Huxley - Assistant Coach

PUCKING SAVED
PLAYLIST

<u>CH. 3</u> - **SEE YOU AGAIN** - Miley Cyrus

<u>CH. 4</u> - **IMPOSSIBLE** - James Arthur

<u>CH. 12</u> - **YOU ARE THE REASON** - Calum Scott

<u>CH. 14</u> - **STARGAZING** - Myles Smith

<u>CH. 21</u> - **HOLD ON** - Chord Overstreet

<u>CH. 24</u> - **SHE'S BEEN THROUGH THE FIRE** - Brian Rhea

<u>CH. 36</u> - **DON'T BLAME ME** - Taylor Swift

<u>CH. 36</u> - **LOVE ME BACK** - Max McNown

<u>CH. 39</u> - **YOUR LOVE IS MY DRUG** - Kesha

<u>CH. 40</u> - **GOODBYE EARL**- The Chicks

<u>CH. 42</u> - **LOOK WHAT YOU MADE ME DO** - Taylor Swift

<u>CH. 43</u> - **RESCUE** - Lauren Diage

<u>E</u> - **CARRY YOU HOME** - Alex Warren

Chapter One
Liliana

Four Years ago (November 30, 2020)

"Get up, bitch. We're going to be late."

My best friend, Morgan, calls from the bottom of my bed. When I don't answer, she grabs the edges of my super comfortable blankets, ripping them from my bed. If I wouldn't be completely lost without her, I'd be tempted to disown her for this atrocity alone. After almost twenty years of friendship, is disownership an option at this point?

Jumping on the bottom of my bed, she bounces up and down, knowing how much it pisses me off to be woken up like this. Peeking at her with one eye, she is ear-to-ear smiles. What a ho.

"Come on, Lily," she whines. "We haven't been dancing in ages, and you finally have a night off. Get up, put on a sexy dress, and get ready to shake your ass. I already have shots lined up in your kitchen. Shots, as in plural, because I need fun Lily tonight, not overthinking Lily."

Groaning, I roll over to check my bedside clock. The same one Morgan calls me an old lady for having. It's not like she's not used to seeing it by now, it's been in every bedroom I've had since middle school, which is around the same time she started practically living at my house.

The first time she went down her stairs, in a sports bra and pajama pants, with serious bedhead and found the living room filled with her brother's high-school friends, that's the day my house became her second home. And we've been inseparable since.

"If you don't get out of that bed in two seconds, I will get a glass of ice water and soak you. That's not the kind of wet a girl desires to be. It's dinner time, and I'm starving and need food to go with my alcohol," she announces, smacking my ass as she crawls off my bed.

I hate that I slept the day away. And a night out does sound fun.

Sitting upright, I groan as every muscle screams in pain. I'll need to stretch at least before we head out, or I'll be walking down the street looking like I have a literal stick up my ass, instead of the imaginary one Morgan insinuates is there. Morgan offers to massage my poor back at least once a week, and maybe one of these days I'll take her up on the offer.

Last night's shift was a rough one. We were searching for a missing boater until two in the morning. Thankfully, they wore a life jacket, so that person was able to go home to their family. That's not usually the case when people are boating and partying on Lake Michigan in late November.

Morgan pulls me from my thoughts with the tapping of her heels. *Tap, tap, tap.* That's when I know I have about two minutes to comply with her demands or she'll literally pounce on me. Again.

"Fine, you win," I huff out, knowing it's easier to give in than to argue. And she was right anyway, not that I'd ever admit that out loud to her, but I have been working too many shifts lately. Reaching into the far corner of my closet, I pull out a dress that has never seen the light of day since leaving the small boutique where I bought it.

The skin-tight, black as sin, mini dress—that I bought on a whim when my mental health needed a boost, and even though it wasn't practical—is gorgeous, despite that it barely covers my ass. But who cares that it cost almost half a month's salary? I was willing to push all self-doubts aside for this one night. Only because I know in a few hours I'll be too drunk to care how much skin I am showing and the hit it took on my wallet.

"Here," I fling the dress behind me, "is this okay?"

Morgan walks up behind me, a glass of wine already in her hand, and slaps my ass. "Yes, girl. Someone is looking to get laid tonight. Let's go!"

Why do I have a feeling I'll live to regret my wardrobe choice? After pulling my hair up into a messy bun, adding a quick layer of makeup, and slipping the dress over my head, I know for a fact tonight is a bad idea. As long as we don't end up in the back of a cop car, I'll consider the night a success. Working with the CPD, I'd never live down having them called on me.

I got picked up after a Yetis game last year when one of the opposing fans couldn't handle their team losing and started a fight. One of the officers drove me home, but not before taking my picture in the back of his cruiser and posting it in the break room. It took six dozen donuts before they agreed to take it down.

I won't allow that to happen again. Especially not in this dress.

Pregame drinks before the club were apparently a must, per Morgan's rules. I would've been more than happy to spend the rest of the night in the dive bar we just left, but in the words of my best friend, "the music wasn't musicing enough to shake my ass and get me laid." So, here we are, walking down Franklin Street, after a few too many drinks, looking for a place for her to shake her ass.

I'm now regretting my choice in footwear, I'll soon be walking barefoot if she makes me walk more than two more blocks. On these streets, that'd be a crime, but what other choice would I have?

There are so many clubs right next to her university, but she always insists on driving the forty-five minutes into the city to my apartment to drag me out. I knew since I was nine years old that the only dream I ever had was to become a search and rescue diver, which didn't require a degree, only lots of other training. So while she was grinding away in college, I was already set in my career.

Morgan explained when she wants a night out to dance and decompress, she doesn't want to run into any classmates or drunk frat guys. Her nursing school is stressful, so I'm more than willing to oblige, because I also feel more comfortable on my home turf. I think it also has to do with the fact that I live close to her brother and our other friend Alex, but I never bring those facts up.

When we go out, we usually stick to the places where other first responders frequent, as a 'just in case'. Two drunk girls alone in a big city... Even though we say we can take care of ourselves, anything can happen. It makes Jordan, Morgan's brother, feel better, and if we don't want him hiring someone to follow us, it's a concession I'm more than happy to make.

"Morgan, if you don't pick a place soon, I'm going back home. The hockey game just got out, and the bars are filling up. I want strong drinks and greasy food in my belly now. You are the one who was *starving*."

Slamming her hand on the crosswalk button again, she grumbles, "Fine, party pooper. Right over there looks to be a fun bar with loud music and a line out the door. We'll head over and finish the night there. Does that sound good, princess?"

"Perfect, my Queen." Looping my arm through hers, we watch the cars zoom past.

As the light turns green and we get our symbols to cross, the most horrific sound echoes through the busy street. Metal contacting metal tears through the night. One block down from us, where the walking trail intersects with the river is only a small railing. That railing allows walkers and runners beautiful views of the river but doesn't offer protection against vehicles going into the water.

When the light turned green, the SUV moved forward. A large truck sped up behind the SUV and slammed into the rear right side, sending the SUV through the less than adequate railing and into the Chicago River.

Ripping off my heels, I push my purse into Morgan's hands. "Call 9-1-1."

"Lily, be careful. You won't be able to see. I'll get help." She is running down the street after me, cell phone to her ear.

Morgan has been my friend for so long, she knows what I am about to do. With no hesitation as I reach the bank's edge, I dive into the freezing water and swim towards the now slowly sinking SUV.

Barely any time has passed since the vehicle entered the water, less than a minute maybe, but the front is already sinking underwater. After a quick assessment, and only being able to see very little in the dark, I am able to tell all the windows are closed.

Thankfully I never leave home without my emergency escape bracelet. It was a gift from my father on my sixteenth birthday, and I promised to never leave home without it, and I never broke that promise. Even after my parents passed away from a drunk driver days after I turned eighteen, I never left the house without it—it was a way of always having a piece of my parents with me.

Not able to see into the heavily tinted windows, I choose the rear driver's side window to enter, crossing my fingers that I'm not about to shatter glass into someone's face. After a quick flick of my bracelet, the glass shatters enough for me to be able to reach inside. When I pull enough glass away, I'm greeted with the crying of a beautiful, though scared, little girl in the rear passenger seat.

"It's okay. I'm here to help," I choke out as I tug on the broken glass, ignoring the feeling of my skin being shredded and the blood staining the water. Normally I'd have gloves on while working, and they'd protect my skin, but I don't even care about that at the moment. "My name's Lily. Can you tell me your name and if you're hurt?"

The little girl stops crying but is still gasping for air. "I'm Julie. Please help my brother, Alex. He's not answering me. Why won't he answer me?"

The water is rising faster now. I need to get her out of here. "Can you unbuckle?"

She shakes her head. "I'm stuck. But get him, and I'll wiggle out." She is breathing heavily but not screaming or panicking like I'd expect a young girl in her situation to be. And she stopped crying the moment I spoke to her.

Looking in the front seat, I know she's right. The front is almost completely underwater, and the man is unconscious. Blood seeps from a cut on his head, but with it being dark, I can't see where it is coming from. If I don't get moving soon, one or both will drown.

"Okay, here's what I'm going to do. There's enough water in here that I'm going to recline your brother's seat and pull him through and out this window. As soon as I get him out, I'm coming back for you, and I'm not leaving without you. I need you to wiggle out of your seat belt while I free your brother, okay?"

"Yes. Just save Alex. He didn't want to take me for ice cream, but I begged him too. We wouldn't be here if not for me," she cries out.

"I got him, Julie. He'll be safe with me. Now wiggle with all your might. I'll be right back."

Damn, this guy is huge. There is no way I'll be able to take him to the surface and have him float enough to come get Julie. I need her to get out of her seat. One thing at a time.

Reaching my hand between the seat and the door, I squeak out a thank you. The power still works in the SUV, or I wouldn't have been able to recline the seat back. Reaching below his arms, I pull him back enough for the water to do its job. At least he drove a large SUV; otherwise, he wouldn't have fit out the windows, and I wouldn't have enough time or equipment to go through the windshield.

Once we are out of the vehicle, the blood on his head is flowing freely and I realize I need to get him to Morgan. Moving through the water, I hear Morgan screaming my name and I use her as a beacon. At least eight other people are standing on the bank, holding their phones' flashlights, guiding me in, and I'm grateful.

Morgan's been in school for nursing, so I can just leave him with her. As soon as I make it to land, and the other people help drag the man up, I'm diving back into the water. The little girl is the only thing on my mind now.

When I'm about five feet from the back window, the SUV shifts and slides underwater. I've seen this before; it means the wheels must have been balancing on a rock or something else, and when the water filled enough of the cab, it shifted the weight and countered the weight.

But Julie, the little girl, hasn't surfaced yet. It's dark, but she isn't in the water splashing around. Without stopping, I take one last breath and dive.

I'm fast underwater, and that isn't a brag. After a few fumbles, I am able to find a tire, and even though it was on the opposite side of where I needed to be, at least I have hands on the vehicle. I was going in blind, and that is never good.

Feeling my way over the roof, I find the back window, squeezing through, I don't take time to run my hand over the frame and a stray piece of glass pierces through my dress and down the length of my thigh. I'll worry about that after I locate and get Julie out.

I feel a leg, and she isn't moving. After a few seconds of tugging on her belt, I am able to pull her loose. She must've wiggled almost all the way out by herself, she just needed one last tug to get all the way out of her seat. But she isn't moving, and that means she isn't breathing.

Pulling her to shore seems like I'm moving against time. It was a known fact that when I worked with my team, my captain tended to keep me away from children when in the field whenever possible, even though I was able to calm them down in high-risk situations; better than some of the men. There was no staying away from it this time since I saw the accident happen, and there was no way I would've been able to stand by and do nothing. Morgan grabs Julie from me while I am still in the water, not waiting for me to ask for help. "She's not breathing, Lily. The ambulance is pulling up in sixty seconds. The man kept coming in and out of it and just yelled for the girl."

"Her name is Julie, and that's Alex. I'm starting CPR. Paramedics can take over as soon as they get here. Why is it taking them so long to get here?"

"Lily, you're a beast, the accident happened less than eight minutes ago."

Without stopping compressions, my eyes whip to her, and she nods. How could that be possible? I could've sworn I was in the water for at least thirty minutes. But I should know better than most people how adrenaline skews time.

Lights floods the area, and sirens descend. "Hey, it's Officer Burke. Lily, I'm here to help. Do you want me to take over compressions? You must be tired."

"I'm fine," I snap, not willing to stop.

I hear my name called out but don't look up from my compressions until a gentle hand comes down on my shoulder. It's Eddie. He is draping his jacket over my lower back, trying to cover my torn dress.

"Lily, your dress is torn to shit, and you are covered in blood. In the little light we have, I can see you're going to need stitches. Blood is also pouring out of your hands with every compression. I'm not sure what happened tonight besides you saving the day like always, but now you need to let us take care of you and let the medics care for the little girl."

"Is that an order, Cap?" Sarcasm is prevalent in my voice, though I never stop my motions, keeping in time with life saving measures.

"Yes, it is. Now switch out on the count of three. Don't make me remove you, because you know I will."

A medic is at my shoulders, arms next to mine, ready to take over. "Ready. One, two, three. Switch." When my arms stop compressions, I am hauled to my feet and into warm waiting arms. As Captain Carlson turns me to lead to another waiting ambulance, my eyes meet those of the man I pulled from the water.

His brown eyes feel like they are trying to pierce my soul, and not in a good way. It feels like he is blaming me for what happened, but he can't blame me anymore than I blame myself. I should've pulled the little girl out first and sent her up. She could've treaded water while I pulled her brother from the car, then we could have all swam out together.

But if looks could kill, his would've done its job. Hopefully we never run into each other again, because I don't think I could handle being on the receiving end of his rage.

Chapter Two
Liliana

This is not the way I wanted to start my morning. Jordan, Morgan's brother, hasn't left my side since driving me and Morgan home from the hospital last night. I would've been totally fine taking a rideshare, but Eddie wouldn't hear of it with the amount of drugs coursing through my system they gave me when I got fifty-six stitches from dragging my body against broken glass.

He told Morgan either he was going to drive us home, or her brother could take us. Jordan apparently pulled Carlson aside and said he'd be sleeping on my couch anyway since Morgan was refusing to leave my side, so he'd take me home. And yeah, she slept in my bed, which meant I didn't sleep worth a crap. She's worse than what I would expect sleeping with a child would be like, she kicked me all night.

Eddie is in my kitchen standing at my coffee machine with Jordan when I stumble out of my bedroom after almost no sleep. So now instead of sleeping in and trying to forget one of the most traumatic days of my life, I have a house full of people I love—but don't want here.

Morgan must have heard me leave the room, because two minutes after I close the door behind me, she's wide awake and standing behind me. I'm grumpy in the morning, and today it's even worse. I want to be alone, but instead, I'm surrounded by two brooding men and one over dramatic best friend as they all read the horrifying facts about last night's accident. Facts that Eddie hasn't stopped bitching should have been told to us before being published in today's paper.

"Like, for fuck's sakes, Eddie. What good is it being attached to the Chicago PD if they won't even share information with their own people? We need to hide Lily. Jordan, you know people. Lily needs to be surrounded," Morgan shouts as she tosses the paper aside.

"Stop being dramatic, Morgan. It can't really be that bad?" I ask. refusing to read the paper until at least one cup of coffee is coursing through my system.

"Yeah, okay. Dramatic? My reaction is mild. Just look at Eddie's face. He wants to murder someone," Morgan mumbles, picking the paper back up and handing it to me.

LAST EVENING, ALEXANDER BENSEN, ROOKIE FOR THE CHICAGO YETIS, AND HIS SISTER WERE IN A HIT AND RUN THAT LEFT THE MINOR BENSEN IN CRITICAL CONDITION AND THE STAR ROOKIE WITH MULTIPLE INJURIES, BUT HE IS EXPECTED TO MAKE A FULL RECOVERY. BENSEN'S VEHICLE, STOPPED DURING THE TIME OF THE ACCIDENT, WAS HIT AT SUCH A HIGH RATE OF SPEED, IT WAS PUSHED INTO THE CHICAGO RIVER, WHERE IT QUICKLY SUBMERGED. "IF IT WASN'T FOR THE QUICK THINKING OF AN UNNAMED BY-

STANDER," A SOURCE STATED, "BOTH BENSEN SIBLINGS MOST LIKELY WOULDN'T HAVE MADE IT OUT OF THE VEHICLE."

THE DRIVER OF THE OTHER VEHICLE FLED THE SCENE ON FOOT, AS THAT VEHICLE WAS DISABLED. WHEN POLICE ARRIVED ON THE SCENE TO INVESTIGATE, EVIDENCE TURNED THIS INTO MORE THAN SIMPLY A HIT AND RUN. INSIDE THE DISABLED VEHICLE, BOUND IN THE TRUCK'S EXTENDED CAB, WAS A YOUNG WOMAN, BLOODY AND BEATEN. SOURCES AT THE HOSPITAL STATE SHE MAY NOT MAKE IT THROUGH THE DAY.

CPD COMMENTED THAT THIS IS AN ONGOING INVESTIGATION INTO FINDING THE DRIVER'S IDENTITY, SO ANYONE WITH ANY INFORMATION IS TO CALL THE TIP LINE IMMEDIATELY.

"Wonderful," I whisper, slamming my coffee hard enough on the table that it splashed out and all over my hand. The pain of the hot coffee doesn't register as dark thoughts race through my head. "So some kidnapper is loose and running the streets of Chicago, possibly looking for another victim? There were so many people in front of those bars last night. And no one saw the person flee the vehicle? Fucking fantastic."

"Lily, if that accident never happened, who knows what would've happened to that girl. The forensic team has a chance of finding genetic evidence and making an identification before he's able to pick another victim. If you think about it, last night, you saved three people's lives," Morgan tries to reason as she wipes my hand with a towel.

Shaking my head, I can't understand why everyone is treating me like some sort of hero. It started when my colleagues arrived at the scene and spouted their bullshit praise. Then, when we arrived at the hospital for me to get stitches, I had doctors and nurses tell me how brave I was to dive into the river and save those two people. I wasn't brave; I was stupid. I acted recklessly and made reckless mistakes. I was intoxicated and listened to a young girl about how to do my job, even though I was second guessing myself, and it resulted in sloppy work and her needing CPR, and I will never be able to get the sound or feel of her little ribs cracking under my compressions out of my head. And the look her brother gave me; he will hate me for as long as he lives.

"Um, yeah," I say, standing so quickly my chair almost overturns. "I think I'm still worn out from last night, or maybe it's all the drugs you all demanded they pump into my system even though I didn't want them, but I'm exhausted. So I'm going to head back to bed, and you can all see yourself out of my apartment. I don't want to hear any of this *"but we're worried about you bullshit,"* get out and don't hover. Or I'll call my landlord today and have him change the locks, and none of you will get a copy of the key."

I can see that Morgan is about to argue. I held up a hand to stop her. "I will message each of you when I wake up later, but right now, I want to sleep." Not waiting for them to agree, I turn and walk back to my bedroom, shutting the door with a defined click so they know I mean what I said.

It still takes them almost a half hour, but the last one finally leaves, and my apartment is silent. Too silent. I wasn't lying when I said I was tired; every muscle in my body is screaming, and my bed sounds like heaven. The only problem is that I can't shake this chill. Walking to my closet, I pull out an old Chicago Yetis hoodie, sweatpants, and some thick socks. The sweats were a gift from Morgan on my last birthday.

Burrowing under the blankets, it doesn't take long for my eyelids to feel heavy and sleep to take me.

Alex

Julie has just fallen back to sleep, yet I can't make myself let go of her hand. It's my fault my little sister is in this hospital bed, hooked up to all these machines. The doctors have run every test, and they've told me and my parents over and over that she will be okay, but my brain still hasn't decided to believe them. She's my baby sister; I'm her protector, and I didn't protect her.

Four broken ribs, which will take time to heal, and mild hypothermia, which has been alleviated; according to the doctors, Julie was lucky. There's nothing lucky about what happened to her—to us. Me, all I got was a seatbelt bruise and a cut on my head where they think I hit the steering wheel. The team doctor will run another exam before I'm allowed on the ice again, which is bullshit.

According to the police report and the pictures I saw of the accident, yes, we are lucky. But Julie shouldn't be in this hospital bed; if anything, it should be me.

The police wouldn't let us read the statement from the woman that pulled us out. My father wanted to know how Julie ended up underwater for so long. We deserve answers. When the police wouldn't answer him, my father raised his voice at the officer.

The officer wasn't phased by Damon Bensen's outburst, but Julie didn't like it one bit. She started crying and stated it was her fault she was left in the water, not the person that saved us. She told everyone that I was hurt, and she begged the woman to take me first since the water still wasn't high in the truck. And that she told the woman she could get out of her seat by herself, but she knew she was stuck.

Julie didn't get to tell us any more, her heart rate went erratic, which triggered a monitor at the nurse's station, and a very angry nurse came barreling in and kicked everyone but my mother out of the room. By the time we were allowed back in, my sister was asleep. And here we are now. That's why I won't let go of her hand, she's in this bed because of me.

I am deep in my dark thoughts and don't hear the knock at the door. A few of my teammates have been circulating through the halls all night. The coaches were here as soon as they found out what happened, wanting to make sure I was okay and to see if my family needed anything.

Even being a rookie and part of the team for only a few short months, everyone in the organization made the team feel like a family.

Like right now, our team captain, Bjorn Olsson—who everyone calls Bear—is standing next to me, coffee and newspaper in hand, still wearing the same clothes he had on last night. That tells me he hasn't left since he came in about an hour after I arrived by ambulance.

"How are you holding up, Alex?" Bear asks, handing me the hot coffee and placing the paper on the bed next to me.

"Fine, man," I grumble. "You should really go home."

"I'm good right where I am. And yeah, you're full of shit about being fine. So drink your coffee, and then you need to read the paper. There's an article about your accident that's disturbing."

"Disturbing? Disturbing how?" My brows raise, searching his face for any sign of answers.

"Just read the damn paper. But keep your cool, you don't want to wake your sister," he instructs as he pulls out his phone and sends off a text. "Knight, Caddel, Hawkins, Kasper, and I are going to be at your penthouse tonight with pizza and beer. Before you say no, just know your mom gave us the key and told us to get you out of here. Mrs. Jade scares the shit out of me, so I won't go against her, so you have no choice."

His words only half register as I read the newspaper article. "What the fuck? There was someone tied up in the truck that hit us?"

"I told you it was disturbing. Hopefully the police find the bastard that hit you guys and kidnapped that poor girl. We don't need trash like that on the streets of Chicago."

"Alex…"

All eyes turn to the little girl in the bed. "Hey, baby girl. How are you feeling?"

"I just want to go home. I want my own bed and my dog," Julie demands.

Bear chuckles. "You tell them, darling. No one comes between a girl and her dog."

I shake my head. "That's not how that works, Bear."

He exaggeratedly gasps for Julie's benefit. "What do you mean? Do I need to squish them? I am a large man. Should I squish them, Julie?"

"No, don't squish anyone," she chuckles. "You would get in trouble."

"I don't mind a little trouble. It keeps me on my toes." Bear smiles at Julie.

He turns and winks at me. "I'm going to let the nurse know she's awake, then rally the guys that are in the hall and tell them to head out and either meet at your place tonight or go home and get some sleep. Let us know if you need anything. If not, your house, six tonight. Don't be late, or I will tell your mother."

All I can do is shake my head as Bear walks out the door.

"I like your friends, Alex. They're nice," Julie whispers.

"Yeah, baby girl. I like them too."

We fall into a comfortable silence as we wait for the nurse; she's flipping through the T.V. channels, and I am flipping through the newspaper. As I scan the article again, a thought comes to mind—I need to find out the name of the woman that saved us. When I close my eyes, I see her face. I need to see her again. I will do anything to see her again.

Chapter Three
Liliana

Two Weeks after accident

*D**ing Dong.*

I swear to everything she holds dear, if that is Morgan ringing my doorbell in the middle of the night instead of using her key, I will take away her key privileges. Yeah, I'm lying to myself, I wouldn't do that. But I will beat her with a pillow.

Ugh. I groan as I pull myself out of bed as the doorbell rings again. "I'm coming, ho, calm your tits."

Looking through the peephole, there's no Morgan. There's no one at my door. Reaching for the baseball bat I keep next to the door at all times, I disengage the deadbolt and slowly open the door. Just like the peephole showed, no one's here. But there is a package on the doormat. Maybe the person ringing the doorbell was one of those all-night delivery services.

A jet black box with a bright red bow sits on the floor at my feet. It's gorgeous, so why am I hesitating to pick it up? Because I've seen too many true crime shows where severed limbs are delivered in boxes just like this—that's why. My nerves are just wild because I was woken up from a restful sleep. At least that's what I keep telling myself.

Picking up the box, I bring it inside, making sure to relock the door behind me. Placing it on the kitchen table, I turn the overhead light on so I can get a better look. Someone took great care in this packaging.

The bow looks professionally made, almost too good to pull open. Almost. I still hesitate. Why does it feel like I'm opening a bomb? I'd feel better about it if there was a label or a note on the outside. Get over yourself, girl, and just open the damn box.

Pulling the beautiful ribbon and lifting the lid of the box, I quickly realize just how foolish I am. This package obviously isn't for me; it has to be for one of my neighbors with children. I will need to ask them in the morning, since there isn't a card or address label anywhere on the box. Too bad. Hopefully I can find the intended owner.

Inside, I gently lift the ornate, handmade doll. Her hair looks to be made from some sort of red silk rope. Kinda like our rappelling rope we have in our rescue kits at work.

Tomorrow I'll post a note next to our mailboxes, letting them know I have the package and they can come pick it up.

Three Weeks after accident

Ding Dong.

No. Whoever's at my door just needs to go away. I haven't been home from work for even ten minutes, I can smell myself, and the water for my bath just finished filling. I need a relaxing night without any interruptions, and I don't have the energy for company. I haven't even taken a sip of my wine yet.

I love my neighbors, but they've been dropping by unannounced more lately the last few weeks, after hearing an argument between Eddie and me about the accident. That man can't keep his voice down for anything. I think he did it on purpose, just so my neighbors would worry about me.

Ding Dong.

Okay, fine, I'm coming. Grabbing the robe from the end of my bed, I tiptoe to my front door and, like always, check the peephole before I answer the door. Seeing which neighbor it is will determine how long I expect them to talk before they let me resume my night. I should've grabbed my wine glass from the bathroom counter.

That's weird. There's no one in the hallway. I check the peephole again. Nope, no one there.

Maybe they got sick of waiting and left. Keeping the safety chain in place, I crack the door open. Right outside is another black box with a bright red ribbon. Freaking hell.

Maybe this one will have a card, because the last one didn't belong to any of my neighbors, and now it's sitting in my guest room closet. Opening the door only far enough to grab the box and bring it inside, this box looks identical in shape and weight. Maybe it's another doll.

Removing the lid and looking inside—nope, not a doll. This time, there are six handmade black fabric roses tied together with the same red silk rope. That's ominous but gorgeous. Someone took a lot of time making these.

Again, the box contains no note. But I'm not going to dwell on it, because my bath is calling my name. I want nothing more than to just wash the day away, then crawl into bed, put on some B-rated horror movie for background noise, and sleep until tomorrow. I'll leave a note at the mailboxes again, asking if anyone is missing the package, but that will be tomorrow's problem.

Three and a half Weeks after accident

"Eddie, I swear I'm going to quit. I'm sick of coming home smelling like something that crawled out of the sewer. How is this even possible?" I say, complaining to my friend and captain as we walk up the stairs to my apartment together.

Teasing, he says, "I don't know how you do it to yourself, Lily, I smell fine."

Would he forgive me if I turned around and Spartan kicked him down the steps, because I'm close to doing just that. "Yeah, you never end up like us because your ass stayed out of the river while I jumped in after the kid that thought he could jump across on a dirt bike. I swear, if my parents were still alive, I'd call them right now and apologize for all the stupid shit I pulled as a kid. And I'd even apologize for all the stuff Morgan pulled me into. Which would be ninety-nine percent of the stuff I got in trouble for."

At the top step, I stop in my tracks. Eddie, not expecting it, bumps into me so hard I fall forward onto my knees.

"Damn it, sorry, Lily. Why did you stop? Are you okay?" He looks around trying to find any danger.

Pulling myself up, "Sorry. It's that box at my door. It's the third one I've had delivered in less than two weeks, and they are obviously not for me, but I can't figure out who they are for."

His brows pull together, and he grabs my shoulder to stop me from grabbing the box. "What do you mean they aren't for you, and this is the third one? What's inside the boxes?"

Waving him off with my right hand, I step around the box and pull out my keys. "Oh, nothing dangerous or anything. Whoever is delivering them just has the wrong address." Walking into my apartment, I place my bag on the couch, expecting Eddie to follow me, but he is still in the doorway looking down at the box, phone in his hand.

"The first one was a beautiful handmade doll. One that you would see made for a little kid. The second box had a bouquet of handmade flowers. See, nothing to be worried about. Stop acting like such a dad and come inside so we can order dinner. I'm starving." Pushing past him, I grab the box from the ground.

Placing the box on the table, I go to the basket I keep in the kitchen that holds all the takeout menus in a four block radius. "Are you feeling Chinese, barbeque, sandwiches, or something else?" I call out from the kitchen. When he doesn't answer, I peek my head back to the dining room. "Eddie?"

"Sorry, something doesn't feel right about these boxes. Were there any notes attached to the other ones?" His eyes haven't moved from the box.

"No, none. And not one of my neighbors is missing a package or has received anything like this."

"I need you to open it up, Lily. Something's off. I can't tell you what, call it the almost thirty years on the job, but I'm thinking we need to call the CPD."

"I love you, Eddie. But I think you are overreacting. So, here, let me prove it to you." Lifting the box lid, I freeze. My chest constricts, and my vision blurs. "Eddie…"

"Lily? What's wrong?" He pulls the box from my hands.

"I was wrong, you need to call the CPD."

"Lily," Eddie is kneeling in front of me. The tears finally stop flowing, and my breath evens out. But it feels like any second I'm going to launch into a full-blown panic attack.

"Officers Burke and Walden are here to take your statement and collect the boxes for evidence. Are you ready to talk to them?" Eddie questions.

"Yes."

Two uniformed officers walk over to my table. "It's nice to see you again, Ms. Sterling. I'm sorry it's under these circumstances. This is my new partner, Officer Walden; he recently transferred from New York. Can we sit?"

"Yes, please," I whisper.

Officer Burke takes the lead. "I'm sure tonight was a shock for you, but can you please tell us about tonight? And Captain Carlson told us you've also received two other packages. We'd like to hear about those as well, and then we'd like you to show us where they are so we can collect those and have them checked for prints or other evidence."

"Okay, I'll try," I say shakily, focusing on my hands in my lap and not the officers in front of me. I close my eyes and pull details from my memory.

I make it through the first two boxes without breaking down, but when I get to tonight, I'm not sure if I'll be able to give them what they need. "Eddie, can you do me a favor?"

He never left my side. "What do you need, Lily?" he gently asks, touching my shoulder for support like he's done a million times.

"Can you call Jordan and have him bring Morgan over? You can tell him what's going on, but tell him not to give Morgan details until they get here. I need her, but I don't need her coming here ready for battle. You know she overreacts."

He sucks in a breath. "Yeah, I'll do that. And I'll make sure Jordan keeps it to himself. Morgan would end up in the back of the cop car if he told her what's going on, and we don't need that headache tonight."

Standing from his chair, he turns to the officers. "I need to make a phone call, and Lily needs a moment alone. When I return, we'll continue with tonight's events. Okay?"

Both officers nod. Officer Burke had to tap Officer Walden on the shoulder to get him to stand and move away from the table. Something about Officer Walden makes me feel like he doesn't believe what I'm telling them, like I'm making it up. But why would I do that? Officer Burke was there the night of the accident, but my name was never released to the papers due to the ongoing investigation into the kidnapper. But everyone in the police department had to know the details of the investigation, right?

A few minutes later, Eddie's back at the table, and so are the officers. "Jordan lost his shit, just want to warn you, Lily. He's upset, like me, that you kept this from us. But he understands you need him to be calm and bring Morgan here as quietly and quickly as possible. But I wouldn't be surprised if he doesn't threaten to lock you in his apartment for the unforeseeable future."

"And who is this Jordan person?" Officer Walden asks, notebook at the ready.

"He'll be here soon. He's her best friend's older brother, and they've been friends for almost twenty years, so he is like her family. Are we ready to continue?" Eddie says curtly to the officer. Then he turns to me and waits for me to answer.

"Yeah, I want to get this over with before Morgan gets here." I walk them through finding the box, joking about it being misdelivered, and finally getting to lifting the lid.

Taking a deep breath, I will myself to continue. "As soon as I lifted the lid, I knew this one was different from the previous two. Inside was a pile of black lace fabric; I didn't pull it out of the box. But I'm guessing it's the same as what's in the photo. On top of the fabric was a picture of a young woman in a black dress holding a bouquet of black flowers, with a doll placed on her chest. I didn't look too close at the picture, but I could tell she was dead."

"How could you tell that, Ms. Sterling?" Officer Burke asks.

"Because her throat was cut, her eyes were wide open, and her head was surrounded by blood. So either she was playing a prank—or she was dead. And written on the picture, it said, 'You took away my plaything, so I need a new one. I'll see you soon.'"

Eddie looks to Officer Burke. "Do you think it's him?"

Officer Burke has a grim expression. "The red rope sounds the same, but we won't know for sure until we get it back to the lab. I was just going to take the boxes with us now, but since it seems to not be just stalking, and is a threat on your life, I'm going to call forensics and have them collect them. Ms. Sterling, I think we need to talk about protective custody."

I just shake my head. "No, absolutely not. I'm not going to trust my safety to someone I don't know. I'll keep my safety in my own hands, thanks." Standing from the table, I turn to Eddie. "I'm going to my room. The other two boxes are in the guest room closet. Can you please show them where they are and let Jordan and Morgan in when they get here? I just need a few minutes to myself."

"Go, I got this. I'll check on you before I leave," he says as he leans in and gives me a hug.

"Lily, sweetheart," Morgan whimpers as she crawls into my bed and pulls me into her arms. "I know you're not okay, so I need you to tell me what you need. Because what I need right now is to commit murder, but I don't look good in orange, and from the way Jordan and Eddie are talking, they may beat me to it."

"Morgan, I've never been scared like this. I don't know what to do."

Someone softly knocks on my bedroom door. "Come in."

It's Jordan, and he does not look happy. "Hey, brat. How are you feeling?"

"I didn't mean to fall asleep and only realized I did when Morgan crawled into bed with me. How long was I out?"

"Only about an hour." He shoves his hands in his pockets and leans back on his heels. He's fidgeting, which is not like him at all.

"What's going on, Jordan?" I sit up in bed, my stress level for the night has hit its limit.

"Something happened. I'll let Eddie explain, why don't you both come out here?"

"Oh, for fuck's sake. What now?" I grumble. "What else could go wrong tonight? Was another box delivered?"

Walking out of my bedroom, Eddie is pacing around the table looking at his phone, and my vodka bottle with two shot glasses sits in the middle.

Not caring whose glass it is, I walk up to the table, pour myself a shot, and slam it back.

"Someone better start talking, or I'll continue drinking," I urge.

Eddie stops pacing, Jordan stands next to him, hands on the back of a chair, and Morgan sits next to me, pouring each of us a shot. Tapping her glass to mine, we each shoot them back. She fills them again while I keep my eyes on the guys.

"Okay," Eddie starts. "I went downstairs to get my gym bag from my trunk because I was going to sleep on your couch tonight, knowing how stubborn you are and knowing you wouldn't want to leave. Well, when I got to the parking lot, I noticed your car was vandalized."

"What?" I yell. "Could this night get any worse?"

"Oh, that's not the worst part," Jordan grumbles.

"Oh, great. What's the worst part, Eddie?"

"Well, the CPD forensics team came back and took some samples from the vehicle, and they said it was covered in blood. Human blood, not animal blood. Jordan and I were speaking, and there's a credible threat on your life. I know you didn't like the idea of police protection, but Chicago isn't safe for you right now. Would you ever consider the idea of leaving, just until it's safe?"

It takes everything in me to hold in the sobs trying to break out of my chest. "And where would I go, Eddie? I have no one else that's not in this room right now. Everyone else is dead."

"If you agree, I know of a place that will keep you safe. It won't be Chicago, but whoever's doing this won't be able to get to you. And once they're caught, you come right back."

"This is my home. My job is here. My friends are here. Everything I know and love is in these city limits. If I stay here, not only am I putting myself at risk, but you assholes as well, because I know for sure you won't stay away from me and let me handle this on my own. So that will put a target on every one of you. Okay, fine, I'll agree for now. Because I don't want anyone near me to get hurt. But promise, promise, I'll be able to come home."

"I promise, Lily. When it's safe, you'll come back home," Eddie tells me. There's so much sincerity in his voice, it's hard to not believe him.

But I hate relying on others, so I'll go along with this plan for now and wait for Eddie to tell me when it's okay to come home—or until at least I determine when I'm coming home, safe or not. But I don't tell them that little tidbit.

Chapter Four
Alex
One month after accident

"What the hell do you mean you can't find out her name?" I growl at my lawyer through the video call on my phone as I pace the living room, looking out at the Chicago streets below.

"Alex, you need to understand, there are some things you can't just throw money at," Lucas, my father's best friend and my lawyer, says, ever trying to be diplomatic.

"All I'm asking for is the name of the woman that saved not just my life but my sister's life. Can't you tell the police that I want to thank her? It's been a month, and I've checked the newspaper every single damn day. Nothing, not another word on the kidnapping. My father has tried to use his connections. Nothing. How hard can it be to find one woman?" I yell, slamming my hand on the table. "Don't those reporter vultures usually pounce on stories like this, the happy-ending, feel good stories? I just need her fucking name."

"Fine, you know what, Alex? I'm going to tell you something, but I need you to keep your head. I've known you since you were born, and I know you are hotheaded and like a rabid dog when you want something. I did find out a little information, but it's secondhand, and I can't confirm it. And you won't drop it, damn it." He sighs so loud through the phone, I know he doesn't want to tell me.

"You sound ominous, Lucas. What is it?"

"The reason they are keeping the woman's name out of the papers, reports, and everywhere else is that she has connections within the police department, and they are making sure that information stays away from the press, but before you go spouting bullshit, it's for good reason."

Lucas goes silent.

"I'm waiting, Lucas. Is she a celebrity or something? Did she pay to keep her name out of the reports?"

"No, you petulant man. She's being targeted by the same person that hit you and your sister. Remember what they said in the paper?" He holds up his hand to shut me up as I open my mouth to ask questions. He knows how my mind works. "She's received several 'gifts,' as this person is calling them. Each gift has had a piece of eight-millimeter soft silk red rope incorporated somehow. Forensics matched it to the exact rope used to tie the girl up in the cab of the vehicle abandoned at your hit and run. The very last gift she received was the first one that had a note attached that said, 'See you soon.' It was not confirmed to me, but I'm getting the impression they want her either moved or placed into protective custody. Which isn't a bad idea. I know you want to know her identity, and I promise I will keep working on it. But please, don't do anything stupid, and know that they are doing this to keep her alive."

My mind is spinning a mile a minute, and I need to sit down. Is she being targeted because she was there that night and helped me and my sister? Of course that's why. That's how they came into contact. So it's my fault my savior with the haunting green eyes is now in a madman's crosshairs. That's not acceptable.

"Lucas, I want you to keep trying to tap any contact and find out her name. Even if it's for me to pay for her protection. You know money isn't an issue. I don't give two shits about fancy things if the people around me aren't safe."

"You got it, Alex. Just let me know if you're going to do something stupid so I can get the bail money ready and prepare your parents. Not that your father wouldn't do that same damn thing. Knowing him, he'd be sitting right next to you in the cell. You Bensen's, y'all are the reason I have gray hair."

I can't help but chuckle. "But you love every single one of us."

"True, but I love your mother and sister more. They never cause me any problems."

"I'm telling my father that one."

"Snitch," he teases. "Just keep your head down." He disconnects without further argument.

If the police won't help me find her, I'll just look for her every place I go. Hockey takes me all over the country; maybe luck will be on my side, and one day fate will help our paths cross again. Either way, I'm not giving up until they do. Our destinies were forged when she saved my life. And I need to know why.

Chapter Five
Liliana

Present Day - Four years later - November 25, 2024

Forty-eight hours. I've been back in town only forty-eight hours, and my best friend is already making me reconsider my decision that it was time to return. As much as Eddie tried to talk me out of it, Chicago is my home, and I wanted to come back. No, I needed to come back. It's been four long years since I was talked into leaving my home for my own safety. Every day that I was gone, it felt like a part of me was being chipped away.

It hurt watching the Chicago news, knowing that it was only a short distance away but out of my reach. Every time I'd watch a Yetis hockey game, I felt two emotions. I felt anxious any time Alexander Bensen was on the screen, knowing I've never seen hatred like I saw in his eyes. And overwhelming sadness that I wasn't in person watching those games.

Now that I'm back, I don't want to be watching over my shoulder for dangers, but I'm still wondering every minute if I'll become a target yet again.

It's true that the kidnapper has yet to be apprehended, but the CPD has not heard a peep from him since I left the city, so what are the chances he stuck around? Once I was gone, he probably took off to other parts unknown, right? At least that's what I've convinced myself when I made the decision I could no longer stay away.

I missed my city—my home. It was time to come back, and I'll handle the consequences. Hopefully.

My phone dings, and I can't help but roll my eyes.

> **Morgan:** Are you on your way?

> **Me:** I can't go.

Yeah, that's not going to work.

> **Morgan:** Bitch, I know you're joking. You better be joking. Jordan gave me his season tickets for tonight because he's going to be out of town. THE SEATS ARE ON THE ICE. You know my brother doesn't do that out of the kindness of his heart. And I'm all dressed up. Plus……I need Lily time. We haven't seen each other, except over video, in four years. So put on your slutty big girl panties and let's go.

> **Me:** I saw you this morning.

> **Morgan:** I mean, we haven't hung out in four years.

> **Me:** We had dinner last night.

I wonder how far I can push her before she snaps and shows up at my door.

> **Morgan:** I will fight you. We haven't been to a hockey game in four fucking years. We are going.

> **Me:** I'm sorry, but HE will be there. I can't go.

> **Morgan:** Sweetie, You know I love you. I'd never force you to do something you didn't want to do, but it's been four years. Do you think he'll recognize you? It was dark when he saw you, and he was probably concussed.

> **Me:** Eddie said they never released my name. And the likelihood he recognizes me is slim, but I don't know if I want to chance it. You didn't see the way he looked at me. His eyes were full of hatred.

> **Morgan:** You're as obsessed with the Yetis as I am. You know you are, you can't lie to me. I know you never missed a game even while you were gone. So take a chance.

It has been years since I've been to a rink. And the Yetis are my team. I wish my dad was here to go with me.

> **Me:** I can't lie. You know I'm obsessed, and no, I didn't miss a game. You know I watched them all. I love that fluffy snowman. Rogue is my favorite. He should win mascot of the year. Do you think Scottie can introduce us?

The idea of meeting Rogue solidifies my decision to give it a chance and go.

> **Morgan:** You won't know unless we go. So, get that fine ass out of bed (I'm your bestie. I know you are still in your pajamas while I'm busting my ass at work) and get dressed.

> **Me:** First off, I'm in my pajamas because I'm a grown ass adult and allowed to be in my pajamas all day if I want to be. I don't start work again until tomorrow, so shut your face. And fine, I'll go. But you are paying for my drinks. And I need lots of drinks to deal with you tonight.

> **Morgan:** Deal! See you in an hour at your place, and we will catch a rideshare from there.

> **Me:** Ugh, fine. Love you.

> **Morgan:** Love me too!

"Damn, Morgan. How much did your brother pay for these season tickets?"

Giggling, she shrugs. "He refuses to tell me. The only thing he'll say is that he'll sell his body on the street before ever giving them up. So anytime he offers them to me for free, be damn sure I'm taking them and bringing my best ho with me." Bouncing up and down next to the glass, Morgan glances all around, taking everything in.

We grew up watching Scottie and Jordan play hockey, so this isn't anything new. It was a sad day when Jordan hung up his skates, but the three of us made a pact to always support Scottie no matter what team he ended up playing for.

"Here they come," Morgan squeals, as both teams take to the ice for warm-ups.

Hiding down in my seat as much as I can, which isn't easy with where we are sitting, I try to make myself invisible. "Has Scottie skated past yet? I haven't seen him in a few years."

"Ugh, girl. Yes, he has. Stand your fine ass up here with me and you can see him for yourself. I had dinner with him and my brother the other night, and I had to remind myself not to stare. He and Jordan were talking about his latest puck bunny escapades. Good thing I'm an amazing actress, or else they'd realize how much their bragging was ripping my heart out. Like seriously, how can he not see that I've been in love with his dumb ass for the last like twenty years? Maybe I just need to move on, but how can I when he's always doing sweet things for me? This other nurse at work, Trevor, has been asking me out lately. And I've been telling him it isn't a good time, but maybe it is a good time. Maybe I need to give someone else a chance."

"Have you ever thought of just telling Scottie how you feel?" I ask, wrapping my arm around her shoulder, not mentioning this Trevor person, but locking that information away for later questioning.

"Yeah, no, girl. Confessing my feelings will be the last thing I'll ever do. That man is a ten, whereas next to him, I'm like a two. And before you go berating me for talking shit about myself, I know I'm smoking hot, like sexy as shit. But standing next to that man, I may as well be invisible." The pain in her eyes breaks my heart.

"Such a dumbass," I say under my breath. Shaking my head, I scan the ice and find the man in question. I can't fault my best friend. I mean, I've been around Scottie and have become tongue-tied, and I'm not even the one in love with him.

As if he knows we're talking about him, he skates over and taps his gloved hand on the glass, scowling.

"What the hell are you wearing?" he yells to Morgan.

His eyes cut over to me, and he waves enthusiastically. "Hey girl, it's great to see you."

He's smiling at me; Morgan's glaring at him, and I'm whipping my eyes between the two of them.

Completely ignoring what he said to me, Morgan throws her hands in the air. "What's wrong with what I'm wearing?" she shouts.

Even I can see the fire in his eyes as they meet hers again. "Where's the rest of it? Does your brother know you leave the house in only half a shirt?"

Every person in our section is watching the exchange, amused, and a few have their phones out. Great.

"Oh, grow up, Scott Kasper. What I'm wearing is fine. Now go win your game and leave me alone."

Without another word, he huffs and skates away.

He gave in way too easily.

The crowd around us is dead quiet until I break the silence by bursting into laughter and nudge Morgan with my elbow. "Yeah, he doesn't care at all." "Oh shut it, you. He was probably just looking for my brother. These are his season ticket seats after all." Pink tints my best friend's cheeks.

"Uh huh. Keep telling yourself that." I smirk at her denial.

"I'm going to run to the restroom before puck-drop. Then I'm going to get another beer. Do you want a refill?"

"Yeah, thanks." Watching her walk away, I can't help but scan the ice. I see Alex a few times and turn my head each time as he skates close by. What would the chances be that after four years he'd even recognize me? Would he be openly hostile towards me in such a crowded place if he did recognize me?

I still can't believe the man I saved that night was Alexander freaking Bensen, six feet-two inches of what wet dreams are made of. Watching him skate by again, the light reflecting off his signature long brown hair, it's hard to pull my gaze away.

I wonder what it would feel like to run my fingers through his hair?

"What the fuck is wrong with me?" I mumble to myself, shaking my head.

A few minutes later, the teams begin to file off the ice and take their last break before puck-drop. The crowd thickens, and cheers fill the stadium. I'm in absolute awe. I missed this. The noise, the chill in the air, the overall atmosphere.

In high school, I'd listen to girls hate on Morgan and me for always being around hockey players. They didn't understand it wasn't the players for us. Well, it was for Morgan, one player to be exact. But for me, it's the game. The rush of hearing the skates connect with the ice and the bodies hitting the boards—it brings back memories of times with my parents before they were killed.

I'm pulled from my memories as the couples behind me let out a gasp. Thinking something happened, I jump from my seat and look around, hoping something didn't happen to Morgan.

When my story is retold, I will forever blame Morgan for the embarrassment I'm about to suffer. Because I wasn't paying attention to my surroundings, I didn't notice that Rogue, the Yeti's mischievous mascot, has made his way down the aisles and is standing only feet from me trying to gain my attention. When I didn't see his waving arms, he took one of the soft snowballs he's known for hurling at unsuspecting fans and threw one at me, hitting me directly in the face.

All of this, of course, is being broadcasted on the jumbotron in the center of the arena.

At initial impact, I whip my head in his direction, immediately fangirling. "Omgoodness, Rogue!"

Here I am, giddy as all can be, and what does he do? He shakes his damn finger at me. Well, that's a disappointing first impression.

I wonder what he'd do if I ran over and gave him a hug?

Morgan decides at that moment to make her appearance, and Rogue turns his attention to her. After a few seconds, it's apparent that she's the one he's after, and I end up hands on my knees, tears streaming down my face, with uncontrollable laughter.

Big bad Rogue is trying to pull my best friend's crop top down to cover the bottom half of her stomach. It hits me instantly that Scottie did something. I'd need to thank him for the entertainment when Morgan isn't around. I spent too many years away from her for her to be mad at me already.

I'm proven correct when Rogue picks up a bag that's at his feet, which I was too distracted to see before, and shoves it into Morgan's waiting arms. She pulls out two Yeti jerseys with Kasper on the back.

"Oh, that fucking asshole."

Rogue tosses a snowball at Morgan, and that only makes her step closer to him. "You go back to the locker room and tell him I don't want his jersey and don't appreciate his caveman antics." Rogue just crosses his arms over his chest, tapping his right foot, and not moving.

A fan right next to us, wanting to get in on the fun, yells, "Put on the jersey." That starts a chant, and soon it sounds like half the arena is repeating it.

Me, I'm still laughing. Morgan whips her head over to me. "Fine, ho, if I'm wearing it, so are you."

I just shrug and put on the jersey she tosses to me. It's not like I don't have a closet full of Scotties jerseys at home, so this doesn't bother me.

After we have them on, everyone around us cheers, and Rogue claps before stalking up the stairs. Morgan, in one last act of defiance, picks up one of the snowballs that's lying between two of the seats and throws it at the mascot, hitting him squarely between the shoulders. Turning, he does the international sign with his two fingers for 'I'm watching you' and walks away.

The jumbotron is still on us until we both take our seats. So much for a quiet game where no one knew I was here. Thanks, Morgan.

That was one hell of a welcome back to Chicago.

Chapter Six
Alex

Every time I step on the ice, a sense of calm washes over me. I tried to explain it to a girlfriend in college, and she acted like I'd lost my mind. Like nothing in the world should come before my feelings for her. She couldn't understand that even though hockey can be a violent, contact sport, the crisp air in my lungs and the feeling of the ice gliding under my skates always felt like home.

If I had a free day, I'd go to the rink, skate laps, and run drills. If I was stressed or upset, I'd go to the rink and shoot pucks at the net until I almost couldn't lift my arm.

My ex thought I should run to her, and looking back, she may have been right. But maybe that's why I haven't found *the one* yet. I need whoever I spend the rest of my life with to understand hockey isn't simply a hobby or a game—it's my passion. That hockey is as much a part of my life as the air in my lungs.

The only person I've ever been more obsessed about than hockey is my mystery woman from years ago. Each month that goes by, I try to convince myself she's gone for good, but my heart and my head aren't communicating. How long will it take for them to get into sync? Ten years? Every month my lawyer sends me a report with no reported sightings, and it's a kick to the chest.

Right now, I need to focus on the game ahead of us. Skating along the boards, I try centering myself. Concentrating on the sound my skates make on the ice, I can feel my heart rate even out.

Warmups are almost over, and as soon as the puck drops, the only thing on my mind will be hockey.

Right as the team is heading back to the locker room, the scene playing out on the jumbotron catches my attention. Normally, the only time I pay attention to the screen is when they are playing back a call that landed me in the penalty box, but not today.

Rogue is messing with the girl my teammate, Scott Kasper, was yelling at during the beginning of warm-ups. A girl I've seen over the last few seasons at a few of our games. But now, standing next to her, is a familiar face. A face that has haunted many of my dreams the last four years. I can't look away as she throws her head back and laughs at our mascot. Could it be her?

Rubbing my chest, right over my heart, I want to rush into the stands. Or at least skate over and confirm if it is in fact her. I need to know.

"Let's go! Locker room before Coach loses his shit," Bear yells, pushing at my shoulder. When I don't move, he says, "Yeah, yeah, she's a pretty girl, but move your ass, Bensen."

Still in shock that she might actually be here, in our stands, I allow Bear to push me to the door.

I need to ask Kasper about the girl. He knows the one with her, so it's a good chance he knows the other one's name. Could this be real? After all these years, will I finally get a name?

We're lined up in the tunnel waiting for our names to be announced, and I can't shake the feeling that she is who I've been looking for. What are the chances she's the girl I've been looking for anytime I was on the streets of Chicago for the past four years? Or is my mind playing tricks on me and just hoping it is her? Lots of women have red, curly hair. But my mind is telling me this is her. Before the night is over, I am determined to find the answer. One last chance before I give up searching.

"Hey, Kasper, who is that girl you were flirting with in the stands?"

Punching me in the shoulder, he growls, "First off, I wasn't flirting. That's my best friend's baby sister, so she's off limits. Why do you want to know?"

Glancing around to see if anyone is paying attention to our exchange, I hold my hands up in surrender. "Hey, hey, hey. I was wondering about the red-haired beauty sitting with her. She reminds me of someone I met a few years ago. Someone I've been looking for."

As soon as my question sinks in, Kasper softens, turning almost sheepish. "Sorry, Alex. I'm a little protective of Morgan, my best friend's sister. I've known her most of my life. And the one sitting with her is her best friend, Liliana. I've known her just as long, so watch what you say about her, too. And do me a favor and leave her alone. She's a sweet girl, but she's had a rough few years. She's not your usual puck bunny, just a huge hockey fan."

"She just... Remember my accident my rookie year?"

"Oh, shit, man." He snaps his fingers. "Yeah, I remember that. I slept in the hallway with half the team that night. You scared the shit out of us, man."

"You know I've been looking for a woman every time we go out and at every home game."

"Yeah, you drive us all crazy, dude. It's been years. You never said you were looking for the girl that saved you. You've never given us details of who you were looking for, so we've been taking bets on a scorned lover or some shit."

I growl in annoyance. "No, asshole. I've been looking for the woman that saved mine and Julie's lives. Her name was never printed. And no matter who I spoke to at the hospital or even the police station, they couldn't or wouldn't give me or my lawyer a name. It was bullshit. I even hired a private investigator, and he came up empty-handed. It's like she disappeared."

Kasper doesn't even try to hold in his laughter, even though he looks nervous. "Like The Little Mermaid? Like she came out of the water and then disappeared."

"Fuck off, Kasper." I lean over to smack him with my glove. "I'm serious. And that girl with your friend looks very similar. If you've known her name this whole time, I may just stab you with my skate."

"After the match I'll ask Morgan to meet us for drinks. Will that get your panties untwisted?" he asks nervously.

"Yeah. Thanks."

"Now get your head in the game, or Coach will have our ass. Cap is already giving us the look that means if we don't win, we'll be skating lines tomorrow, so I'll blame that on you if it happens."

"Yeah, let's go."

There are two minutes left in the third period, and it's tied one-one. Our goalie, Knight, is on fire, and it was only because of a dirty hit to Hawkins on defense that the Saint Louis Devils were able to get that one goal.

As time counts down, it takes all my willpower to stop glancing to the stands, hoping to catch the eye of a certain red-headed beauty.

"Let's fucking go," Knight yells as we line up for a face-off in the Devil's end zone.

On defense, Caddel and I are ready to go.

Bear wins the face-off, and the puck snaps to me on the other side of the rink. The Devil's forwards are occupied, so I take the puck and fly down the rink. Everything seems to move in slow motion. A quick deke around their defenseman and it's me versus the goalie. With a quick flick of my wrist, I execute the perfect slap shot. With being a defenseman, I don't normally take it all the way down the ice, but I got a mean slap shot.

The goalie tries to reach for the puck, but it sails into the top corner, out of his reach. The red light flashes, and the crowd and my team erupt. Even Knight comes out of his goal to celebrate.

Once back on my feet, I skate along the boards, looking for the redhead that I can't get out of my head. *It is her.* I slow my speed as I come to her seat. Locking eyes, she looks shocked to see me, but it is her; there's no doubt about it. Now to convince Scottie to give me more information about her. I don't even think he's aware he let her name slip.

Now that I've found her again, I won't let her go, even if Scottie refuses to help me.

Chapter Seven
Alex

O nce again, I'm one of the last ones in the locker room. Pulling off my shirt, my phone starts to blow up.

Hawkins: Yo, Scottie, who were the hotties in the stands Rogue was messing with? The ones that he gave your jerseys to?

Scottie: Fuck off, Hawkins.

Knight: Inquiring minds would like to know.

Scottie: Really, Knight?

Me: I'd really like to know the name of her friend.

Scottie: Fuck off, Alex. Both of them are off limits.

Caddel: Forbidden fruit always tastes the best.

Hawkins: Oh yeah, I saw them on the jumbotron. I'd show either one a good time. But you know what they say about redheads...

Me: Hawkins, you finish that phrase and I will shove my stick up your ass.

Bear has left the chat.
Caddel added Bear to the chat.

Caddel: Stop pissing off Daddy.

Bear: 20 extra laps for everyone tomorrow.

Scottie: What the fuck did I do?

Chapter Eight
Alex

After hitting the showers, Scottie comes up to me and says he sent his friend a text warning her that I'm asking questions about their friend and want to meet for drinks after the showers.

"My friend has agreed to meet with you. But our other friend is exhausted and just wanted to go home, so she put her in a rideshare, and she won't be joining us. But Morgan has agreed to meet us at the bar and hear you out. Just letting you know, Morgan is beyond protective. You won't get to the girl you are asking about without Morgan's permission. So make a good impression. Yeah?"

"Best behavior, scouts honor."

Shaking his head as he walks away, "We'll see. We'll meet you at Sticks."

I'm sitting at a table with a few other guys when Scottie and his friend walk through the door. Here we go. Best behavior. Right. I needed to remind myself to take it slow and not come off too strong. Just because I've been waiting to find my mystery woman for four years, it means they've been protecting her just as long.

Seeing them walk through the door, I jump up and look around for a quiet place to move to, not wanting to have this conversation where my teammates are in the process of getting drunk.

Maybe this was a bad idea. Scottie's friend looks like she wants to tear me to pieces.

Walking right over to me, not intimidated by our height difference, she looks up at me. "Listen, this is how it's going to go. You and I are going to go sit at the table over there, alone. You are going to answer my questions. If I don't like what you have to say, I won't give you my friend's name. Period. Do you understand?"

Turning to look at Scottie for assistance, Scottie crosses his arms over his chest and nods. "I told you, it's up to her. You're my boy, Alex, but I've known them for about twenty years. Talk to Morgan, and just a warning, she can smell a lie a mile away."

"I'm no threat to your friend." I try to keep the annoyance out of my voice. Do they think I'm a bad person?

Rolling her eyes, she walks away. "Let's go. Scottie, can you please order me a drink? Something very strong? I have a feeling I might need it."

"You got it, Morgan. And only because you played nice with Rogue tonight. Well, mostly, he told me you threw one of his snowballs back at him. In all the years he's been our mascot, you are the first person to do that. Even little kids don't do that to him," he laughs as he walks away.

"Yeah, asshole. You're so lucky I don't rip your balls off right now for the stunt you pulled. But we'll talk about that later, I won't forget. The only reason I'm not going to rip your balls off is because it made our girl laugh."

Putting his hands up in surrender, Scottie slowly walks backwards towards the bar.

We head to a four person table in the back corner of the bar, away from everyone else.

The staredown begins as soon as we sit down. If I knew how to start my questions without the possibility of pissing her off, I'd jump into it. But the look she's giving me—I'm scared. And that's crazy, because I could squash her like a bug. Maybe I should call Bear over for backup.

"Okay, so talk. Why were you asking Scott about my friend? And just to put all the cards on the table, I know who you are, but I want to hear your side," she all but growls, not breaking her stare.

"Four years ago, my sister and I were in a major accident. We were leaving one of my hockey games when my SUV was hit and pushed into the river. I was knocked unconscious. A woman risked her own life to save both mine and my sister's lives. We heard the man that hit us is a dangerous man, still on the loose, and targeted the woman that saved us. I've been looking for her every day since the day of the accident. So has my lawyer. I want to… No, I need to thank her for what she did for my family. Without her selflessness, my parents could have lost one or both of their children that night. And because she helped us, her life has been turned upside down. It's not right, and I want to help her.

Continuing, I lay it all out on the table, I say, "I see her face in my dreams almost every night. My lawyer was told she was forced out of Chicago because her life was in danger, and so I looked for her everywhere I went. In every city we had a game, I looked in the stands for her. I never believed in fate until that night, until she saved us. I mean her no harm, but please, if your friend is the one that saved my sister, please let me talk to her. Thank her. I'll never be able to repay her, but I'd like to try."

Scottie comes over with her drink. "Can I trust him, Scottie?"

He looks down at me, his friend and teammate, and nods. "He's good people, Morgan. You can trust him. I've known he's been looking for someone, I just didn't know it was her. I knew she was the one that saved him, but I figured he knew who she was because he never talked about the night."

"Scottie, please stay and be my witness," she asks. "Now, you listen to me. It's bound to come out some time, so you keep your fucking mouth shut until I talk to her. Yes, my friend is the one that pulled you out of the river that night. I was with her, I saw everything. She's had nightmares about it every night since. Not to mention she'll wear the scars for the rest of her life."

"Scars?" I mumble. Literal or figurative?

Her head tilts as she looks at me. "You don't know? She had to get fifty-six stitches from dragging her body against the broken glass from your window because her stubborn ass didn't want to wait to clear the window properly because your truck was sinking. Not to mention the ones on the palms of her hands from pulling away the broken glass to get to you both."

I feel devastated. "I didn't know."

"Why would you know? How could you? You didn't even know her name, so why would you have access to her medical records? Anyway, she blames herself for your sister's injuries. She knew she should've unbuckled your sister, but your sister was screaming at her to save you, and she had a few drinks that night, so she wasn't thinking one hundred percent clearly. We were out together when we witnessed the accident, and she knew she couldn't wait for other responders to arrive. Her supervisor confirmed that she was correct. If she would've waited, you both would have drowned, but her being intoxicated caused her to make mistakes. She will never allow herself forgiveness. Unless... you can give her that."

She turns to Scottie, he nods. "Can you do that for her? Can you clear her mind of all the burden and let her finally move on from the accident? Well, as much as she can move on."

"There's nothing to forgive. And I will help her in any way she needs me. My parents are so thankful for her and would love to meet her. My sister screamed at my father for demanding more details from a police officer because she didn't want your friend to get in trouble for leaving her in her seat, so she has a supporter with her, and me—I'll get on my knees and thank her every day for saving my sister. Have I proven that I don't mean her harm?"

Grabbing the back of my neck, it's hard to keep my cool. I'm so close, after all these years, to finding her.

"Yes. You have. But I still need to get her okay. You understand, right? But I'll tell her everything you've said tonight, and I'll have Scottie with me when I talk to her. That's why I asked him to sit down. She'll be relieved that you don't hold her responsible, and maybe that will allow her to heal. Scottie can be your character reference."

Scottie stands and reaches a hand down to Morgan. I know it's time to get out of here. There isn't anything else I can say that can help sway them. I can only hope that the girl I've been looking for will agree to meet.

Lily

He remembered me. At least he didn't come off the ice and yell at me or have security escort me out of the arena. That was no doubt recognition that crossed his face, but I was confused because I didn't really see anger.

Maybe in a few days Morgan can ask Scottie to get a sense if he remembered me or if I'm just freaking out for nothing. I don't want to give up going to the games, but I will if I need to. I wouldn't be able to handle seeing the same look on his face that I saw the night of the accident. The hatred would be too much. And what if he had the Yeti's management ban me from the arena? That would be the ultimate embarrassment for a fan like me. What would Scottie think if that happened?

Making it up the last few steps to my door, I freeze in my tracks. "No, no, no, no, no. This can't be fucking happening." Right on my doorstep is a jet-black box with a blood-red ribbon. The only difference between this one and the ones I received years ago is this one has a note on the top.

I have two options: I can handle this myself, or I can call Eddie. If I call Eddie, he will try to talk me into leaving again. I decide to see what's in the box before I make my decision. Pulling the note out from under the ribbon, I turn it over.

WELCOME HOME! IT WAS A SURPRISE TO SEE YOU ON TV TONIGHT ENJOYING THE HOCKEY GAME. REMEMBER TO KEEP YOUR HANDS TO YOURSELF—YOU BELONG TO ME.

Dropping the card at my feet, the temperature drops about twenty degrees. Lifting the lid from the box, inside is a pair of handcuffs and a rose, tied together with a length of eight-millimeter soft silk red rope. His signature. He's making sure I know it's him and not some other stalker psychopath.

I don't want to leave Chicago again. Hiding out for the past four years while waiting for word that this kidnapper has been arrested was the most mind-numbing time of my life. I wasn't able to continue my search and rescue position, so I took a position as an EMT. It wasn't the same. Eddie hid me in a small town in Michigan, not far from where he grew up, with one of his family friends. They were amazing and super sweet, but I missed my independence and my home. I missed Chicago.

No, for now I will keep this to myself. Gathering the notecard and the box, I unlock my apartment, grab the bat I placed next to the door as soon as I moved in, and walk room by room, making sure I have no unwanted visitors. Stopping in the guest bedroom, I push the box into the back of the closet. The last thing I need is for Morgan to find it and run to Eddie. I love her, but she worries too much. Should I be worried? Probably. But I'll stay in da loo loo land for a little while. What's that saying? Out of sight, out of mind?

What I need now is to just crawl into bed and get ready to face Eddie in the morning. Tomorrow I get back to work, something I need desperately. After walking through my apartment and making sure every door and window is secure, I burrow under my blanket and make every negative thought in my head tomorrow's problem.

Chapter Nine
Lily

As the sun streams through my blinds, the realization that sleep isn't coming hits me. Why can't I turn my brain off? A hot shower and then an IV of coffee is what I need before Eddie arrives in, oh, an hour and a half.

The hot water pouring over my tense muscles helps my mind to calm down, but not enough to stop the images from last night. All night, as I tossed and turned, I kept replaying the last four years of my life and where it went so wrong. Before the accident, I had a promising career, a healthy social life, and felt fulfilled. After that night, I was no longer able to do my job, being shuttled to small-town America to hide out. Because of the scar that lined the length of my right leg, I haven't let anyone see me in minimal clothing, let alone naked.

Do I regret going into the water to save them? Not for a single second.

Do I wish that saving them wouldn't have put me in some sick man's targets? Well, yes.

But I would not change my decision to jump into the water to save them that night. Even knowing the course it would push my life onto.

I'm pulled from my thoughts as the alarm on my cell phone chimes, reminding me to hurry my ass up or I won't be ready when Eddie shows up.

Eight a.m. on the dot, ever the punctual supervisor, the doorbell rings and I'm still in the middle of brushing my hair; it's not like he can really expect me to be ready on time for my first day back.

Knock. Knock. Knock. "Open up, Liliana."

"So impatient. I'm coming," I yell across the apartment. Even though I know who is on the other side of the door, I'm still compelled to check the peephole. Not that I don't trust Eddie—I trust him with my life—but it's muscle memory.

"You are way too chipper this early in the morning, Eddie," I yell through the door.

"It's not early, lazybones. And if you don't open the door, I can't give you the extra-large double espresso caramel macchiato I picked up on the way over."

Damn near ripping the door off the hinges, I lunge at Eddie with grabby hands. "Give me, give me, give me." I'm waving my hands in his face like a toddler looking for a toy.

"Someone's excited to get back to her training."

"No. Wrong. This girl's excited for the coffee in your hands. And maybe a little excited for the training, but wait to ask me that until after the caffeine hits my bloodstream." Pulling the coffee close to my chest, the moment the scent hits my nose, my morning feels a little brighter.

"Well then, you'll be happy to know that I have a full day of training and recertification scheduled."

And my buzz is ruined.

"Oh yay. Are you trying to get everything done in a single day? Trying to kill me?"

"I figured one day of hell, then we can get back to saving lives. Get the dream team back together. Isn't that why we all do this job?"

"Yeah, okay. I understand why you did it. I'll still be cussing you out all day, though. But don't take it personally."

"Not personally at all. Let's go, Lily. I missed working with you. This is going to be fun."

Today was anything but fun. Morgan wanted everyone to get together for dinner to celebrate my first day back to work, but after literally crawling on my hands and knees up the stairs to my apartment, I told her if anyone shows up to my door, I will Spartan kick them down the flight of stairs and not feel one fragment of remorse.

That's a lie, of course, because right now, I can't lift my leg that high. She tried to guilt me with the whole 'I miss you bullshit.' That's how I ended up soaking in the tub with the water as hot as it could go, phone on speaker with Morgan, Jordan, and Scottie, and a glass of wine.

"You didn't drown, did you?" I hear Morgan yell as I'm enjoying just closing my eyes, listening to her and Scottie go at it over the phone, waiting for Jordan to break them up.

"Oh, shit. Sorry, no. I was just thinking. So tell me about last night after the game."

"Girl, if you don't go out with Alex, I think I might," Morgan gushes.

"The fuck you will," Scottie barks.

Jordan snickers.

"You really think he doesn't hold what happened to his sister against me?" I ask unsurely.

"He's a really good guy, Lily; you know I wouldn't lie to you. I'm on your side, always. Any time I've heard him talk about you the last four years, there was never any malice," Scottie explains.

"In the last four years, he never asked you who I was, Scottie?"

"This is where I'm going to sound like an absolute moron. So no judging."

"Oh, we are going to judge," Jordan heckles.

Morgan laughs. "I second that."

"Whatever, y'all love me. So, I knew Alex had been looking for someone for the last four years, but he never said it was the woman who saved him from the accident. Just at every arena and bar we'd go to as a team, he'd be searching for… someone. Some of the guys on the team and I assumed it was an old girlfriend or something. Boy, we were wrong. It wasn't until the game last night when he saw you and Morgan that he mentioned the accident. If he had mentioned it years ago, I would have called you while you were away. I knew you blamed yourself unnecessarily about the little girl, and this could have saved you worry."

"He's smitten if you ask me, Lily. If anything, he wants to get you into bed and have you ride his stick," Morgan adds.

"Ugh, I don't need to hear my sister talk about a guy's stick. Shut it, Morgan," Jordan chastises.

"With that, guys, I'm going to bed. Eddie proved to me today how out of shape I am, and I need my bed. So I will talk to you all tomorrow."

"Let me know if you'd agree to talk to Alex, Lily, and I will pass on the message. Unless you want his phone number, then I'll text it over," Scottie says.

"Yeah, maybe tell him to send you a picture or two. And one for your friend," Morgan chuckles.

"For fuck's sake, Morgan. I'm never giving you my tickets again," Jordan groans.

"I'll let you know soon, Scottie. Promise. And Jordan, don't punish me because your sister's horny and can't get laid. Night, everyone. Love you guys."

There's rounds of groans, love yous, and good nights before everyone disconnects.

That's what I needed—to talk to my friends. I was serious about going straight to bed, I don't even have the energy for dinner.

Lying in bed, all I can think about is what Morgan and Scottie said about Alex. For four years the night of the accident has haunted my dreams. Could Alex make my nightmare go away? Maybe meeting him and talking to him wouldn't be the worst thing. I have a few days to think about it and let Scottie know. What's the worst thing that could happen?

Chapter Ten
Lily

Last night was another damn near sleepless night, but not for the normal reasons. After speaking to Morgan, Jordan, and Scott, everything I've thought about the possibility of Alex and his family blaming me for the little girl's injuries has been wrong. That is if Alex told Morgan the truth. What if what I saw in his eyes that night wasn't hatred and I was just imagining it? There have been too many nights to count that I've seen those blazing eyes in my sleep.

If he lied to Morgan, he better run very, very far, because she even scares the shit out of me. She watches true crime to fall asleep and wouldn't think twice about making him disappear. I once listened to her list off ten ways to make a body disappear to a guy that was rude to a waitress in a restaurant we were at. It was magnificent.

Anyway, I told Scott I'd let him know by the end of the week if I feel comfortable meeting Alex face-to-face. Most women would jump at the chance to have the attention of *the* Alexander Bensen, defenseman for the Chicago Yetis.

I'd be lying if I said I didn't enjoy the physical physique of the male hockey player. But I grew up with hockey, so my heart races as the puck glides down the ice and the bodies slam into the boards just as much as it does being in the proximity of the players.

Before my parents were killed by a drunk driver, my father instilled into my head that athletes and other celebrities are people first and foremost and want to be treated as such. Some love the spotlight, but for others, the lack of privacy makes it hard for them to trust the intentions of others.

With the exception of Rogue, the Yeti's mascot, I've always tried to follow my father's advice and never make someone uncomfortable just because of their status. Rogue, I just can't help myself—I have to fangirl when I'm around the fluffy mascot.

If I decide to sit down with Alex, maybe I can convince him I will only do it somewhere private. Being spotted with him is a surefire way to see my picture, if not my name, in the newspaper and gossip columns. If that happens, my stalker will not be happy, and the last thing I need is for him to escalate his threats. I don't want to live in fear, and I really don't want Alex involved in whatever this is either.

Feeling like I'm going to crawl out of my skin, and knowing there's no way I'm going to be able to fall back asleep, I decide that maybe a run will help clear my head.

Pulling up my weather app, I'm excited to see no rain today. Currently it's a warm forty-two degrees outside. Most would think that is insanely cold, but not for late November in Chicago; I'll take it. In a few weeks, when the snow comes, I'll be missing the forty-degree weather like crazy.

With the mild weather, I pull out an old Team USA NHL long-sleeve shirt and black running leggings. By the front door are my favorite pair of HOKA running shoes. Morgan teases me because I have four of the same pair, but hey, they feel like I'm running on a cloud, so why not?

There's about an hour left until sunrise, so about an hour until the city comes alive. Should I be running the streets of the city alone at this time of morning? No. But grabbing my pepper spray and leaving my headphones at home, I decide to take my chances. I feel like I'm coming out of my skin, and if I don't expel some of this tension, I will be on edge the rest of the day.

Morgan likes to make fun of me for my running obsession. It's something she's never understood. In high school, she'd take a beach chair, sit next to the track with an iced coffee, and cheer me on.

But running does something to my mind. As my feet slap the pavement, the wind slaps against my face, and my lungs burn with lack of oxygen, it's like everything I was stressing about is seeping out of my body. It's hard to explain to someone that's not a runner, but even through all the blisters and chafing, every mile logged is worth it because it helps my mental health.

My body is on autopilot, knowing the route I want it to take without having to think about each turn. One of the first things I did after signing my lease was map out the best running route around my apartment. When choosing my routes, I look for things like safety while also keeping away from congested areas.

The last turn on my route comes into view, and I finally allow myself to glance at my watch. Realizing I pushed myself harder than ever and beat my best time, a sense of accomplishment flows through me.

Now to shower and get ready for another day of work. Feeling the burn as I make my way up to my second floor apartment, I'm feeling amazing until I hit the last step. The moment my eyes land on my doorstep, my heart drops into my stomach, and all the water I drank before my run tries to come back up.

There is yet another jet-black box with a blood-red ribbon waiting for me. "Motherfucker," I hiss to myself. The audacity of this bastard. After work tonight, I'm going to the hardware store and purchasing a doorbell camera. I'm going to have fun explaining that to Morgan and Eddie. But maybe I'll just say it's a precaution. I'm becoming quite the liar, and I hate it. I don't like this version of myself I'm becoming, and all because I'm keeping the danger away from the people that care about me.

Grabbing the box, I move it inside, not wanting to be vulnerable outside a moment longer. Who knows if he's able to see me when I step out of my sanctuary. Placing the box on the table, I take no care with removing the bow and the lid. Inside are binoculars, with a note card attached to them with a length of red silk rope. He's so freaking predictable. The note card says,

I'm always watching!

Gathering everything up, I toss it in the back of the spare room closet with the rest of the crap he's been taunting me with. If I were smart, I'd grab this one and the last one he sent me and take them right down to the dumpster. But something inside me is saying he'd know, and that would escalate his aggression.

He won't win. I won't let him. Yes, I need to be honest with myself, he is terrifying me, but I'm not oblivious to what he is. So if he comes for me, I won't be some helpless victim. I just need to stay on my toes and be vigilant. I won't put my life on hold for him again. I just need to be prepared.

Chapter Eleven
Lily

Morgan: What are you doing tonight?

Me: Sleeping! I'm exhausted.

Morgan: Boring. No, you are going out with me.

Me: But I don't want to.

Morgan: Yes, you do. Get dressed.

Me: Did anyone ever tell you that you are annoying?

Morgan: All the time.

Me: Good, so at least you know it. Where are we going?

Morgan: Promise me you'll go first, and then I'll tell you.

Me: No.

Morgan: Okay, then it's a surprise.

Me: No.

Morgan: Fine, biotch. Jordan is stuck in another meeting and gave me his tickets again. Plz, plz, plz, come with me???

Me: Are you paying for all my drinks? And snacks. I want nachos.

Morgan: Of course.

Me: Fine.

Morgan: Are you feeling okay? That was too easy.

Me: I changed my mind. I'm going to bed.

Morgan: No, you don't! I'm on my way, and I will bring wine to pre-game.

Me: Fine. But you better bring the good shit. I have muscles I didn't even know I had that hurt.

> **Morgan:** I will stop at Jordan's and raid his wine fridge first. He has the expensive shit. See you soon, and you love me.

> **Me:** Jury's out on that.

It's been three days since I received the last gift. My nerves are shot, and my sleep is almost nonexistent. Maybe what I need is a night out with my best friend, enjoying a sport that gets my heart racing and throwing back some much-needed alcohol. Lots and lots of alcohol.

Arriving at the arena, the seats are still as amazing as I remembered. Growing up, my parents couldn't afford glass seats, and we preferred to attend more matches in cheaper seats. My father did surprise me for my sixteenth birthday with glass seats, and that's a night I will never forget.

Morgan picked me up early enough so we could be here for warm-ups. She swears it's so she has more time to get snacks and drinks before the game starts, but I know the truth—she'd never miss an opportunity to watch Scottie stretch and warm up on the ice. That girl has it hard for him, and he's completely oblivious.

As warmups start, Hawkins, one of the assistant captains, makes it to the ice first, knocking over the stack of pucks, scattering them onto the ice. Morgan, clapping her hands together, jumps up and down, squealing, "Here we go."

All I can do is roll my eyes, even though I'm just as excited for the game as she is. "I'm going for the first round. I'll be right back." The only reason I know she was somewhat paying attention to me is by the wave of her hand. Her eyes won't leave the ice the entire time I'm gone, of that I am sure. But she'd still expect alcohol when I return.

The seats we're in have their own snack and bar section, so the lines aren't crazy. I'm able to use the restroom, grab drinks and snacks, and be back in my seat and next to my crazy friend in less than ten minutes.

As I walk up, my eyes find Alex. As he's talking to his goalie, he lifts his jersey, swiping at the sweat on his face. Holy abs. I can hear the girls near me practically swooning, and all I feel is jealous. But why? It's not like I have a claim on him, I just don't like women sexualizing him.

Back at our seats, Scottie and Morgan are arguing, which isn't uncommon. They normally couldn't be within five feet of each other without the sexual tension exploding. If she couldn't see he wanted her as much as she wanted him, I wouldn't be the one to tell her. I'll just enjoy the show until it blows up in both their faces. I wonder if Jordan sees what I do and he is just keeping it to himself? Hmm, maybe one of these nights we are watching an away game at his apartment, I'll corner him and let something slip.

"Of course I didn't wear your jersey," Morgan yells through the glass. All eyes in our section are watching the interaction, just like last time. With it being a season ticket holder section, they could guarantee this will happen almost every time we are here.

"Why the hell not? I gave it to you for a reason," Scottie yells back, pounding his fist on the glass.

"You gave that to me because you didn't like my shirt that night. I'm wearing a respectable shirt tonight. See." She spins around, trying to prove her point. "Plus, you didn't ask me to wear your jersey, so how was I supposed to know you wanted me to?"

He tilts his head and just stares at her. "Just… assume you should always wear my jersey when you come here, damn it."

He skates off before she can yell back a retort. "That man is the most confusing and exhausting human being." "Uh huh," I chuckle.

"What's that supposed to mean, Lily?" she gasps.

"Absolutely nothing, Morgan. Absolutely nothing."

"Oh darling," an older woman sitting behind us calls out. "When a man gives you his number to wear, that means he's smitten." The man in the seat next to her nods in agreement.

Morgan scoffs and crosses her arms over her chest. "Men are stupid."

A chorus of 'agreed' rings out around us. I don't even try to hide my smile.

Warm-ups are almost over when both Scottie and Alex slowly skate by our seats, heads together, looking directly at us. They don't stop, but we can tell they were talking about us.

"Do they think they're being inconspicuous or something?" Morgan asks, throwing her hands in the air.

Laughing, I say, "It kinda looks like it, doesn't it? From what I've learned working in a ninety-nine percent male dominated profession, is that men gossip more than females. So it makes me wonder what they're talking about. Us, of course, but what exactly?"

"Oh, whatever. Warm-ups are over. Let's go stock up on more alcohol and your damn nachos, and maybe some popcorn before puck drop. They are playing Seattle, and if it's anything like the last time they played them, it's going to be a bloodbath, so I don't want to miss a moment."

"But I just got back from the drink stand. See," I say, pointing to both cup holders and the full cups, "new drinks."

"I'm going to need more than that. Let's go get more." She doesn't wait for my response before she is rushing up the aisle. Yep, Scottie riled her up something good, and I'm here for all of it.

Five minutes until puck drop, Morgan and I are settled in our seats, munching away on nachos, popcorn, and beer, and out of nowhere, a barrage of snowballs comes raining down on our unsuspecting heads. I'm barely able to cover my nachos so they won't land in my cheese.

Jumping to our feet, we come face-to-face with none other than Mr. Rogue himself.

"What the fudge, dude?"

Those aren't the words I wanted to use, but at the last second, I noticed a set of young children two rows away. I can control my mouth when I need to. Most of the time.

Rogue shrugs his shoulders, then points to the lady waiting next to him. Morgan looks at me with confusion on her face and shakes her head. Neither of us knows who she is, but she's dressed in a Yeti polo, so she is obviously part of the staff. Rogue taps her shoulder and nudges her towards us. She glares at him. Good for her.

"Here you ladies go. I'm supposed to deliver these to Morgan and Lily and make sure you open them and see what's inside."

Morgan loses it. "That conceded, asshat. Freaking Scottie." Inside her bag, of course, was another one of Scottie's jerseys. Like that man would let her wear any other number but his. Maybe one of these days, I can convince her to test a theory and wear another player's jersey and see what happens. Fireworks—that's what would happen.

Opening my bag, there is a jersey inside, but not just any jersey—it's Alex's jersey. "You've gotta be kidding me." Also inside is a stuffed version of Rogue and a handwritten note. Unfolding it, it reads,

Lily - Please meet me after the game for drinks. Bring Morgan, and I'll bring Kasper and the rest of the team. I don't want you to feel uncomfortable or pressured to be alone with me. Please say yes?

"Sorry, Ms. Lily, but I'm not allowed to leave until you give Mr. Bensen your answer," the Yeti's staff member said.

"What? Now?" I ask.

Morgan looks at me, confused.

"Morgan, drinks after the game? Alex is asking."

"Really?" she asks skeptically.

"Yeah, will you go with me? Scottie will be there."

She rips her attention from the jersey she holds in her hand long enough to glance at me. "Sure, yeah. Sounds like fun," she says, acting like it was even an option she'd say no to.

"Fine. Tell Alex as long as they win, I will go. But he needs to score, and they need to win."

Rogue's shoulders shake like he's laughing. And the woman looks shocked that I would give an ultimatum. "Okay, I'll tell Mr. Bensen your terms."

Both Morgan and I track the young woman as she moves across the bleachers, through a locked gate, and over to where the players are standing, waiting to take the ice. A few seconds later, both Scottie and Alex poke their heads just far enough over to lock eyes with us. And the looks on their faces are priceless.

Scottie's eyes are wide, like he is trying to guess what game I am playing, but Alex, the left side of his mouth pulls up in a sexy smirk and he squints his eyes. I know that look—it means challenge accepted.

Damn, I'm in trouble. But Alex is a defenseman, it's more uncommon for the defense to score, but not unheard of. And with Scottie being an assistant captain, I'm sure he'll help him achieve my ultimatum.

With them playing Seattle, I just wanted to give them a little extra motivation to win.

Seattle was supposed to deliver a bloodbath, not allow them a shutout. Final score, four to zero. And not only one, but two of those goals came from none other than Alexander Bensen. What the fuck? His team captain was even in on it. How rude of all of them. Each time he scored, the team would look in our direction and laugh, so I knew Alex or Scottie told them of our bet.

Right after the final buzzer, Morgan and I are gathering our belongings and decide not to wait for them to shower and change but to catch a rideshare to the bar and start pregaming before the team arrives.

The more alcohol I have in my system, the easier it will be to sit down with Alex. Those plans are squashed when we turn to head up the aisle, and who is standing in our way? Rogue. Didn't this guy have anything else to do? Waving a hand, he wants us to follow.

"You know what, Rogue? You used to be my favorite, now I'm going to have to reevaluate. What do those guys want now?" I grumble, standing my ground.

Rogue, reaching into his pocket, pulls out a snowball and tosses it in the air, patiently waiting for us.

Morgan just shrugs. "It's not like he didn't complete your ultimatum. And we've already consumed a fair share of alcohol, so let's just see what these jackasses want, then we can make them drive us to the bar. It's probably safer than the rideshare anyway. Like really, what's the worst that could happen to us at the arena?"

Rogue leads us to a door that needs keycode access. Once inside, we descend a few flights of stairs and come out right next to the home locker room. Great, all eyes are on us when Rogue puts our backs to the wall and points down like he is telling children to stay put. The other women in the hallway, most likely the WAGs of the team, look at Morgan and me like we don't belong. And honestly, we don't.

Bjorn Olsson, AKA Bear, the team's captain, is the first to emerge from the locker room. "Little Hawthorne, what did you get yourself into?"

Morgan, obviously knowing who Bear is, rushes over and gives him a hug. "Bear, don't start your shit. And it wasn't me. It was my bestie, Lily, over here that's been the bad girl tonight. Blame her."

"Oh, I've heard all about her," he laughs. "For the past four years, I've been hearing all about you, without knowing it was you."

"What?" I gasp, feeling the heat creeping up my neck.

"Nothing, nothing," he waves off, "let me introduce myself. I'm Bjorn Olsson, but everyone calls me Bear. I'm friends with this brat's older brother, that's why she feels free to sass me."

"Oh, that, and I have so many embarrassing stories about him that he wouldn't dare berate me for my sass," Morgan beams with pride.

"Now those I need to hear," Scottie yells as he and Alex walk up behind us. "Hey Cap, are you heading to Sticks with us to celebrate the win?"

"Yeah, sure, let's go," Bear agrees.

Squeezing between everyone to get to us, Scottie throws his arms around mine and Morgan's shoulders. "You ladies are riding with me. I know how handsy these assholes can get when the adrenaline is pumping, and I don't feel like murdering anyone tonight. So we'll meet you all at Sticks."

Alex's shoulders drop, a look of disappointment on his face. Bear notices too and laughs as he slaps his shoulder. "Let's go, grump-a-puss. My car's faster. I bet we can beat them there and have a table waiting. Loser buys everyone a round."

That seems to perk him up. Bouncing on his toes, little by little, the corners of his mouth turn up.

"Oh hell no. Let's go!" Scottie yells. "I'll never live it down if they beat us. Move those asses, ladies."

Chapter Twelve
Lily

Alex, Bear, and half the team did in fact beat us to the bar. By a lot, actually. From the looks of the tables as we walk into the bar, they are already done with a round or two. Morgan held us up, and knowing my best friend, it was totally on purpose to mess with Scottie.

First, right before we made it to the arena exit, she ducked into the restroom. When Scottie yelled into the restroom that she could pee at the bar, she yelled back, "I wouldn't have made it to the bar, so hold your tits."

Watching him pace outside the restroom, grumbling under his breath about Morgan being an ungrateful little shit, was by far the highlight of my night. And so far the night has been pretty great. But watching these two drive each other crazy is always comedic gold.

It's like everyone can see the sexual tension from a mile away except Morgan, Scottie, and I'm assuming her brother Jordan. Because I don't know if Scottie would be breathing if Jordan knew his best friend wanted to fuck his little sister. I could be wrong, and he wouldn't have an issue with them being together. But everyone else knows, and that's what makes their interactions hilarious.

After Morgan left the restroom, she was walking so slow that Scottie threatened to toss her over his shoulder. He would've done it too, but she reluctantly gave in.

And here we are, at Sticks, standing in front of half the Chicago Yetis hockey team, where I'm freaking the fuck out. Yes, I grew up around hockey. Yes, I could tell you the player stats with more accuracy than probably half the men in this bar. But there's a player that makes my heart race that's only across the room, and I'm not sure if even after four years I'm ready to come face-to-face with him.

"I can't do this." Turning to leave, Morgan grabs my shoulders.

"You good?" Her eyes search mine.

"No. Not at all. They are all staring at me." Knowing she could feel me trembling, she looks back towards the exit. She'd remove me from the situation if I needed her too, even without me asking, because we know each other that well.

A hand comes down on my shoulder as I'm focusing on Morgan. Not expecting the contact, I let out a screech and jump. "It's okay, Lily, it's just Scottie," Morgan says, lunging for me, gripping my waist.

There's no way for her to know how on edge I've been lately with the return of my stalker. It's not like I've told anyone, not even the police. Eddie has questioned my behavior, but I've always been able to come up with a quick excuse.

This week, the excuse was I got caught up with binge-watching a new T.V. series and haven't been getting much sleep. I'm not going to be able to keep it from Morgan much longer, she's too perceptive.

Something over my shoulder catches Morgan's attention. Scrunching her nose, she gets a stupid smile on her face. "I think someone's waiting to talk to you. But only if you feel comfortable."

Turning around, I lock eyes with the man I've been actively trying to avoid for the past four years, Alexander Bensen. He's more intimidating than I remember. He walks the few steps over until he's at Scottie's side. Damn, he's gorgeous. And tall. So fucking tall.

Keeping his hands down at his sides, like he's afraid to spook me, he says, "Lily, you have no idea how long I've been wanting to meet you so I could thank you for saving mine and my sister's lives years ago. Do you want to sit down and have a drink? We can either sit with the team, or," he points back to a corner, "over there it should be a little more quiet."

Morgan looks at me and shrugs. "It's up to you, cupcake. I threatened his balls if he hurt you, and I'll keep an eye out, so why don't you guys go over where this rowdy bunch won't disturb you as much?"

There's something about the way he's looking at me that has my heart aching. It's like he's expecting me to tell him no or turn and walk away. "Yeah, the table in the back sounds good."

Alex reaches out and gently places his hand on my lower back. Even though there was barely any contact, it makes my heart race as we walk through the crowded bar.

Sliding into opposite sides of the booth, drinks are delivered to us before I could even remove my jacket. Looking over at the team table, Morgan lifts her glass in salute, and I know they came from her.

"So..." I hesitate.

"I have looked for you everywhere," he rushes out.

Gasping, I look up at him, and his eyes are locked on mine. Too stunned to say anything else, I just ask, "What?"

"Sorry. I didn't mean for it to come out like that." Pausing, he downs about half his beer. "Let me start over without sounding like a complete creep."

I can't help but chuckle. "You didn't sound like a creep."

He sounds so unsure of himself, so anxious. I'm the one that's been distressed that he'd blame me for what happened with his sister. Reaching across the table, I give his hand a quick squeeze before pulling back and shoving my hands back to my lap.

A small smile spread across his lips. Taking a deep breath, he continues.

"But yes, for the last four years, I haven't stopped trying to find you. I never gave up hope that one day we'd be reunited. After the accident, when my head started to clear, I wanted... no, I needed to find you to thank you for what you did for Julie, my sister. The newspaper didn't release your name, my lawyer wasn't able to find out your name nor any other information that would lead us to you, and the police wouldn't tell us anything. Later, we found out it was because the person that hit us was a psychotic bastard and turned his attention to you, and then you fled Chicago. I asked my lawyer to find you so my family could offer you protection.

"After what you did for us, my mother would've loved nothing more than to put you in bubble wrap and keep you hidden. When I told her I've finally found you after all these years, it took my father threatening to lock her in a closet to keep her from coming to my game and hugging you to death. Just to warn you, I won't be able to keep her away forever. So if you see a five-foot-six-inch hurricane running towards you, hopefully it's my mother. But if it's her, an older version of me will be chasing her, because my father never lets her out of his sight."

I don't know whether to laugh or cry. All these years, I thought his family would hate me, and here he's telling me they want to thank me?

"But about what I said about looking for you. I mean it. Every away game for the last four years, I'd be searching the stands for you. I couldn't get you out of my head. Every night when I closed my eyes, those haunting green eyes and that fiery red hair dominated my dreams.

"Sorry, sorry. I'm being too intense." He downs the rest of his beer and jumps out of his seat. "I'm going to go grab another round. I'll be right back."

The second he is out of his chair, a familiar body slams into my side.

"Okay, ho, spill. You look ready to bolt. Do I need to follow him, push him into the alleyway, shank him, and throw him into the dumpster?"

Turning to her, I can't tell if she is serious. "You scare me sometimes. So I'm glad I'm your favorite person and never on your bad side."

The way I'm able to tell she's had more than a few drinks is that she leans over and kisses my cheek. "Scottie, come get your girl," I yell across the bar.

Seconds later, both Scottie and Bear join us. Bear chuckles at Morgan hanging all over me, and Scottie just shakes his head. It's nothing he's not used to. "So, how's my boy doing?" Bear asks.

"Honestly," I start, glancing over at the bar to make sure he's still out of earshot. "I thought after what happened with his sister, he was going to hate me, never in any scenario I imagined over the years did I expect that he'd been looking for me all this time to thank me."

Bear looks over at his friend and sighs, "Yeah, I was there in the hospital with him the night of the accident. Julie is his world. When she told the police and their father she begged you to save him because he was unconscious and underwater and she was fine, he lost it with guilt. Even though the doctors explained if you would've saved him last, because he was already underwater when you got to them, he probably wouldn't have survived, it took him a while to come to terms with them. He never blamed you for what happened to Julie either, Lily. Not ever. Neither does Julie nor their parents. For the last four years, he's been driving me nuts looking for you everywhere. I just want you to know that he comes off intense, but he's a good guy. He'll protect you with everything he has, and loves even stronger. That's a warning."

A warning? I'm just about to ask questions when Alex comes back to the table with drinks, like lots of drinks. Or two drinks and lots of shots.

The rest of the evening passes with nice conversation and friendly competition. Charlie Hawkins and Axel Caddel, two teammates, are doing a shot for shot competition. Bear just shakes his head, convinced he'll be the one to make sure they'll get home okay and not die of alcohol poisoning. Always the captain on duty. It must be exhausting, but by the way he is looking at his teammate, it was not a duty he'd give up for anything.

The bartender makes the last call, and everyone groans out their disappointments. Morgan is passed out in a booth with her head in Scottie's lap. I watch as he strokes her hair, every few minutes looking down at her face with such care. Yeah, those two need to figure out their feelings before I sit them down and shove them down their throats.

"You almost ready to go home, Lily?" Scottie asks in a hushed voice.

Alex, who has been tearing a cocktail napkin into tiny pieces, stops and looks between the two of us. "I'm going to call a driver, and he can take her home."

Reaching over and placing my hand on top of his, I tell him, "That's really sweet, but Morgan's going to stay with me tonight. I need to make sure she's okay. She can't go back to her house like this, and my guest room is practically her other bedroom, so if it's okay, Scottie will take us home so he can carry her because I'm not going to attempt to lug her up to my second-story apartment."

At least he doesn't look offended. "I understand. Would I be able to get your phone number at least? I had a great time tonight, and hopefully we can see each other again soon?"

"I'd love that, Alex." Leaning into his shoulder, I feel him relax around me. I haven't felt this free in years. Who knew just a few words would be able to lift so much pressure off my shoulders?

Unlocking my phone, I hand it to him so he can program in his number. A few moments later, his phone buzzes on the table. "I texted myself from your phone so I have your number."

Scottie didn't drink, he never does when we are with him and not staying at home, so we were good to go home in his SUV. Alex grabs my jacket from the booth and helps me into it, then throws his arm around me, leading me outside as Scottie carries a still half-asleep Morgan and places her in the front seat.

"Will you message me when you get home so I'm not up all night worrying?" Alex asks, pulling me close.

"And why would you worry, Mr. Hockey player?" I chuckle. Now that I'm up and moving, the alcohol seems to be hitting me a little more. My head is swimming, but in the best way.

"There's just something about you, spitfire, that I can't get out of my head. I have this need to make sure you're safe. So will you message me, or do I need to call Scottie in like thirty minutes?"

Pulling back so I could see his face, I feign offense and ask, "Did you just call me spitfire?"

His grin makes me swoon, or maybe it is the alcohol. "Yeah, spitfire. I called you that because you are feisty."

"You are ridiculous," I tell him as I burrow into his warm sweatshirt. Even wearing my jacket, it doesn't protect me against the winter temperatures of Chicago. That will teach me to dress for fashion, not warmth.

"So, will you text me, or should I just follow you home?"

Looking up at his eyes, we just stare at each other, not moving. I don't think he's joking. "Fine, as soon as I get Morgan to bed, I will message you. Don't freak out if it takes me a bit, she can sometimes get frisky when I'm helping her out of her bar clothes."

"Huh, who can get frisky?" Scottie asks, popping his head out of the car.

"Of course you would hear that. You know who, you shit. Morgan gets frisky when she's drunk and I try to put her to bed. She tries to fight me when putting her in pajamas and just wants to sleep naked. But I'd really rather she didn't defile my guest bed. Both you and Jordan have slept in there, and I don't think Jordan would appreciate knowing his sister sleeps naked in that bed. Yet, I don't think you would mind. But I've seen her naked more times than I can count. So let's go so you can help me carry your girlfriend up to my apartment."

"Not my girlfriend," Scottie huffs.

Alex laughs and gets a nasty look from Scottie.

"Night, Alex. I'm glad I made it out tonight. And I forgot to thank you for my gifts. I can't wait to sleep with Rogue tonight. I've been wanting him in my bed for such a long time." I make that comment right before closing the door in his shocked face. I can hear Alex cursing Rogue out, threatening to kill him, and Scottie has tears streaming down his face from laughing so hard.

Scottie gets in and closes the door, looking out the window at Alex still standing there with a heated expression on his face. "You really are a brat, you know that? I've never seen Alex so flustered. I wish I had that on video. Now let's get you girls home."

Me: I'm home and was only groped twice.

Alex: Oh, the images you just gave me. You are being extra naughty tonight, spitfire. Are you trying to make me jealous?

Me: Maybe?????

Alex: Hmmm. Are you in bed?

Me: Yes

Alex: Alone?

Me: No

Alex: Who's with you?

Me: Rogue

Alex: How long have you had the hots for our mascot?

Me: Years

Alex: So when I sent him to you with gifts, it was like sending an extra gift?

Me: You have no idea that you made my dreams come true.

Alex: He will disappear.

Me: Don't you dare!

Alex: Poof, gone.

Me: Alexander, I've had too much to drink for macho caveman jealousy.

Alex: Hmmm…

Me: Goodnight, Alex. Sweet dreams.

Alex: They will be the sweetest, spitfire.

Chapter Thirteen
Alex

Last night was everything I'd hoped it would be. After years of wondering what Lily would be like when we met, she's all that and more. Now that she's in my life, I'm not letting her go.

Did I cross a line when I added the tracking app and cloning software my parents' IT company created to her phone when she gave it to me to add my phone number? Yes, I absolutely crossed that line. But in my defense, Lily and I would've met four years ago if she wasn't targeted by the man that almost killed my sister and me.

Is that a healthy way to defend my actions? No. But at least I can admit that to myself.

The guilt I've lived with for the last four years that she was on his radar because of me has been ripping me apart, turning me into someone I don't recognize. So a little illegal software on her phone to make sure she is safe should be considered endearing, right?

It's because of that software that I know where her apartment is, and why first thing this morning I parked down the block but in view of her front door.

> **Me:** Good morning, spitfire.

Lily: Morning, Alex.

Me: What? Not a good morning?

Lily: Not until I've had my coffee, it won't be.

Lily: Ask me again in like twenty minutes, once the caffeine has hit my bloodstream.

Oh, that's adorable. I'll need to remember that. She might be grumpy-cute until caffeine.

Me: What are your plans for the day?

Lily: Oh, you know. Take over the world.

Me: You're adorable.

Lily: You wouldn't be saying I was adorable if you could see me now.

If only she knew all she had to do was step out her door and I'd be able to see her. Hmm.

Me: I'm sure you are cute no matter what.

Lily: (Incoming picture)

The blood races to my cock at the sight of her mussed hair and tank top pajama top without a bra.

Me: Are you trying to kill me this early in the morning?

Lily: Now who's adorable?

Me: Still you, I promise.

Lily: (Incoming picture)

Me: Hmmmmmm. I don't like seeing another man in your arms, Lily.

Lily: Jealous, Alex?

Me: You have no idea.

Lily: Well then, I shouldn't tell you that I fell asleep cuddling Rogue, and when I woke up, he was between my legs.

Me: That's it. I'm on my way to the rink to kill him.

Lily: Oh, stop it, you caveman.

Me: I'll get you a little hockey player to sleep with, and I'll make sure he has my jersey on.

> **Lily:** So you want me to sleep with two men? Got it. I might be able to get behind that.

> **Me:** You really are sassy in the morning, spitfire.

I need to see her again, maybe find a way to steal Rogue from her bed. Could Scottie be bribed to do it?

> **Me:** We are going to be leaving Wednesday for a seven-day away game stretch. I'd love to see you before we go. Maybe dinner?

I'm not a patient man. So when the seconds tick by and still no response, I'm convinced she's going to say no. Did I push too fast?

> **Lily:** Dinner sounds great. I'm off at three on Tuesday, so I'm free anytime after that if that works.

> **Me:** Great. I only have morning skate that day, so how about I pick you up at four?

> **Lily:** I can't wait. Just let me know the dress code.

She sends me her address, not knowing I'm already sitting outside.

> **Me:** Well, if I get to pick… (wink)

> **Lily:** Freaking men. Fine, I'll wear what I want, and you can deal with it.

> **Me:** Dang it, okay.

> **Lily:** I need to go make Morgan a hangover breakfast. You have a good day, Alex.

> **Me:** I will, now that I talked to you, Lily.

She doesn't message the rest of the day, but I know she's hanging out with Morgan, so I don't want to act like a stalker. I try to use that time to figure out a date for Tuesday, but even after hours of searching online, I got nothing.

At Monday morning skate practice all I can think about still is this damn date. Most people think of a professional hockey player and think of someone that is out with a new girl every night and sleeping around. Yes, that was me in college. I hate to admit that I was a man whore. But the moment I was pulled from the water four years ago and looked into those green eyes, the only action I've had was from my hand. Four years without so much as looking at another woman, and I regret nothing.

"Bensen, if you don't get your head out of your ass, you'll be skating lines for the rest of practice," Coach screams.

"What the fuck is wrong with you?" Bear calls out as he skates up next to me. "You've missed three passes so far, and I've never seen that happen. You good?"

"He's thinking with his dick, that's what's wrong," Knight calls from behind us as he continues telescoping in his crease as some of the guys take shots on him.

"Oooo, you got called out," Caddel heckles as he skates past, working a drill.

As we continue practice, I continue to be sloppy, stuck in my head.

I see the puck heading my way, but right before it hits my stick, Scottie body-checks me from the left and right into the boards.

"Enough," Coach booms. "It looks like you all forgot how to play hockey today, so I'm done wasting my time. Hit the showers, and we are on the road in two days. You better come ready. Because next time you all show up to practice and perform like this, you'll be skating lines until every single one of you are puking." He turns and skates off the ice without another word.

"Alex, start talking," Bear huffs, his chest heaving, tapping his stick to the ice in front of me.

"I'm taking Lily out on our first date tomorrow, and I can't figure out where to take her."

Every single person stops moving towards the locker room, and all eyes are on me.

"You've got to be shitting me. That's what got you skating like you're back in Mini Mites?" Bear grumbles.

"Where do you take the other girls you've dated?" Knight asks, skating up next to me.

Not even thinking about the words before I speak, I accidentally confess, "I haven't dated in years. Four years, to be exact. Not since the night of the accident my rookie year. It was the night Lily pulled me and my sister, Julie, from the water and saved our lives."

"Damn, Bensen. You've been whipped for four years, and you didn't even know her name until recently?" Hawkins confirms. "That's commitment, Bro."

"Yeah, pathetic, right?" I murmur. "But I don't care. When I saw her, I knew. So you fuckers can make fun of me all you want, I can take it."

"Yeah, yeah, we get it. You're in love. So what do you need help with? There's enough man whores on the team, ask your questions," Scottie teases.

Knowing that Scottie has known Lily since they were kids gives me hope he can help me out. He'd know what her interests are.

"I need date ideas. How can I make our first date special?"

Looking around the ice, most of my friends and teammates either avoid my gaze or just shrug their shoulders.

"Sorry, dude," Caddel calls out, "I normally just take my bunnies back to my place, but I don't think that will work with Lily."

"Call her a bunny again and I will shove Knight's goalie stick up your ass," Scottie threatens before I have the chance.

"Whoa, whoa, whoa. Why does it need to be my stick? Why can't it be yours?" Knight throws his hands up in protest.

Scottie waves his hands all around. "Because yours is bigger and will hurt more."

"Okay, fair. Yeah, I'd let you use it as long as you sanitize it after," Knight nonchalantly says.

"Back to me, please," I groan.

"Hey Alex," Assistant Coach Jameson, who's been leaning against the boards, laughing at my pain, calls out, "Your girl likes the water, right?"

"She loves it, Coach. Why?" I look at Bear, and he just shrugs his shoulders.

"None of you assholes pay attention to anyone but yourselves, do you? Do any of you know what my wife's job is? Here's a hint... they are a major donor of the Yetis."

Everyone looks around, but no one knows who he is talking about.

"Maybe I shouldn't help you out," Coach accuses.

"Sorry, Coach. We don't mean to be assholes, we'll pay more attention," Hawkins apologizes, standing next to me. "But can you take a little pity on our boy here? He's about to bomb this date he's waited four years for and needs help."

"Fine. Let me talk to my wife, and I'll text you tonight. If she comes through for you, I expect you, and maybe some of your teammates, to help her out at her next event. And before the next practice, do your research and find out what she does. Alex, if I help you out, you don't give them any hints."

"Yes, Coach," we call out around the ice.

"Man, I really feel like shit," Caddel says, sitting on the bench next to me. "I didn't even know Coach was married."

"That's it. I'm having HR put together a packet, and we are going to learn the basics about our Yeti family," Bear chastises. "You know why?"

No one answers, but we all feel like Dad is educating us.

"This team has had our backs more times than I can even count, so the least we can do is show them we aren't just conceited athletes. Let's not be the assholes we were just accused of being."

Chapter Fourteen
Lily

Alex will be here soon for our date, and I've never been this nervous. He wouldn't tell me where we were going, but to dress comfortably and that we would be indoors. Yeah, that tells me absolutely nothing.

After trying on half my closet, I can't see my bed anymore from all the discarded clothes. Screw it, I'm just going to wear an oversized sweater, black leggings, and my Chucks. If he shows up in a suit, I don't care. He can just be embarrassed with my outfit; it would be his fault for not giving me a dress code.

Four o'clock on the dot, my doorbell rings. I'm not going to lie, I stand frozen in place, heart racing at the thought we'll be alone tonight, without Morgan or his teammates as a buffer.

Get out of your fucking head, Lily. He's just another person. A famous person, but a person. It will all be fine.

Opening the door, my breath catches in my chest. Standing a few feet away, he is wearing black jeans and a long-sleeve grey Henley. It takes all my restraint not to reach up and touch the corners of my mouth to check for drool.

"Hey," he says softly.

"Hi, sorry. Don't mind me." I move back to hold the door open. "Come on in. I just need to grab my purse and shoes, and I'll be ready to go."

"Take your time," he calls out.

Walking out of my room, I catch him looking at the pictures lining my living room wall. The pictures of me and my parents and me and Morgan in high school.

"I'm ready," I sigh.

"Is this your scary friend?" he asks, pointing to a picture of me and Morgan on ice skates on the pond behind my childhood home.

"Yeah, that's Morgan and me freshman year in high school. She wanted me to teach her how to skate so she could impress a certain someone."

"Scottie, right?" He gives me a cocky grin.

"See, even you see that there's something going on between those two. Right?" I huff out as I bend over to put on my shoes.

"Everyone can see the sexual tension between those two, I'm guessing except those two. And the way he's defensive about her is like a macho caveman. Some of the guys on the team rile him up about it any chance they get. So if you see any of them hitting on her, know it's because they want a reaction from Scott. Unless it's Hawkins or Caddel, then your friend might want to watch out."

"That's awesome. I've been trying to get her to open her mouth and tell him for years, but she's stubborn. Maybe seeing his friends openly hit on her will give him the... push he needs."

Biting his bottom lip, he tries to hold in his laugh.

"So, are you ready to tell me where we're going yet?"

He shakes his head. "Nope, it's a surprise."

"For future reference, I hate surprises."

"Noted."

Locking the door behind us, he places his hand on the small of my back as we make our way down the flight of stairs to the road. Looking around, I expect to see a flashy sports car. I'm pleasantly surprised when he leads me to a black Lincoln Navigator. Still expensive, but not 'flash my money in your face' flashy.

Opening my door and holding out his hand, he helps me into the SUV. And even leans over, buckling me in, like I'm not capable of doing it myself before we take off. I have mixed feelings about this. I've seen it done in movies, and the woman swooned, but it only happened to me when I had too much to drink, and this is not one of those times. For now, I'd try to put it out of my mind and enjoy the evening.

"So, are you going to tell me where we're going yet?" I know I've already asked him, but I really do hate surprises, now more than ever with my stalker having returned and leaving "gifts" for me again. Turning in my seat, I watch his face for any clues. But nothing.

"Nope, like I said, it's a surprise. Do you trust me?"

"Okay. But just so you know, Morgan knows about this date, so if I disappear, you will have her to deal with," I tell him after hesitating for a second.

Reaching into the center console, he pulls out a blindfold. "Would you put this on?"

"Okay, Alex, now I need you to swear to me that you don't plan to take me somewhere and murder me."

Hitting a button on his steering wheel, a phone ringing connects through the speakers.

"Hey, dude, aren't you supposed to be on a date? Don't tell me you chickened out."

I immediately recognize the voice as Scottie.

"You're on speaker, Kasper, so don't give anything away. I asked Lily to put on a blindfold, and she's worried I'm taking her somewhere to murder her. Can you reassure her for me?"

"Hey, brat," Scottie laughs. "Alex told me all about what he has planned. I know it will be hard, but put your trust in him for tonight. You won't regret it."

"Fine. But if you don't hear from me tomorrow, you get to be the one to explain to Morgan and Jordan you said it was okay."

"I can't handle you sometimes, Lily. You need to lay off the true crime documentaries."

"You love me, Scottie."

"Bye, Kasper." Alex disconnects, cutting Scottie off. "Will you put it on now, please? We are close, and I don't want the surprise ruined."

"Yes, I guess."

"Good girl."

"Hmmmm. You really need to stop saying that to me." I breathe, hoping he can't see how the phrase physically affected me.

It was hard to tell time being blindfolded, but not too long later, we pull into a parking garage.

"Stay there, I'll come get you."

"Good, because I don't feel like falling on my face," I chide.

"Sassy, I love it," he chuckles.

Opening my door, he runs his hand down my arm before grasping my hand. Lifting me from the SUV, when both feet touch the ground, he slides an arm around my waist and guides me.

When we stop, a door opens. "Bensen, everything's all set."

"Thanks, Coach." I can feel him shifting around. "Here's a donation for your wife. Please express to her how thankful I am that she was able to make this happen on such short notice. And as we spoke about, just have her email me the details of her next fundraiser, and I'll make sure I'm available."

"Much appreciated, Bensen. Follow me, I'll take you the back way so you aren't disturbed. She was able to have the area blocked off. And the meal will be served in about thirty minutes."

Color me intrigued.

We walk for a while, and there is familiar noise all around, but I'm not able to place where we are.

When we stop, I hear a hushed conversation between Alex and, I assume, his coach. They aren't speaking loud enough for me to hear them this time.

His arm lets go of my waist, and both hands move to my shoulders. "Are you ready for me to remove your blindfold?"

"Please." The anticipation is exciting, but I'm ready to see where we are.

I prepare for my eyes to be blinded by harsh lights, but instead, I find the dim lights of a place I come to often but am normally surrounded by so many people.

"Alex, the Wild Reef? We're at the Shedd Aquarium? And alone? But how?"

He's smiling, and it melts my heart.

"The man you heard was Coach Jameson, one of our assistant coaches. His wife helps run the aquarium. So we are going to have dinner here, and you can watch the sharks for as long as you want. I thought you'd like this more than just going out to a restaurant where we'd be surrounded by people."

Unable to help myself, I launch myself into him and wrap my arms around his waist. "Thank you, Alex. No one's ever done anything like this for me before."

Rubbing his fingers down my spine, I can't help but shiver. He places his chin on my head and chuckles. "You're special, Lily, and I wanted to do something special for you. So let's just enjoy the night and each other's company."

"Okay."

Breaking apart, he takes my hand and leads me to the glass just as a sandbar shark swims by. I can't help but giggle because I'm so excited. I'm so focused on watching the sharks glide through the water that I didn't even hear that our meal was brought to the table set up a few feet from us, also near the glass.

"Lily, dinner is ready," Alex whispers in my ear.

Still keeping hold of my hand, he leads me to the table that is covered in different plates.

"I didn't know what you'd want to eat, and I didn't want to ask and ruin the surprise, so I ordered a variety."

"Everything is amazing, Alex. It's perfect."

The conversation over dinner is light and just what I needed. We talk about my job and about the hockey season. We keep away from talking about the accident or my time away from Chicago, which I appreciate.

When the plates are being cleared, Alex stands and holds out his hand. "Will you tell me about some of the animals? I was going to read up on them today, but I thought learning about them from you would be better."

That's how we spend the next hour. And he seems genuinely interested in everything I am saying, not bored at all. It is refreshing and melts my heart a little more.

"I know they said we could stay as long as we wanted, but it looks like we are holding up the cleaning crew." He points to the entrance, where two cleaning carts are sitting, waiting.

It's sweet how he thought of other people, especially knowing that he probably paid an insane amount for this date to happen.

"Yeah, let's let them do their jobs." Stopping in my tracks, he turns to look at me, confusion in his eyes.

"Everything okay?"

"I just want to thank you for this, Alex. It was perfect. It was... just perfect." Sighing, I can't believe I am suddenly tongue-tied.

Pulling me in for a hug, he kisses the top of my head. "Anything for you, Lily. You'll see. Now I need to find a way to top this."

"Yeah, right," I huff playfully.

"Challenge accepted." He smirks, and I can start to feel the walls that I spent the last four years putting up come down.

Pulling up to my apartment, I realize I don't want the night to end. When he walks away, will he come back? This is too good to be true, right? Things like this don't happen to people like me.

I turn in my seat to look at him. "Thank you for tonight, Alex. It was a night that I'll never forget."

His brows furrow. "Why does that sound like the start of a goodbye?"

Shaking my head, I try to work through my thoughts and doubts. How can I say what's on my mind without it coming out all wrong? "It's not a goodbye, Alex. But I'm a realist. You're… you, and I'm just me."

His Adam's apple bobs as he swallows. "Listen, Lily. There isn't anything "just" about you. I wish, for just a moment, that you'd be able to see yourself through my eyes. You are strong, intelligent, brave, sassy, and so much more. If anything, I'm "just" a hockey player. Nothing special."

"Alex," I whisper as I stare into his eyes, feeling like they are trying to devour me.

"Stay right there." He breaks our stare and points to my seat. Jumping out of the SUV, he's around to my door before I unbuckle my belt.

Opening my door and holding out his hand, he pulls me to his chest as my feet hit the ground. "Come on, spitfire, I'll walk you to your door."

"You don't have to," I start to protest but stop when he pulls me in tighter, reaches up, and tilts my chin so our eyes meet. "Okay," I say in an almost whisper, conceding when I see the look in his eyes.

"Good girl," he whispers right next to my ear, close enough I can feel his hot breath.

Yep, I'll be taking a long, cold shower tonight.

We stop in front of my door, standing in silence for a few seconds before Alex reaches down and grabs the keys from my hands, then unlocks my door and hands my keys back to me.

"Do you want to come in?"

"More than anything, Lily. But not tonight?"

Nodding, I don't trust myself to respond, because I feel hurt, or embarrassed, or both?

Then, I swear he mutters, "Oh, what the hell?" And his hands slide around my waist, and he pushes me against the door, mouth crashing to mine.

My brain takes a second to compute what is going on. Alex freaking Bensen is kissing me. *Me!* I want more, and apparently so does he.

Pulling my bottom lip into his mouth, he gives it a little bite. Letting out a gasp, I open, and our tongues slide together.

He moans and pushes me harder against the door.

I have no idea how long we've been pressed against my door, holding each other, in no rush to end our kiss. But when the door on the lower level slams shut, we slowly drift apart.

Dropping my head to his chest, I'm sure he feels me shiver in his embrace.

"I have a six am flight, I should probably go," he says, sounding reluctant.

"Yeah. Yeah, okay."

He places a kiss on my forehead before releasing me. "Good night, Lily."

"Good night, Alex."

As he walks away, I wonder if that kiss affected him as much as it did me.

Chapter Fifteen
Lily

> **Morgan:** You better have your ass in a cab, or you're going to miss puck drop.

> **Me:** Almost. I had to shower until my hot water ran out. I had a water rescue tonight and couldn't warm up. Leaving now.

> **Morgan:** Hurry, bitch!

Chuckling, I pull up my phone and check the status of my rideshare. They are two minutes out, so I grab my purse, lock the door behind me, and rush down the stairs. Right on time. They pull up just as I'm leaving the front door to my building.

Since all the Chicago teams are somehow all on an away schedule this week, the traffic is almost nonexistent. I just might make puck drop after all.

> **Me:** I know you won't get this until after the game, but good luck tonight. I'll be watching. (Selfie picture)

I pull up to Jordan's apartment with ten minutes to spare. "Thank you!" I yell to the driver as I hardly wait for him to come to a complete stop before jumping out of his car. I'll give him a nice tip and a five-star rating, so it will make up for my rudeness.

Thankfully, no one else is in the lobby waiting for the elevator. It's six fifty-three on a Tuesday night, so normal people are probably eating dinner.

> **Me:** I'm in the elevator.

I shoot a quick text to Morgan, and I know she's seen it because the second the elevator doors open, she's yelling down the hall, waving her arms all around.

"Let's goooooooo. They are on the ice, and it's about to start."

She's jumping up and down in the doorway to her brother's apartment, and I can hear him grumbling inside and his friends laughing.

Coming to Jordan's place has never felt like I had to dress to impress, and tonight is no different. Dressed in my Bensen jersey, black leggings, black and white Hokas, and no makeup, I walk through the front door and am greeted by the room of Jordan's friends; not one of them looks at me like I don't belong.

I hate that my mind jumps right back to the other women at the arena the other night and how they looked like they belonged on the runway and not at a hockey game. Oh, how they'd have the jokes now if they could see me. That would never be me, judging other women, or people, by how they dressed to impress the people around them.

Tattoo-covered, tree-trunk arms wrap around my waist and lift me off my feet, pulling me from my thoughts. "There she is," Jordan announces. "I swear, if you would've taken much longer, Morgan would've sent out a search party. And that's your job, not hers," he laughs.

"Don't mind him." Morgan walks up, Pina Colada in hand, "He and his friends were playing some sort of shot game where they needed to take a shot every time the female announcer said Scottie's name. So... They may be halfway to hammered, and the game hasn't even started yet. Yay."

Morgan is jealous the female announcer on the TV seems smitten with Scottie, and it's cute to see my friend riled up.

"One minute until puck drop, people," someone yells from across the room.

"Let's get a seat, ho." Morgan latches onto my arm and pulls me in front of the TV. For living alone, Jordan has a lot of seating in his living room. For as long as he's had this apartment, it's been the place we've always gone to to watch sporting events.

The puck drops, and Bear wins the face-off against the Florida Twisters, and it's off to a heated start.

Alex

Road trips used to be fun. The idea of a new city with the boys, and the adrenaline of playing in the enemies' arena, is a rush. Some players can't handle the crowd booing their names; me, I thrive on that shit, and it makes me push my body harder to prove to them

I deserve to be on the ice. That no matter how much the fans hate us, their opinions don't mean shit when it comes to how we play. We don't let the heckling get to us, unless it's from other players.

I used to search every arena for the red-headed siren that haunted my dreams. Now that I've finally found her, and she is back in Chicago and I'm going to be all over the country for the next seven days, road trips don't have the same appeal.

She did let it slip that she'd be watching all my games with Morgan and Jordan, so that made my heart race just a little. The idea of her watching my games, even if only on TV, makes me want to play harder—for her.

Game one of a seven-day road trip, and the Yetis are starting off strong. I've already made one assist, and it's only a few minutes into the first period. As a defenseman, my main job is to defend my goalie, but anytime I can help the offense score, it gets my body soaring.

Hawkins and I have been skating on the same line together for three years and can anticipate each other's moves without talking. Tonight, the Twisters are on the warpath.

With five minutes left in the second period, we are up 3-0, which has spurred the Twisters to play dirty. Tallen, the Twisters' enforcer, makes a break for our goal. Hawkins makes the charge, and I drop back to defend Knight. Tallen dekes around Hawkins, and I'm blocked by their captain, Jacobson. That's when the hit happens. Tallen doesn't take a shot; he takes the puck all the way through the net—and Knight.

Even his own home crowd doesn't know whether to cheer or stay silent as he barrels into Knight, knocking him and the net into the boards.

Chaos ensues. Not only Hawkins and I, but every Yeti sitting on the bench descends onto the ice, and a team-on-team brawl is on. The referees can't do anything but blow their whistles and pull us apart one by one.

Once everyone is separated, it takes the referees fifteen minutes to review the footage and determine that Tallen will receive a game misconduct for intentionally slamming into our goalie. He's lucky he's ejected from the game, because Caddel, our enforcer, wants blood.

Our backup goalie, O'Reilly, will be starting the third period while Knight is in the back being checked out by the medical team.

Lily

"What the fuck was that?" Jordan screams, jumping up and down on his sofa.

Morgan gasps and crawls closer to the TV to track the guys during the brawl.

And me, I half cover my eyes and try not to throw up until I know our guys are okay.

"That guy's lucky he got kicked out. Did you see Caddel? He was being held back by two coaches and Hawkins. Damn. I wouldn't want to meet him in a dark alley," Jordan blurts. "This calls for shots." He runs to the kitchen and returns with a new bottle of tequila and a line of shot glasses.

There's only forty-five seconds left in the second period.

"Hey Morgan, take a picture of me." I chuckle, tossing my phone at her.

"Ooh, ooh, ooh, if this is for Alex, lift your shirt up. I think after that fight he needs some boob action," she yells, a little too loud.

"For fuck's sake, you'll make the man forget how to skate if you do that," Jordan ribs from across the room. "Unless you want them to lose, just take a normal picture, but show off the jersey. That will give him motivation, trust me."

"Aww, look at my big brother with the wisdom."

I smooth down the jersey, turn so she could see the name on the back, and look over my shoulder. "Here." I smile.

"Work it, ho. Perfect. He's going to come in his pants," Morgan squeals.

"My classy sister, everyone," Jordan jokes.

Me: Picture sent

"Here," Morgan thrusts another shot in front of my face. "My nerves can't take this game, so more tequila."

Oh, what the hell. She has a point. Throwing back the shot, the end-of-the-period buzzer rings.

Alex: Wow, you look perfect in my jersey, spitfire.

> **Me:** Put your phone away before you get in trouble. I wanted you to see it after the game.

> **Alex:** It's sweet you worry about me. It's intermission, the only one that's going to yell at me is Bear. And yeah, he's staring at me, so I'm in trouble.

> **Me:** Naughty, naughty, man.

> **Alex:** Hmmmm. Maybe I like to be naughty.

> **Me:** Maybe I like to be naughty too.

> **Alex:** You are killing me, woman.

> **Me:** Get your head in the game, Alex. And no more fighting. I don't like to see you bloody.

> **Alex:** No promises, but I will do my best.

"What had you grinning like a fool over there?" Morgan asks, plopping down next to me, handing me another drink. I'm so going to be sick later.

"Alex was texting me. But I think he got caught by Bear, so now he's in trouble." I chuckle.

"That man has it hard for you, girl." She puts her head on my shoulder. "I'm so happy for you. Are you happy for you?"

Some people might not understand her, but I speak fluent Morgan, drunk or not. "Yeah, babe, I'm happy about it." Sighing, I can't help but let the intrusive thoughts about how he's completely out of my league run rampant through my tipsy head. I'll blame it on the tequila.

It was a good night. The guys won their game, I hung out with friends, and flirted with Alex. Nothing can ruin this high I am feeling.

Jordan orders a car to bring me home because of the amount of alcohol we consumed. He doesn't want me riding in a rideshare alone, and I appreciate his concern. Both he and Morgan beg me to just spend the night, but I just want to be back in my own apartment, and even though the bed in Jordan's guest room feels like a cloud, there's nothing like sleeping in your own bed.

As the driver pulls up to my building, I notice the light above the door is out and need to remember to email the superintendent about it in the morning. "Thank you for the ride," I tell the driver as he opens the door for me.

"Miss, would you like me to walk you to your door? Mr. Hawthorne wanted me to let you know that it is completely your choice."

"Bloody hell, that man," I groan. "No, it is okay. I will be fine. He worries too much. Go home, it's late. I'm just right upstairs. Thank you for the ride."

He nods and walks back to the driver's side door. I notice, however, that he doesn't get back into the car until I am inside my building. I will be having a conversation with Jordan about this later.

When did they add more stairs to my apartment? I want to vomit with every step. "Damn, I need some water."

Finally making it to the top, my heart threatens to stop. "I don't want to deal with this bullshit tonight."

There, right next to my door, is a fucking black box. I don't want to even look inside of it right now, but I know I have to. I wish this psychopath would just drop dead. Is that the alcohol talking? No. Well... Yes, actually. But it's true.

I never even interacted with him, and he still has a fixation on me. What the fuck? Whatever. I can't change anything in his demented brain, right?

I don't even pick the damn box up. As I open the door, I kick it inside. If it's a bomb, fuck it, it can blow up. "Hmmm. Well, look at that. I don't even need to open it up." When I kicked the box, the lid flew off, saving me the effort.

Pictures. That's what's inside this time. The pervert has been following me, taking pictures of me running, at the coffee shop with Morgan, on my date with Alex, and sitting in my seat at the stadium. That means he was that close to me.

Running to the kitchen, I'm only able to make it to the sink before all the alcohol of the night comes back up. For the record, tequila does not taste any better coming up than it did going down. Yuck.

I look back over at the box and photos now littering my living room floor. Nope, I don't have the mental capacity to analyze this tonight. I need to be sober for this, and that is not right now. I will leave all these pictures right here and deal with them in the morning.

Stumbling down the hall, I make it to my bed. I would've just slept on my sofa, but I don't want to be in the same room as the pictures. Crawling up my bed, the last thought I have is—how can I keep all this crazy away from Alex?

Chapter Sixteen
Lily

D^{*ing.*}

Ugh. Nope, nope. It's too early for whoever is messaging me. I swear, I'm never drinking tequila again. At least not finishing a bottle between Morgan and me. Why did Jordan let us drink so much?

Right. Like Jordan could stop either of us from doing anything. He learned long ago not to even try, that's why. He just gives us a safe place to be stupid.

Ding.

Oh yeah, that's why I'm awake at stupid o'clock.

Reaching around my bed, I finally find my phone in the middle under the covers.

> **Alex:** Good morning, beautiful.

> **Alex:** I just wanted to let you know I was thinking about you.

With those two text messages, my entire morning has changed. I went from wanting to hide under my covers all day to feeling like I could actually be a functioning adult. After lots of coffee, of course. And maybe a donut.

Me: Morning, Mr. Too Wide Awake.

Me: Now that I'm awake, I'm thinking about you too.

Alex: I'm sorry. Did I wake you?

Me: Yes, and now you owe me.

Alex: Hmm, what do you want, spitfire?

Me: I need to think about it. What are you willing to give me for the inconvenience?

Alex: The world. Me. Whatever you want.

Me: Stop. You can't be so sweet. Especially when you aren't here.

Alex: Our plane is about to take off, I will message you when we land.

Alex: Think about what you want. (Wink).

Me: (Kiss)

A sassy thought comes to me as I'm pouring my first cup of coffee. Knowing he's in the air and won't be able to respond for a few hours, I feel kind of safe sending the message I know won't go over well at all.

> **Me:** I thought of the FIRST way you can make it up to me for waking me up after a night of tequila with Morgan. I'd like a picture from the locker room tonight. Tell the guys towels are optional but strongly discouraged.

Four hours, one nap, and a few episodes of Criminal Minds later, and my phone starts ringing.

It's Alex. I'm not sure if I should answer it, but I know he'll just keep calling and calling if I don't.

"Hey, Alex. How was the flight?" I answer, trying to act as casual as possible.

"Don't you, 'Hey Alex' me, Liliana Sterling."

"Wow, okay. You really just full named me. What's going on, Alex?"

"You... Hmmm, minx."

I can hear him take a deep breath through the phone, and I bite the inside of my cheeks to keep from laughing. "You good, Alex? Rough flight?"

"You like to push my buttons, don't you, spitfire?"

"Whatever do you mean?"

"I'm sure I'm going to need to remind you, but I'm a jealous person, Lily. I don't share what I consider to be mine. And before you threaten to break off my balls, yes, you are a strong, independent woman, but you are *my* strong, independent woman, and I don't share. So if you think for a second I'm going to send you a picture of my friends and teammates in towels, you are playing with their lives."

"Oh, Alex. You are cute when you're jealous. But to correct you, I did say towels were optional. But will you do me a favor?"

"Anything, Lily."

"Will you growl again for me?"

"Fuck's sake. I'm not a dog, Lily. I'm on a bus on the way to the hotel, sitting next to Knight, who's looking at me like he's keeping track of our conversation so he can mock me for the rest of my life. So no, I will not do that right now."

"What do you want him to do, Lily?" Knight yells, drawing the attention of a few other teammates, who join in yelling through the phone.

"See what you started?"

"All I asked for was a little growl."

"I'll call you tonight after dinner, then I'll give you what you want."

"Yes, sir. Thank you, sir. I'll be waiting."

"Hmmm. Bye, Lily."

"Bye, handsome."

> **Scottie:** So what did you ask Alex to do? Knight wanted me to ask.

> **Me:** Fuck off, Scottie.

> **Scottie:** Love you, Lily.

Alex

After we all check into our rooms, we agree to meet downstairs for dinner before turning in for the night. Some of the other younger guys went out to a local bar; most of us have strict personal rules about game nights.

By the time I make it downstairs, Bear, Knight, Scottie, Hawkins, and Caddel are already at a table.

"Yo, Bensen, over here," Knight yells. "I was just telling the guys about your phone call from the bus. So are you going to tell us what your girl wanted you to do? Scottie tried to get it out of her, and she wouldn't tell him."

One or more of them aren't going to make it to the arena tomorrow.

"Can't you fuckers mind your own business?" Scottie grumbles into his beer. "Remember, I've known her for almost twenty years, so I'll kick your ass if you speak disrespectfully of her. And really, Knight, throwing me under the bus like that?"

"Ohhhh, we have Daddy in the group," Caddel chirps.

"I'm going back to my room," I say with a scowl, crossing my arms and looking back towards the elevators.

"Sit down, Bensen," Bear calls out as I've already turned and am a few steps away. "Caddel, next round's on you."

"Fine." He smirks as he flags down the waiter. "Worth it."

"Let's cut the shit and order food, or I'm going to go back to my room and order room service."

We order almost the entire appetizer menu. Per usual, we'd all just end up sharing everything. We've been friends long enough and done this enough times that sharing food isn't awkward.

As the food is delivered, conversation flows effortlessly.

"So, Alex, how is it going with Lily?" Knight probes, seeming genuinely interested.

"It's going well. The date the other night was a success. Coach really came through for me."

"I'm happy for you, man. And good for us, because you're not grumpy anymore," Hawkins jokes.

I pick up a fry and throw it at his head, hitting him square on the forehead.

"If y'all start a food fight in here, I'm out. I want no part of that headline and Coach's wrath," Bear clarifies.

"At least you found your girl," Knight mumbles.

"What, Knight?" Scottie asks.

"Nothing," he grumbles again.

"No, talk to us," Bear urges, pushing the wings closer to him as if that would persuade him to talk.

"Fine. While Alex has been looking for his girl everywhere we go, I've also been looking for someone. He's just been lucky to find his. I'm not jealous, man. Really," he says, turning to me. "She's out there, and I won't give up looking."

"Well, fuck, Knight," Hawkins sighs. "How long have you been looking for her?"

He looks at each of us, like he is checking to see if we are judging him. "Since we were ten years old, and her father took her away. Her name is Kinsley, and when I find her, I'm not letting her go."

"Damn, dude. That's deep. I never knew you had a heart, goalie daddy," Caddel consoles.

"I'm going to bed. That's too much emotion for me. Only my brothers have ever gotten me to talk about Kinsley, so I don't know how you fuckers got me to. See you all in the morning."

"I'll head up with you," I call out. "It's been a long day." Pulling out my wallet, I throw a pile of bills on the table. "Dinner's on me. Night, boys."

The ride in the elevator is silent. When we reach our floor, Knight clasps my shoulder, stopping me. "You know I'm not jealous of Lily, right? And I'm happy for you guys."

"You have nothing to worry about. You are my brother. If there's anything I can do to help you, just let me know. My parent's company has tech that might be able to help. Just think about it."

"Yeah. Yeah, I'll do that. Thanks, Bensen."

"See you tomorrow, Knight."

He nods his head and walks away. Once we are done with this away stretch, I'll give my dad a call and talk options to help Knight out. Just because they couldn't find Lily doesn't mean they can't find this Kinsley person. The difference is that Knight has a name, whereas I didn't.

Looking at my phone, I realize how late it is. Damn it. I stayed down with the guys longer than I expected to, so I hope Lily didn't go to sleep.

> **Me:** Are you awake?

> **Lily:** (Incoming picture)

She's lying in bed, in a Yetis hoodie, no makeup, looking so beautiful.

Hitting her number, she picks up on the first ring.

"Hello, beautiful."

"Hey, did you have a good night with the guys? Take any pictures?"

"Oh, so that's how it is? Jumping right in with the jokes?"

She laughs, "That's how it is. I need something to fantasize about while you are gone. That kiss did something to me, then you walked away."

"Lily," I growl.

"Yay, I got you to growl at me. Mission success."

"Oh, you brat." There is silence on the line. "So, what did that kiss do for you, spitfire?"

"Hmm, maybe when you get home I can show you."

"I'm going to hold you to that."

"Promise?" She yawns.

"Promise, promise, pretty girl. Now why don't you get some sleep?"

"Okay, I do have an early shift tomorrow, and Eddie will kick my ass if I fall asleep in the back room."

"If he gives you crap, just let me know. I think I can take him."

"Oh, Alex. You're adorable."
"Goodnight, Lily."
"Goodnight, Alex."

Chapter Seventeen
Lily

How did I get here? All these years, I've been fine with the idea that I didn't need a man in my life to make me happy. Now, it's only been six days without seeing Alex in person, and I feel incomplete. I'm pathetic.

The quiet used to be my solace, but now, I realize what I was feeling was loneliness, and I'd just adapted to be okay with it. I don't want just anyone to fill the void in my life—I think I want Alex. And that idea scares the hell out of me.

> **Morgan:** I'm apartment sitting for Jordan. Come watch the game with me… I have tequila.

> **Me:** You spoke the magic word. I'm grabbing my stuff and will be there soon.

Yeah, I lied to myself when I said no more tequila after the last time. Tequila never lets me down, so my relationship with her is still solid.

Having girls' night is just what I need to get my mind away from the dark thoughts.

Throwing on my Bensen jersey and grabbing my bag, I'm out the door in less than fifteen minutes and meeting the rideshare right outside the door. With two hours until puck drop, Alex will be heading to the arena with the team. Snapping a quick selfie, I send it to him.

Me: Image sent

Me: Good luck tonight.

Alex: Damn, girl, did I ever tell you how good you look in my jersey?

Me: Maybe once or twice.

Alex: Are you going to be watching tonight?

Me: Of course, I wouldn't miss it. I'm on my way to Jordan's now. Morgan is apartment sitting, and we are going to raid his liquor cabinet.

Alex: You two and all the liquor you can drink. (Insert face palm emoji) Promise me you'll be safe?

Alex: And no other boys allowed.

Me: Yes, sir. And I love your jealous side, FYI.

Alex: Lily…

> **Me:** Hmmm

> **Alex:** Call me sir next time we're together and see what happens.

> **Me:** Oh, now I'm intrigued.

> **Alex:** You may be over my knee.

> **Me:** ALEX!

> **Alex:** What? You started it.

> **Me:** Good luck tonight, you deviant.

> **Alex:** Thanks, spitfire. I'll message you after the game to see how much of Jordan's cabinet you and Morgan drank.

> **Me:** *Wink*

"It's not fair how hot he looks even in those bulky hockey pants." Morgan huffs as she lies on the floor, feet up on the sofa. Why she's looking at the TV upside down complaining, I have no idea.

"Do you ever think to just, I don't know, tell him you've been in love with him since middle school?" I chuckle and bring the cocktail to my lips, completely unphased by not only the glare my best friend is sending my way but also the pillow she whips at my head, but misses me by at least ten feet.

"You shut your mouth. He can never know. Right?" Her eyes are wide and cheeks bright red. But the redness could be from the alcohol.

If I wasn't three sheets to the wind, I would argue that she woman up and go for it. I've seen the way he looks at her when he thinks no one else is watching. I've seen it for years. They just aren't ready to admit it to each other yet, but one day they will be.

Calloway on a breakaway. It's just him against Atlanta's goaltender. And GOAL!

"Thirty seconds until the second intermission, where the hell is that pizza? And why is it so hot in here? Can we open a window?" Pulling at the jersey, I'm tempted to pull it over my head. Why are these things so damn hot?

> **Me:** FYI, tequila makes Lily's clothes come off. See.

> **Me:** Sent image.

> **Alex:** Hello, Morgan.

> **Me:** Hello, Mr. Hockey Man. Why aren't you on the ice?

> **Alex:** It's intermission. I shouldn't have my phone, but I heard a message. Are you both being safe?

> **Me:** Safe, yes, booooooo. Good??? That's relative.
>
> **Me:** Is Scottie naked?
>
> **Alex:** Well... He took his jersey off.
>
> **Me:** SEND ME A PICTURE!!!
>
> **Alex:** No, sorry. I don't want a picture of a half naked man on Lily's phone.
>
> **Me:** You suck. I'm going to get her drunker. Byyyyyee.

"Morgan, have you seen my phone?"

"Nope. Not me," she calls from the kitchen, a piece of pizza half hanging out of her mouth.

I narrow my eyes at her. "Yeah, that wasn't convincing. Ho, where is it? I want to make sure it's charged for the end of the game."

Morgan laughs. "Because you are in love with Alex and want to see his beautiful face? Or is it his dick you want to see? Do you guys have phone sex?"

"What?!" I yell at my piss drunk best friend, whipping my head to the side, seeing her sitting on the sofa. "How did you get there when you were just in the kitchen? And shut your face about phone sex."

"That wasn't a noooo," she giggles.

"Girl, I wish," I huff. "That man turns me on more than I'll ever admit."

"Jump him already. I need to live vicariously through you." Cocking her head to the side, she bats her lashes.

"I don't know if I'm ready for all that yet." What I really mean is that I'm not sure if I want him pulled into my messed up life, and the idea of the darkness surrounding me touching him in any way makes me want to disappear.

"You good, Lily?" Morgan asks with concern in her voice. When I don't answer quickly enough, she crawls across the couch and onto my lap.

"Really, Morgan?" I flick her forehead.

"Hey!"

And we're back. It's a tied game, folks. Who will take home the win?

"Let's go, boys," Morgan yells at the TV.

With the announcement of the return of the game, my chance to confess to my best friend that I'm being targeted again went out the window.

"You're right, Morgan, their asses look amazing, even in those padded pants."

"That's my girl." She jumps up and kisses my cheek.

Alex

The last game of this road trip is done, and we ended on a win. We head off the ice and down into the locker room with Coach following behind. "Bus leaves in thirty, and be in the lobby at five am for our flight home. I know most of you are as ready as I am to get home. Great job tonight, boys. It was too close for a while, but you showed them you are the superior players and deserved the win. Go celebrate, but don't be late for the checkout in the morning."

"Hell yeah, I'm ready for my own bed," Bear yells out as he's stripping for a quick shower. "Now if only we were able to get a flight out tonight."

"Anyone wanna meet at the hotel bar for a late dinner?" Hawkins calls out, already in the showers.

"I'm game," Caddel says back.

"I'm just going to order room service and go to bed. I'm beat," Knight grumbles.

Digging in my bag, I see a text from Lily. Before answering, I yell out, "Yeah, room service sounds good. That's what I'm going to do too."

Knowing that Lily and Morgan were on their way to being over the top drunk, I'm going to wait until I'm showered and dressed to respond to her. Once I message her, I'm not going to want to stop to wash my ass.

Making it the quickest shower, I'm washed and dressed in five minutes and packing my bag to load into the bus to make it back to the hotel. Pulling out my phone, I finally respond to my message.

Lily: Nice win tonight, sexy hockey man.

Me: Are you drunk, spitfire?

Lily: What? No.

Me: Send photo proof.

Lily: Image sent.

Me: Fuuuuck... Where are your pants, pretty girl?

Lily: Oh. Those things? They are going to get in the way.

Me: In the way of what?

If she says what I think she's going to say, I might cum in my pants.

Lily: In the way of me getting myself off in nothing but your jersey.

Me: I'm calling in twenty minutes. Don't you dare touch yourself before I call. We are almost to the hotel. Be a good girl.

Lily: Maybe. But no promises, sir. I really want to touch myself.

Me: Hmmm.

"Whatcha looking at?" Hawkins leans over the bus seat, trying to see my phone.

"Fuck off, Charlie, and mind your own business," I snap.

"You were looking like a kid in a candy store. I was just wondering what had you making that face." He chuckles as he sits back down.

The second the bus stops, I'm pushing my way to the front. Bear shakes his head at me but has a knowing smirk.

"Come on, come on, come on," I chant as I push the button for the elevator over and over again, knowing that it won't make it move any faster. Checking my phone for the hundredth time, I have two minutes left of the twenty I gave Lily to wait for me.

After waiting *ages* for the elevator, I finally reach my floor, only to drop my keycard four times before successfully opening my hotel room door.

The door doesn't even click shut before I send a video request.

"To what do I owe the pleasure, Mr. Bensen?" she purrs.

"Don't play with me, spitfire. I'm hanging on by a thread."

"Ooh, so what would happen if I told you I took off my panties?"

"Uggghhhh," I groan. "I need to see. Please let me see. I'll beg."

"If I show you mine, will you show me yours?" She giggles. Twisting a strand of hair around her finger.

I love seeing Lily with liquid courage. After tonight, hopefully she won't need alcohol to open up with me. "You don't need to ask me twice, darling."

She snickers, "What are you doing?"

"Getting naked." My suit jacket, shoes, and tie were discarded the second I was through the door. A few of the buttons of my dress shirt are now missing in my haste to remove it, and I end up on my floor when my foot gets caught in my pants.

"Alex!" Lily yells when my phone goes flying, landing across the room with a loud thud.

"I'm okay. One... second." Crawling across the room, I'm still kicking off my pants. "There, boxers only. Your turn, let me see those clothes go bye-bye."

With a flick of her wrist, the jersey's gone. "What clothes?"

"Fuck. Me." Running a hand over my face, I groan. "Prop your phone up, spitfire, I need to see you, and you'll need your hands."

"Yes, sir."

I watch her shift on the bed, adjusting until she's in view of her camera.

"Um, Alex. This feels a little one-sided. I'm naked, and you, sir, still have your boxers on. Not fair."

A shiver rocks through my body every time she calls me, sir. Staying where she can see me, I push my black boxers down my thighs until I'm able to use one foot to flick them all the way off.

"Better?" I ask as I wrap my fist around my cock and pump it a few times.

Her mouth drops open. "Yes, keep doing that, Alex. I want to watch."

"Fairs, fair, spitfire, I need to see you too. Let me see how wet that pussy is for me."

Smirking at the camera, she takes two of her fingers, sucks them into her mouth, and spreads her legs wide. After she removes her fingers, she runs them up the inside of her right thigh before sinking both fingers inside. Arching her back off the bed, she lets out a moan that has me increasing my speed.

"Fuck, Lily. That's so hot. Don't stop. Tell me how it feels."

"Oh, Alex. Your fingers feel so good."

"That's right, those are my fingers making you feel so good. Go a little faster, baby."

She obeys, without question.

"Alex, I need you right with me," she moans. "These are your fingers inside me, so that's my mouth on you."

She arches into her palm, breath panting, and her legs shaking. She's so close. "Come on, baby. Eyes on me."

Her heated stare locks on my hand, pumping harder on my cock. "That's it, watch me, watch you. But get there, Lily. I'm close and won't be able to hold on."

"Alex," she whimpers, "I'm coming."

"Fuck, Lily. So am I. Watch me, spitfire. This is what you wanted."

She giggles as the hot liquid covers my stomach. "That's so hot. I wish I was there to lick it off your abs."

"You'll get your chance, baby girl. I guarantee it. When I get home, the gloves come off. I'm going to show you how good we will be together." My eyes never leave the screen as I watch the sweat glisten on her skin.

"That sounds perfect. I can't wait to see you, Alex. Now go clean up before that dries on your stomach, or you fall asleep."

"Damn, how I wish you were here to help lather me up. But I'll be counting the minutes until I get back." Wagging my eyebrows at her, she giggles.

"Such a smooth talker. Good night, hockey man."

"Good night, spitfire. Dream of me."

"Like I'd dare to do anything else," she whispers before disconnecting the call.

I have her right where I want her, falling for me like I am her. This road trip is going to be a trial of my self-control, but if I play my cards right, we'll both be so hot for each other in the next few days. I can't wait to see the need in her eyes when I make her scream my name.

Chapter Eighteen
Alex

After being on a seven day road trip, the last thing I want to do is spend the evening at our favorite bar when I could be spending it alone with Lily. But after six hours of flight delays, when Bear announced dinner and beer were on him, my stomach thought it was a good idea.

"Hey, Alex, Morgan and Lily are going to meet us at Sticks. You're welcome," Scottie booms from a few aisles back.

"Yo, Scottie, when are you going to hit that?" Caddel yells from the first row of the bus.

"What the fuck did you say, Axel?" Scottie drops his bag and tries to climb over the seat to get to the young player.

"He's just joking, man," Hawkins tries to interject, popping up right next to Caddel. "But, yeah, Morgan's a hottie. Is she single? Caddel and I could show her a good time."

It's been rumored that Caddel and Hawkins have occasionally shared a puck bunny or two.

The bus is silent for three seconds before it erupts in laughter. Scottie looks like he is about to have either a heart attack or murder Caddel and Hawkins.

Caddel and Hawkins each have beaming smiles, so proud of themselves for riling up Scottie.

"Get to the restaurant, all you fuckers, or next practice will be lines until you puke," Bear roars with promise.

Bear is in the seat behind me waiting his turn to exit the bus, so I lean in close to him. "When do you think Scottie will get his head out of his ass and finally ask out Morgan?"

He doesn't even look at me when he answers. "Never. That's his best friend's little sister. He'll just torture himself, and us, for the rest of his life. Fucking idiot," Bear sighs. "Let's go. I need a drink after dealing with you children all day."

For a Tuesday night non-game night, Sticks is busy. At least Bear called and gave them a heads up that we were coming in. Reid, the owner, is a Chicago native and wanted to create an environment where athletes can feel like the regular people we are, so he opened his bar/restaurant. He prides himself on his security and allows us to have as normal of a night out as possible.

No matter where we go, we are always treated like bugs under a microscope, but here, we have tables behind a roped-off area where we can enjoy our meals without being flocked by fans. Once we leave the roped-off area, it is a fend-for-yourself situation, but at least there are boundaries. We don't always sit in this area, and some of the guys prefer the attention, but it's nice to be able to eat without having random women trying to sit in your lap.

Walking through the door with Bear and Knight, my vision goes red. "What the fuck?"

Next to me, Knight howls, having to lean over and grab his knees for support.

Bear grabs my shoulders. "Don't kill them. They are doing it to rile you up."

Lily and Morgan are sitting at the table in our area, and next to them, with their arms draped over their shoulders, are Hawkins and Caddel. Lily won't meet my eyes, but Morgan has a knowing grin.

"Lily," I rasp through gritted teeth.

"Alex. It's so nice to see you." She beams back at me.

"Can I speak to you for a minute? Alone." I reach out my hand to her.

"Of course. I'll be right back, gentlemen." She giggles as she stands and takes my hand.

Pulling her to my side, Bear calls out for me to behave. Unlikely.

"I missed you," Lily squeals as I drag her down the hall towards the restrooms.

"What are you doing, Alex?" Lily whispers as I check the door on the furthest restroom. Single stall restrooms are the best.

Pulling her through the door, I kick it shut and click the lock.

Pushing her up against the wall, my hand curves around her throat, and my thumb finds the pulse point thumping violently against her flushed skin. "You know you are playing with their lives, allowing them to put their hands on you. Did you enjoy teasing me out there, spitfire?"

"Hmmm," she moans, eyes glossing over.

"I take that as a yes. Just like you enjoyed teasing me last night on the video call, when I couldn't touch you—couldn't taste you."

"Oh, Alex," she gasps as I lift her into my arms and move across the room.

Our mouths slam together, her fingers digging into my hair, as our kiss deepens.

Placing Lily on the counter, I push back just enough to marvel at how gorgeous she looks with flushed cheeks, swollen rosy lips, and lust-filled eyes.

"We're going to need to be quick, love. So take off your pants, and lean back."

"Alex?"

"Lily. I can only take so much teasing before I snap. Now, I'm going to make you moan my name, and then we can go back out with the rest of my team and have dinner. But I'm going to have my dessert before my dinner, so take off your damn pants and get back on the counter. I won't ask again."

She hasn't moved, either because she's too turned on or shocked at what we are about to do. I choose to believe the former.

I wrap my arm around her, nuzzling her neck. "Fuck, you smell good." Trailing kisses down her neck, she shudders in my arms.

Lifting her hips, she grinds against me before wrapping her legs around me and jerking me in tight against her body. I know she can feel how hard I am through my jeans, because the second we connect, she lets out a gasp.

"This isn't going to work," I groan, pulling her off the counter and placing her on her feet.

"What..."

Before she can finish her question, I have her leggings and panties down around her ankles. "Hands on the counter, spitfire. You're going to look in the mirror and watch yourself fall apart on my fingers. Then I'm going to suck them clean, and we are going to walk back out to my team like nothing ever happened. So you're going to need to be a good girl and not scream—this time. Unless you want everyone in the bar to know what I'm doing to you."

"Alex." Her mouth opens, and she pants as I drop down to my knees. Starting from the bottom, I run both my hands up the insides of her ankles, then calves, finally to her thighs. Moving painstakingly slow. I watch her eyes grow wide in the mirror and feel her try to control her hips and keep them from grinding against me.

Reaching behind her and grasping my shirt, she tosses her head back in frustration when I skip the very heat of her and continue up her body. Wrapping my right arm around her stomach, my left hand wraps around the base of her throat.

"What do you want, Lily?"

"More. I want more."

"I need more specifics, spitfire. Do you want to fuck my hand?"

Her eyes meet mine in the mirror, hips bucking back.

"Yes, Alex. Fuck me already."

"I love it when you beg."

My right hand slides down her body, her eyes following it in the mirror. "Eyes on me, spitfire."

Trailing my mouth along the column of her throat, along her jaw, and stopping at her ear, I whisper, "You make a noise, and I'll have to stop. You drop your eyes, and I'll have to stop. Tell me you understand."

She nods.

"I need the words, Lily."

"Yes, sir."

"Hmmmm. Good girl, now eyes on me."

Her hips buck as I slide my fingers through her soaked warmth. Biting her bottom lip, she's taking my threat to heart. Not that I'd be able to stop. I knew that was a lie the moment I touched her.

Sinking one finger inside her, her head drops back against my chest. She still hasn't made a sound. Pumping slowly, a purr emanates from her chest, but I'll allow it.

I plunge a second finger, and her knees nearly buckle. "We're going to have to speed this along, Lils. We don't need anyone coming to look for us."

Hearing her take a deep breath, I pump faster and harder. Moving my left hand from her throat down to cup her breast. My thumb finds her clit, pressing.

Her walls clench my fingers, her knees shake, and I know she's close. "Let go, Lily. I can't wait to lick my fingers clean and taste you."

My words push her over the edge. "Alex," she moans, falling apart in my arms.

Keeping our eyes locked in the mirror, I remove my fingers and, one by one, lay them on my tongue, sucking them clean. "Delicious. Now let's get you cleaned up and rejoin everyone."

"Do you think they'll know what we did?" she sighs.

"Oh, no, Lily. They'll never guess," I lie, because they'll absolutely know.

Chapter Nineteen
Alex

Hawkins: Did anyone else notice Alex disappeared for a long time at dinner last night?

Caddel: Yeah, him and his red-headed hottie were gone a long time.

Bear: Thin ice, guys.

Knight: Come on, Bear, I want them to keep talking so Alex kicks their asses.

Knight: Maybe Scottie too.

Me: If you both don't shut up, you won't see next season.

Hawkins: He mustn't have gotten laid, he's grumpy.

Caddel: I swore I heard noises coming from the bathroom.

Scottie: I have a shovel and a large trunk.

Bear: No murdering the teammates.

Alex has left the chat
Scottie has left the chat
Caddel added Alex to the chat
Caddel added Scottie to the chat

Me: You are both fuckers that will have matching black eyes if you mention her again.

Caddel: Daddy Bear, will you protect us?

Bear: No.

Hawkins: Rude.

Me: Scottie, I'll pick you up in ten. Hawkins and Caddel, that means you have about twenty minutes to hide.

Knight: Run, run, as fast as you can…

Bear: You better hide the bodies. I don't want to explain to Coach why you murdered two of our own.

Caddel: Rude.

Hawkins: Yeah, rude.

Chapter Twenty
Lily

I've been anxiously waiting for tonight's game since this is the first one after the Yetis' long away game streak. Watching them on the ice, live, is just what I need. I don't know how to describe how I've been feeling lately, except that I've been more anxious than normal. Is it because I'm becoming closer to Alex? Or is it that psycho that keeps leaving me fucked-up gift boxes? If I'm honest with myself, it's probably both.

Ding.

This better be Morgan telling me she's on her way with alcohol.

> **Eddie:** Emergency. The family went down in the lake, we were called in. I'm on my way, be downstairs. Time—now.

Shit. Ripping off my jersey and jeans, I throw on leggings that I can wear under my dry suit and a few layers of long-sleeve shirts. Grabbing my purse and my shoes, I'm out the door. I put my shoes on right before I walk out the outer door and pull my phone out to start sending messages.

> **Me:** I'm sorry, I won't be able to make the game tonight.
>
> **Alex:** Are you okay?
>
> **Me:** Work emergency. Boating accident. Family. Good luck.
>
> **Alex:** Be careful.
>
> **Me:** Always.

One more message.

> **Me:** Ho, work calls, I won't be able to make it tonight.
>
> **Morgan:** Boooo, you suck.
>
> **Me:** Boating accident, family down.
>
> **Morgan:** Shit, my bad. Go save lives. Let me know you are out safe.
>
> **Me:** Always do.

And I do. Ever since Morgan witnessed what happened to me as a child, she worries constantly. Rightfully so. So to ease her worries, I've always let her know before I go into the water and the moment I'm out. If I can't do it, Eddie lets her know. Because Eddie saw how she reacted to the accident when we were eleven.

Eddie picks me up less than five minutes later. "What do we know?"

"A mayday call came in from a small vessel about a mile from Crib Lighthouse. They were taking on water. A family of five. The Coast Guard was called, but we are closer. Our boat is ready and waiting on us. All our gear is loaded and checked."

"Okay. Hopefully they aren't completely submerged by the time we get out there. But we will plan for the worst."

"This is the worst-case scenario. Let's go!" I yell over the chaos of the scene. We are the second boat on location, and the vessel that made the mayday call is almost completely submerged.

"I need to know if anyone is still missing," Eddie calls out to the other team. One child and a woman were on the other boat; a man was grabbing onto the sinking boat like he could hold it up.

"My babies are in there. Two baby girls," the frantic man calls out across, going under the water after every few words.

"Fuck," I grumble. "Give me a preserver. I'll put it over his head, then I'm going in after them."

"Lily, it won't stay afloat long. They had to have hit something for it to go down this quickly," Eddie warns. "You won't have much time. Let us anchor it, then you move."

He knew I wouldn't agree to that, even before I shake my head no. "I know the dangers, Eddie. I'll be careful. But it's little kids. This is what we are trained to do—save lives. Right?" I argue as I finish donning all my gear.

"Yeah. But I should go," he argues, looking around for his gear.

"Bullshit. You lead up here, I go down there. I can't do what you do, so let me do what I do. You know how fast I am, you made sure I'm ready. I'll get them; you trained me well. Trust me." I give him a quick hug before grabbing the life ring he's holding, and then I am falling backwards into the water.

The man in the water sees me coming. "Help them, please."

"I will, but you need to go to that boat. Put this over your head. Where in the boat are your daughters, how old are they, and are they together?" I ask in quick procession.

"They are six; they are together sleeping in the room at the front of the boat. Take the steps down and go straight. It's the door straight at the end of the hall."

"Okay, I will get them, but you need to go back."

"But..."

"No," I yell. "I can't go get them if I'm here arguing with you."

"I'm their father, they need me. They are so little and can't swim." His voice cracks with desperation.

"Listen," I order, "I, not you, am your daughters' best chance right now. I have the equipment to save them, not you. You need to get on that boat and stay safe so you can take care of them when I bring them up because they are going to be terrified and need their father. Okay?"

He rapidly nods. "Okay. Okay."

Not waiting for him to argue again, I shove the ring over his head and release the air from my vest, sinking into the darkening water, leaving him in the hands of the crew above.

Cracking a glowstick, my pulse quickens. The door the father indicated the girls were in is almost completely submerged. Thankfully, the door is a slide door, making breaching possible without going back for equipment.

Pushing the door open against the water still uses most of my energy, but the moment I break two more glow sticks, toss them inside the room, and they catch the glowing eyes of two little girls, I catch my second wind. I'd use every ounce of energy I have left to get these girls to the surface.

The second I have them in my arms, the worst thing that could happen happens—the boat takes on water in a way that throws off its vertical stability, and it begins to tip. Being submerged straight down with two little girls is already going to be a challenge, but if the boat completely tips, I don't know if I can get them out on my own.

Alex

It was another shutout, one step closer to securing our spot in the playoffs. The only thing that could've made it sweeter would've been having Lily in the stands.

"Scottie," a woman screams from the door. Not waiting for anyone to respond, Morgan comes rushing into the locker room as half the team is stepping out of the shower. "Dicks. That's a lot of dicks." She doesn't stop walking or leave; she continues looking for Scottie's locker.

"Morgan, what the fuck?" Bear yells from across the room.

"I need Scottie's car keys. My rideshare will take too long. Someone get me Scottie or his fucking keys!" she yells.

"Damn it, Morgan. I'm right here," Scottie yells, coming from the shower with a towel hanging off his waist. "Why are you in the locker room?"

"I need your keys, Scottie. Lily's missing. One of the EMTs sent me a message. She went in the water to save some children that were stuck in an overturned boat, the boat sank, and none of them came back up. Now I'm driving out to the pier. So give me the keys before I just go through your locker. You are wasting time." Morgan is now frantic.

As soon as I heard Lily's name and missing in the same sentence, I didn't care about a shower anymore. I throw on my jeans and hoodie, grab my wallet, phone, and keys, and rush over to her, grabbing her arm. "Let's go, I'll drive."

"Send me the address of which pier they're at. I'll be right behind you!" Scottie yells as we turn the corner out the door.

Chapter Twenty-One
Lily

Time is running out. I have plenty of air left in my tank, but if I don't get these girls out of the water in the next few minutes, they'll be too hypothermic and won't make it. Their little bodies can't take the temperatures. And the boat sank further than I'd anticipated. My depth gauge reads thirty feet. How the hell did this happen so quickly?

They had to have hit something for them to have sunk so quickly. Normally, they'd float due to air pockets, but that isn't the case here. We were lucky enough to find a small air pocket in the bedroom the girls were sleeping in, where I found them.

"Okay, girls. I know you are scared, but we need to go. We can't stay here any longer; it's not safe. I'm going to get you out of here so you can see your mom and dad. Okay?"

"We're scared," the one girl cried, pulling her sister into a tight hug.

"I know, baby. But listen," I gently say, pulling the tank off my back, "this is filled with oxygen. It's how you breathe underwater. These right here," I pointed to the two mouthpieces, "you place in your mouth, and you will be able to breathe. So, here's what we're going to do: I'm going to put this on my back, you will put these in your mouth, you will hold onto each other, plug your noses, close your eyes, and try to stay calm until we reach the surface. Do you think you both can do that? Be brave for me?"

They both nod. Hopefully they'll listen and not freak out as soon as their heads are under water. I'm not going to stress about something until it happens; I can't in this situation.

"Okay, I'm going to hit a button on my vest, and it's going to flash a bright light. I don't want it to frighten you; it's so the people in the boat can see us coming and grab us up when we get to the top. They will be ready to pull us out of the water. Okay?"

Again, they both nod. "You are both being so brave. You will see your parents soon. Let's go." Attaching the tank again to my back, I give them each a mouthpiece and have them test them a few times to make sure they have the hang of it. "Okay," I drop low in the water, "climb on, and each of you hold on to my vest as tight as you can with your strong arm. Don't let go no matter what. It may feel like you are being pulled in another direction, but that's just because I'm going to be swimming. Okay?"

They nod.

"Okay. Remember, eyes closed, and hold your nose closed. That will help with your breathing. Here we go."

Years of training, and it still causes me anxiety to be without the regulator in my mouth. But then again, anyone would be anxious not being able to breathe. Breaking a glow stick—that is the only light I have to navigate out from inside the boat—I start the swim to the surface. Once I clear the side, looking around, I can barely make out the spotlights being used on the boats above, watching for me to surface. That is my target. At least I am able to use the lights to tell up from down. That is the hardest part of scuba diving in the dark.

Knowing I can't rise too quickly because of the girls' little lungs, I keep my eyes on my gauge. I've been free diving for years, but never carrying two children on my back. But we'll make it. I hope.

When my gauge reads ten feet, my vision tunnels. I'm moving too slow. No, I can make it. The darkness is closing in fast. At the last second, when I know it is safe for their little lungs, I inflate my vest to full capacity, shooting us to the surface.

It's too late for me, but the girls will make it.

Alex

"Here comes a boat," I yell to Morgan, who has her back to the water, as she speaks on the phone with Scottie, telling him where we are.

"Oh no," she cries out when she turns around.

Moments later, the ambulance that has been waiting at the dock's door burst open, and two EMTs rush down the dock with a gurney, waiting for the boat to arrive.

"Morgan, what do the lights mean?" I ask, new to all this.

"Someone on the boat is injured and needs medical attention," she announces seconds before running through the parking lot and to the edge of the gated-off dock.

Eddie is the first person we see, and he has someone in his lap. Someone with long red hair, and that person isn't moving.

"Lily," Morgan wails. I've never heard such a desperate cry. The sound of Morgan's cries has my brain trying to tell my heart that this means that Lily is gone. But that is wrong, right? I just spoke to her a few hours ago.

Car doors slam behind us, but my focus won't move from the boat pulling up to the dock.

Scottie runs around me and puts his arms around Morgan just as her legs give out. Jordan runs up to me and grabs my arm. "Follow me," he commands, breaking through my fog.

We watch silently as Eddie places Lily on the gurney, and the EMTs rush her towards the ambulance waiting at the other side of the locked gate. The locked gate that separates me from the woman that owns my heart.

"Elijah," Jordan yells out. The EMT doesn't stop moving towards the ambulance, but he waves his hand so we know we can move closer. It is nice to be surrounded by people that have been in Lily's life for years.

"Jordan," Eddie calls out. I just now notice he is only steps behind the EMTs. The second I see Lily, my gaze never leaves her.

"What happened, Eddie?" Morgan demands as she and Scottie stand on Jordan's other side.

"She's going to be fine. She suffered what's called shallow water blackout. She rescued two little girls from a sunken boat by giving them her breathing supply. The girls said she was awake until right before they reached the top of the water, which is when she ran out of air and blacked out. We got her out quickly enough that she didn't stop breathing or need CPR. She woke up and was talking to us for a few seconds but was so exhausted because her body is recovering from the lack of oxygen that she fell into a deep sleep. She's going to the hospital, where she'll be at least overnight. This isn't the first time someone from the team has had this happen, and unfortunately it won't be the last."

The EMT, Elijah, explains this as they are loading her into the ambulance, but it doesn't make me feel any less terrified.

"I'm going with her," I demand, not giving them a chance to argue before I'm climbing into the back. Pulling my keys from my pocket, I toss them to Scottie. "Can you or one of the guys bring my car to the hospital?"

"Yeah, don't worry about it. Let me know what room she's in. We'll be there as soon as we run back to her apartment and pick her up some things."

"We are leaving," Elijah calls around from the driver's side door, prompting Eddie to close the door, but not before giving me a nod.

The other EMT doesn't stop moving around Lily as she speaks to me. "My name's Tess, and I'll take care of your girl. Okay?" she assures me, searching my face for approval.

"Can I hold her hand?"

"If you can give me just two minutes to get her hooked up to everything we need, then I'm sure holding her hand would bring her comfort."

Watching her place an oxygen mask, little patches on her chest, and a monitor on her finger is hard. Seeing Lily hurt and unable to help is tearing me apart. I wish there was a way to take away her pain.

My eyes never leave her face the entire time the medic works on Lily.

"You can hold her hand now." Tess's voice is soft.

Lacing my fingers through hers, I never want to let go. If it were possible to pass my strength to her, I'd give her every last drop I have. "Hold on, baby. Rest and come back to me."

Being a first responder brings different attention at the hospital than if you were just a normal person off the street. And because it got Lily the help she needed the moment she was wheeled in the doors, I'll be forever grateful they hold the people that put their lives on the line for the people of Chicago in such high regard.

There was no waiting in the emergency room for us. I was shown right to a room, while Lily was wheeled to have a cardiac MRI completed. I tried to argue that I wasn't going to leave her side, but I lost that fight when the doctor said he'd have security remove me from the hospital grounds if I didn't let them do their jobs. The threat of not being by her side made the fight leave me.

The doctors saw how hard it was for me to leave her side and promised that all other tests that could be done in her room, like the EKG, would be done there so I could be with her. Knowing

I had someone on my side made the dark thoughts I was feeling recede just a little.

Unable to sit down while she is gone, I just pace the room. It took them just over an hour to complete the MRI and bring Lily back to me. She looks so small, so fragile in the hospital bed. I hate it.

Eddie is following behind the bed, talking to the doctor. I watch the nurse hook Lily's oxygen to the wall and plug in all the other monitors.

Once the nurse is done, both she and the doctor leave the room, leaving me and Eddie alone with Lily.

"How are you doing, Alex?" Eddie inquires.

My chest feels like Bear is sitting on top of me. "Why won't she open her eyes?"

"She will, Alex, she will. Her body is tired and took a shock tonight, but she'll be okay. She's been in worse situations than this and pulled through."

Whipping my head to his, "You think that makes me feel better? That she's been hurt worse and survived? She should be treated like a goddess, my goddess, not lying in this hospital bed."

"Man, you have it bad. Does she know that you love her?"

Shaking my head, I rub the spot over my heart. "No, but I think I have for the last four years. From the moment I looked into her eyes as I laid on that bank after she pulled us from the water. There was a spark, or something; I don't know how to describe it."

"Then tell her, Alex. Make sure she knows. She's had a rough life. She's survived more pain than any one person deserves to have thrown at them. She deserves all the love she can get. You treat her right, you hear? She's like a daughter to me, and I protect her like one. I know how to make you disappear. I can make you sink faster than if you were wearing concrete shoes, so keep that in mind."

Taking in his words, I can't tell if he is joking. I kinda hope he isn't, because that would mean more protection for Lily. "I understand, and I agree. You never need to worry about me being the one to hurt her."

He takes the seat across from me, and we sit in comfortable silence for a while until he gets a call. He holds up a finger to me and quietly leaves the room.

> **Bear:** Scottie filled us in, let us know what you need. We will be at the hospital soon.

> **Me:** She still hasn't woken up.

> **Knight:** Me, Hawkins, and Axel are twenty minutes out.

> **Me:** Guys, you really don't have to come.

> **Bear:** You're our brother.

> **Hawkins:** Wait until you see what Knight got your girl. You may be second in line now.

> **Scottie:** You all better behave and not disturb her, or Morgan will cut off your balls.
>
> **Caddel:** Yes! The hottie will be there. I'll keep her calm.
>
> **Bear:** For fuck's sake.

Alex removed himself from chat
Caddel added Alex to chat

> **Caddel:** Sorry, Broski, I was just trying to make someone smile.
>
> **Scottie:** Imma punch him, Bear.
>
> **Bear:** In this case, I'll allow it.
>
> **Caddel:** Rude.
>
> **Me:** Room 1218.

Eddie left the room a little while ago to take a call and returns as I'm putting my phone away. "Has she woken up yet?"

"No. Does that mean the doctor was wrong and she's not okay?" Anxiety rips through my body.

Wiping at my face, I don't want him to see the tears I am unable to stop from coming. I'm supposed to be strong, not emotional. "Why does she do this job, Eddie? Why put herself in danger? She had to have known what could have happened when she went into the water."

"She knew, but that didn't stop her. We go over the risks before every dive. Ask her; she will tell you why she does the job. We each have our own reasons for it. But I can tell you for a fact that tonight, there are two six-year-old little girls that are alive because of her. Yes, one of us could've gone down, but the moment our boat made it out to the accident, Lily geared up and demanded she go in. She has a gift with children. One of my men, or even me for that matter, may not have been able to calm them enough to get them to the surface safely when the boat tipped and went under with them inside. But she knew how to handle the situation. And just a warning, when she wakes up and you guys talk, don't go giving her ultimatums about having her choose you or the job. Because you will not like her answer."

There is a soft knock on the door, breaking off our conversation. Morgan, Scottie, Jordan, and the rest of the team have arrived.

Morgan rushes past everyone and goes right for the computer. Probably against hospital protocol, she uses her hospital credential to pull up Lily's chart and reads through her notes. Scottie has a stupid grin on his face. "What?" I ask.

He just shakes his head and points over his shoulder at the procession of our teammates. "Oh freaking hell, guys. What did you do?"

"Do you think she'll like it?" Knight asks, holding up a four-foot Rogue stuffed animal.

"Where did you get that?"

"Well, they had one on display in the arena gift shop that wasn't really for sale. But I know how much your girl has a crush on Rogue, so I told Archie, the social media manager, that if he got it for me, we'd all do some shirtless promos and not bitch about it. So be prepared for that. I already warned the other guys; they bitched, but it's for Lily, so they'll suck it up."

"And Hawkins, what about you? What's in the bag?"

"Umm. Kinda like four different flavors of cupcakes and six other pastries. I always bring my sister baked stuff when she's sick, so I asked Knight to swing by the bakery. And since we didn't know what Lily likes, Axel and I just decided to get a bunch of stuff. I hope that's okay?"

My friend is kicking his foot around like he is embarrassed; it's adorable to see one of the fiercest hockey players in the NHL acting unsure of himself.

"Thank you, all of you. For everything. Mostly for being here and showing Lily your support when she wakes up. Why don't you put your stuff over on the table, and..."

Lily

"Do I smell chocolate?"

"Lily," Morgan screeches for a fraction of a second before landing almost in my lap. "You scared the shit out of us again."

"Huh?" I groan, straining to open my eyes against the bright lights. I was just enjoying a nap. Right? "Too bright."

"Someone turn the lights down," a strange male voice calls out from somewhere in the room.

Shooting up in the bed, everything comes back to me. The water rescue, the girls, and now I'm in the hospital surrounded by my friends and apparently half of Chicago's hockey team. I've never been more embarrassed.

A machine starts beeping erratically, the door bursts open, and a cheery looking nurse rushes in. "Oh, Nurse Hawthorne, get off my patient's bed." She shooed Morgan away from my side. "Ms. Sterling, how are you feeling? It's so nice to see you awake. Captain Carlson has been driving everyone crazy walking up and down the hall tonight," she chuckles.

Of course Eddie would still be here. "I'm fine, can I go home?"

"Oh dear, no. Not until morning I'm afraid," she tells me, as she types away on the bedside computer.

My head is swimming, but out of the corner of my eye, I see Alex, standing a few feet from my bed. "Hi."

"Hey, spitfire," he mouths. "How are you feeling?"

"I'd like my own bed, but I know they won't let me go home."

"No, probably not. You scared us, so let them make sure you're okay, and I promise I'll spring you as soon as possible."

"Deal."

"Do you need anything?"

"Um, yeah. I swore I smelled chocolate."

"I got chocolate," Hawkins yells from across the room, while Axel rushes to the table to get the bag of treats.

"Wait! I have something too!" Knight exclaims.

And so starts the fight of who brought the best gift.

Chapter Twenty-Two
Lily

It feels so good to be out of the hospital and in my own home. The support from my friends was expected, but having Alex's teammates there overwhelmed my emotions. Did I expect anyone but Morgan and Jordan to be at the hospital? No. So, when I opened my eyes and my room's every space was filled, it was a feeling of support I'd never had before.

This morning when I was released, after the doctor and Morgan, of course, confirmed my oxygen levels were holding, Alex won the argument to bring me home. Apparently, I didn't have a say in the decision, because I just wanted to grab a rideshare and not bother anyone.

I'm not sure which one, but one of his teammates brought him a duffel bag of his stuff, so after carrying me up the flight of stairs to my apartment, back down the hallway to my bedroom, picking out my pajamas, and leaving me alone only long enough to use the bathroom and change, he tucked me into bed and is now using my shower.

The idea of him naked, only feet from me, is the reason I'm unable to relax enough to fall back asleep. My body is telling me to rest, but my brain is saying to join him. The thought of paying him back for what he did to me in the bathroom at Sticks has been running on repeat since that night. What would he do if I walked into my shower and dropped to my knees?

Lost in my thoughts, I don't even hear the water shut off. Still thinking about him, water running down his chest, I'm startled when the bathroom door connected to my bedroom opens and a half-naked Alex steps into my room, towel drying his shoulder length hair. Oh, my.

"I thought you'd be sleeping by now. I tried to be quiet, so I hope I didn't keep you awake. I just didn't shower after the game last night, so I was beyond rank and don't want to stink up your apartment."

Chuckling, I force myself to look him in the eyes and not let my gaze linger. "No, I was just thinking about the rescue, and my brain wouldn't shut off." Lies, of course. I was thinking about him naked. But as I say the words, images of last night flood my vision.

"Do you want to talk about it? I'm a good listener."

"Yeah, maybe then it will stop replaying in my head." Twenty minutes later, I am in Alex's lap, his arms around me, and he is squeezing me tight.

"Can I ask you a question?"

"You can ask me anything."

"Out of all the jobs out there, why this one? I asked Eddie the same question in the hospital before you woke up, and he told me I had to ask you and that every search and rescuer has their own reasons for the job."

His fingers run up and down my arms, leaving goosebumps everywhere they touch.

Clearing my throat, I try to focus on his question instead of his touch. "He's right, we do this job for a reason. For me, this was the only job I ever wanted. When I was eleven, I fell through the ice a half mile from my house. I know I shouldn't have been playing on it, but I never listened. I wanted to go skating and didn't want to wait for my parents to get home from work. We were on the ice the week before, so surely it was still frozen solid, right? Wrong."

His grip on me tightens, like he knows where my story is going.

"Morgan was sitting on the bank and saw the ice break and my legs fall in. She couldn't get to me because the ice was cracking all around, so she ran home and told her parents what happened. Their house was closer, and unlike my parents, hers were home. They called 9-1-1, and the Search and Rescue Department came to save me. Just as I saw the lights of everyone pulling up to the pond where I was pathetically holding on by my fingertips, I remember having no more strength and letting go. As my head was fighting to stay above the water, I remember seeing a man running across the ice with a rope tied around his waist, and he dove headfirst into the hole as I sank below. I woke up in the hospital the next day. That man came to visit me in the hospital, and every day on that anniversary, I sent him a card thanking him for saving my life. He pinned the badge on my chest when I became part of the CPD Search and Rescue Team. Any guess who that man was?"

Alex shook his head.

"It was Eddie. He's the one that saved me when I was a child, and the reason I've dedicated my professional career to saving others. Am I scared every time we have a call? Hell yes. I still have flashbacks of myself going under the water, scared out of my mind, fighting to breathe. But like last night, I saved two little girls, and that makes the fear I live with worth it in my eyes."

He pulls me tight and kisses the top of my head. "Has anyone ever told you how amazing you are?"

"Maybe a few times, but it means more coming from you." Yawning, I curl into his chest.

"Why don't you lie down and get some rest?"

"Will you lie with me, Alex? I mean, if it's not too much trouble?"

"Only if I can hold you, because, well, I can't lie next to you without having you in my arms. I don't have that kind of self-control."

Slowly climbing off his lap, I stand next to the bed as he pulls the covers back. Once we are both settled, facing each other, he pulls me in tight. Arm under my shoulder, I rest my head on his chest, focusing on the beat of his heart.

"I thought I almost lost you, Lily," he whispers as I'm drifting off. "Seeing you lifeless in Eddie's arms, I was terrified."

"I'm sorry, Alex. I thought you almost lost me too. When my vision was going black, all I could think about was you."

"We need more time; I care about you so much. You're mine, right? Please let me call you mine."

"Am I? Just yours?"

"Four years ago, you became mine, Lily. Whether you know it or not."

"Okay, Alex. I'm yours, and you're mine." Snuggling down into the blankets, closing my eyes, I whisper, "Just know I'm a jealous person and will stab a bitch if they touch you. That's what it means if you call yourself mine."

"Hmmm, I like the sound of that, my little spitfire. Now sleep. I'm here with you."

Chapter Twenty-Three
Lily

"Alex, I am coming to the game, and that is final. I'd think you'd want me there," I protest, trying not to throw the chocolate chip muffin that is sitting on the plate in front of me at him.

"It's not that I don't want you there, Lily. Fuck." Running his hands through his hair, he turns to the coffee pot, pouring us each a cup, before turning back to finish his argument. "But you were in the hospital only last week. Are you really up for going?"

"I swear on all your hockey equipment that if you continue to treat me like a damsel in distress, I will burn my Bensen jersey and wear Hawkins instead. How about that?"

His nostrils flare as he stalks around the island.

Maybe I pushed a little too far?

"Now listen closely, Liliana Sterling, if you ever wear any other man's jersey besides mine, you are playing with their lives. Do you understand?"

Biting my lower lip, I try not to laugh. "Well then, you better not look in the back of my closet."

"What the hell do you mean?" he practically shouts, whipping his head towards my room.

"You need to understand, Alex, I grew up being a fan of the Yetis. I've been a fan longer than you've been on the team. So I may have some other players' jerseys. But I promise, I haven't worn anyone else's since you gave me yours." I bat my eyelashes at him, trying to act innocent.

"Who's?" He leans around me and looks back at the hallway.

"What?"

"Whose jerseys are in your closet? Or should I just go look?"

"Fine." I sigh loudly. "Of course I have Scottie's, I've known him for ages."

He nods and shrugs his shoulders like he expected that one.

"I also have Bear's, Knight's, Coach Reyes's from when he played, oh, and Calloway's."

"But not Hawkin's or Caddel's, right?"

I give him a bright smile. "Would it make you jealous if I did?"

"I would kill them if you did," he says matter-of-factly. "They came to the team after me."

"No, Alex, I don't have either of theirs. I promise."

"Hmmm. Okay. But I still don't like the idea of you coming tonight unless you are one hundred percent sure you are okay."

"Alex, I'm going to work tomorrow, so yeah, I'm sure I can go to a game tonight. I'm just going to sit my butt in the seat and cheer you on. Okay?"

"Work? No, Lily."

"Yes, Alex. It's been a week; I can't sit in this apartment and watch TV anymore. I'm going out of my mind."

Not saying another word, he pinches his lips together and just stares into my eyes. "I'm going to drink my coffee, then jump into the shower. I need to head to the arena soon."

"Fine, Mr. Grumpy Pants."

"I'll show you grumpy pants," he grumbles under his breath. I let it go, wanting this to just be over and done with. He doesn't need the added stress on game day.

We finish breakfast in silence. I can see his eyes darting to mine every few seconds, and it takes everything I have, but I hold in my smile.

After taking his last sip of coffee, he stands and moves to place the mug in the dishwasher. "Are you sure you don't want to join me for a quick shower?" He smirks, lifting his eyebrows.

"There would be nothing quick about it if I joined you. So you go, babe. I need to call Morgan and confirm she's going to pick me up for the game tonight."

Walking down the hall, I lean against the wall outside my own bedroom door. Once I hear the water turn on, I pull my phone out and give it sixty seconds. Once that time is up, I walk into my bedroom, strip my tank top and sleep shorts, and push through the bathroom door.

"Lily," he says my name softly, peeking over his shoulder at me standing just inside the door. "What are you doing, spitfire?"

Padding deeper into the bathroom, I don't say anything until I'm standing right next to the glass door. "I thought I'd join you."

"Well, get in here then, gorgeous. I'll wash your back."

"That's not what I had in mind."

"Hmmm. Is that so?" His voice is rough and deep. "What did you have in mind then?"

Dropping to my knees in front of him, I don't give him a chance to stop me. I wrap my hand around his length and slide my tongue from shaft to tip.

"Lily," he growls, placing one hand on the back of my head and the other against the wall.

His growl is like music to my ears, and it spurs me on. Closing my mouth over the head of his cock and circling my tongue on the underside, Alex pulls back slightly, but I won't let him pull out. Digging my nails into his ass, I moan against his cock, and he groans. Letting me know he's enjoying it.

Taking him further down my throat, I swallow more of him. His fingers weave through my hair, giving a little tug.

"Lily, I'm not going to last."

Reluctantly pulling my mouth off him, I huskily tell him, "Take over, Alex."

"I don't know, Lily. I might not be able to be gentle."

I reach back and squeeze his hand. "Fuck. My. Face. Alex."

His eyes are full of lust as he lets go, shoving his cock down my throat. I choke, but I don't tell him to stop. Tears spring to my eyes, I can't breathe, but somehow I feel cherished.

The grip on my hair tightens as the hand that was on the wall moves down to cup my cheek. As I swallow around him one last time, he lets out a guttural sound as he spills down my throat.

"Fuuuuuuucking helllll," he moans.

His thrusts slow as I swallow everything he has to give me. Coming down from his high, his chest heaves.

Pulling me to my feet, he kisses me hard, taking my breath away. "Your turn, spitfire."

"Nope." That was just for you. It's game time, remember. I gotta go call Morgan. I'll see you when you get out." I tap his chest and rush out of the shower all bubbly before he can process what I did.

"You fucking brat," he calls out behind me, and I can't help but smile.

You know what they say about hockey players and pre-game superstitions, right? If they change one thing, and they play one of their best games, they need to keep doing that one thing. So I'm just waiting for Alex to tell me he now needs pre-game blow jobs.

It would be my pleasure, sir.

Morgan and I are sitting in Jordan's season ticket seats again. I asked him why he even got them if he wouldn't have been able to make so many. But he just gave me a long speech about being on a list and blah, blah, blah. Whatever. At least Morgan and I benefit from them. Not like neither Alex nor Scottie wouldn't have given us their player seats if we needed them, but Jordan's seats are better.

The Yetis have been on fire tonight. Alex and Hawkins haven't let a single player near Knight during their shifts, and there's only three minutes left in the game. It's not like they are playing a low ranking team either. This team from North Carolina is only seated two ranks below Chicago, so it should've been a closer game.

As it stands, the score is 4-0, and the Yetis aren't letting up. Determined to have a shutout game, every player is giving it their all.

Every time Alex skates past our seats, we lock eyes, and he gives me the cheekiest grin. I know exactly what he's thinking about, because it's what I'm thinking about.

"Will you pick your jaw off the ground? It's embarrassing. What did you do to that poor man?" Morgan groans, disgusted, but I know it's all an act.

"No can do, sweet cheeks." Smacking her ass, I draw the attention of a group of college guys sitting behind us.

"That was hot, do it again," one of them yells.

"Yeah, grab her ass," another one yells, this time tossing popcorn all over us.

The spectacle draws the unwanted attention of the jumbotron attendant, which has the crowd riled up, and as the end-of-the-game buzzer rings, instead of the team celebrating, they are skating over to the glass next to our seats to come to our unneeded rescue.

"Come on, smack her ass," two of the drunk morons try to chant but are cut off by another one of their friends when they see what is on the other side of the glass.

"Dude—look."

"Hey, do you think they'll toss me a puck?"

Turning around and pulling my attention from the frat boys, I see not only Alex and Scottie, but also Bear, Knight, Hawkins, Caddel, and three other players standing there with murderous glares, eyes locking on the guys behind us.

Tapping Morgan on the shoulder, she whips around and starts laughing. "It was fun, boys. Y'all have a good night." She bends to pick up her stuff; I do the same.

The frat boys are still locked in place.

We make our way across the glass to where a Yetis employee calls out our names. I recognize him as the social media manager. "Evening, ladies. Coach Reyes asked me to rush over here and escort you back and away from those... fans. He's worried that if they continue to be in your proximity, one or more of his players may want to talk to them with their fists. And he doesn't feel like making a trip downtown to post bail tonight. So, yeah. Here I am. Please follow me."

Morgan, sassy as ever, and probably because she saw Scottie standing only a few feet away, throws her arms around this poor man's neck and shouts, "My knight in shining armor. Oh, how can I ever thank you for saving the day?"

He looks like he is going to throw up. His eyes lock with the hockey players, and his arms shoot to the sky. "You are going to get me killed, darling."

"It's okay, Archie. That's just Morgan," Scottie remarks, and he passes them and makes his way to the locker room. "She's just trying to rile us up."

Smirking, Morgan nods, confirming what Scottie said is true.

"Hey, spitfire," Alex whispers in my ear.

"Hmmm. Great game, Alex. You all did amazing."

"Thanks, baby." His grin immediately makes my panties wet. "Hey, my parents and sister are here and want to take us to dinner. What do you say?"

His sister? Oh, no. It feels like all the air is sucked from my lungs.

"Bensen, stop flirting with your girl and get your ass in the locker room," Coach Reyes shouts from the door.

"Wait for me, Lily."

"I…" I gasp. "I have work really early; I should go home. I'm sorry. It was a great game. Amazing. I'll call you later."

He can see the panic in my eyes and hear it in my voice. "Lily, please," he calls out. But I don't turn or stop. Picking up the pace, I am practically running by the time I make it to the parking lot. Knowing Morgan will be worried about me, I shot off a text that I caught a ride home and would talk to her when I got home. She messages back that Scottie will give her a ride, because he's just going to head home too.

Game nights are always harder to get a rideshare, so I start walking down the street, hoping to be out of sight before Alex comes out looking for me. Was it fair that I freaked out and ran away? No, it really wasn't. He's told me so many times that his sister doesn't blame me for what happened that night, but the thought of seeing her in person made me feel like I was about to have a panic attack.

My phone beeps, letting me know my ride is about to pull up.

Tomorrow I'll call Alex and try to explain my reaction and hope that he can forgive me.

"Thank you," I say to my rideshare driver. Looking up at my apartment, I am wondering if it is too late to text Alex and let him know I changed my mind about dinner. I could see hurt in his eyes when I panicked about dinner with his parents and sister, but after the team's over-the-top display against the frat boys that is already trending on social media and will no doubt be on ESPN in the morning, my nerves are a little tight.

I should've told Morgan about my visitor. She said she was just heading home because she had a stupid early nurses meeting, so maybe I'll give her a call right now, while I have the nerve.

My legs feel like lead as I start up my flight of steps, pulling out my phone. I swear, when I find something permanent, it will either have an elevator or be on the first floor. Morgan answers on the first ring, "Hey, ho, what's up?"

"Hey, girl. I'm just getting home, and I have something I need to talk to you about."

"That sounds ominous. Do I need wine for this talk?" She lets out a nervous laugh.

"Well, you'll probably need something stronger once I tell you what I've been keeping from you."

"Girl, are you going to have baby Bensens running around? OMG! Please tell me yes. Those would be some gorgeous ass babies, and I would make the best Auntie Morgan."

"Fuck you, Morgan. I'm not pregnant. This is serious."

"Okay, okay, I'm just joking. So what do you need to tell me?" Silence. "Hello, Lily?"

"Uh, Morgan... I think someone broke into my apartment. I just got home, and the door is open."

I can hear a lot of noise on the other end, but I'm focusing on it. "Lily, did you hear what I said? I'm calling the police. Get out of there and get outside. LILY!"

A shadow rushes out of my apartment door, and before I can turn and run, a blinding pain sears through my head, and I go down hard.

"You tell that little hockey player to keep his hands to himself. You don't belong to him. You belong to me."

"The police are coming, asshole. You leave her alone. They are less than a minute away. Do you hear me? You leave her alone," Morgan screams through the phone. I try to focus on her voice and not the hands that are on my body. My vision is going black, and I know once I am out, I will be at his mercy. I need to stay conscious as long as possible. Don't any of my neighbors hear the commotion?

Finally, I hear the sirens, and so does my attacker.

"I'll be back for you. I'll be watching."

When the door at the bottom of the stairs slams shut, only then do I allow myself to close my eyes and rest.

Chapter Twenty-Four
Alex

> **Scottie:** Missed Call

> **Scottie:** Missed Call

> **Scottie:** Hey man, where are you at? Call me.

Pulling my phone from my pocket for the third time in two minutes, I silence it again. I never answer my phone when I'm having dinner with my family. It's a respect thing.

"Everything okay, son?" my dad asks.

"Yeah, I'm sure it is. It's one of my teammates. They're probably at the bar, wanting me to come out with them. I'll call him when I'm done here. No rush."

Just as I'm about to ask my sister about school, my phone goes off again. I'm about to just turn it off until I see the message and my blood turns cold.

> **Bear:** Call Scottie, 911.

"Mom, Dad, I need to step out and make a call really quick; I'll be right back."

I can see the concern on their faces, but right now, I just need to get outside. Something is terribly wrong; I can just feel it now.

Hitting Scottie's number, it only rings once before his frantic voice is on the line.

"Alex, where are you right now?"

"Scottie, I'm at dinner with my parents. Breathe and tell me what's going on."

"Send me your address. Bear is going to pick you up."

"Tell me what's going on."

"Address first. Or I won't tell you anything."

"Scottie, you are pissing me the fuck off. What's going on?"

"I'm not playing games, Alex. Text me the address now, or I'll hang up. I don't have time for this."

"Fine." Typing out the name of the restaurant and looking at the door for the street number, I send the message. "There, dick."

"One second." I can hear him typing. "Okay, Bear is five minutes out. Get your shit, say goodbye to your parents, and wait for him by the curb."

"I'm done with your word game bullshit, dude. Tell me what the fuck's going on."

"Do you promise not to get into your car, and you'll wait for Bear? Bear said he will knock you the fuck out if you try to drive."

"Who was hurt, Scottie? Tell me."

"It was Lily. She was attacked tonight. But I'm not telling you where she is. Bear has the address. I don't need you killing yourself getting to her. You know Bear will break every traffic law to get you here, but we need you alive. She needs you, and she needs you in one piece."

"How bad is she, Scottie? I need the truth."

"Morgan is with her. She was on the phone with her when it happened. She said she's hurt but more scared. Just get your shit and watch for Bear."

Stumbling into the restaurant, my parents stand as soon as they see me coming. "Son, what's wrong?" Dad asks, trying to stay calm.

"It's Lily," I moan, almost sounding in pain.

A hand comes down on my shoulder. "What about her, Alex?"

"She was attacked." Ripping my jacket off the chair, I turn to rush out.

"You can't drive like this. Wait for me," Dad argues.

"Bear's on his way to pick me up. Scottie wouldn't tell me where she is, because he knew I'd do anything to get to her." Tears roll down my face. "Dad, she's hurt. Someone hurt her."

"Go, Alex. Let us know that she's okay and what we can do to help," Mom whispers and gives me a hug. "We love you. Go."

Running out the door, ignoring the disgruntled looks from the other diners, Bear is waiting at the curb for me.

We make it a few blocks before my choked back sob breaks the silence. "Scottie called me as soon as he hung up with you. They are still at her apartment. She's refusing to go to the hospital, and against medical advice, she signed a refusal of care. Her boss showed up and brought one of their co-workers; he's fixing her up inside. That was her compromise."

When I don't say anything, he puts his hand on my shoulder. "Did you hear me, Alex? If it was life-threatening, they would've taken her to the hospital anyway. She's going to be okay. Everyone that cares about her will make sure of it."

"How Bear? How did it happen?"

"Morgan said he was inside her apartment when she came home."

"He was inside her home? The place she's supposed to feel safe? He touched her, hurt her. I want to kill him," I roar, slamming my fists against my thighs.

"I'm saying this as someone that's been your friend for years. Do not go in there acting like an overprotective asshole. That's not what Lily is going to need right now. She's going to need support, understanding of her decisions, and validation. Inside, you can be rebelling against everything she's saying, but those words better not come out of your mouth."

He continues, his voice hardening. "Her sanctuary was violated today, and you will be there to help pick up the pieces, but only if you can keep your anger in check. You lean on your brothers, and we will help avenge her. You got it?"

I swallow hard, feeling my heart thump hard in my chest. Can I stand back and accept help from my brothers when I want them as far away from this as possible? Yes, because I'd do it for them, and they won't let me push them all the way out.

"Fine," my voice drops, "thank you, Bear."

"No thanks needed between family. We're here. Take a breath and get your head on straight, then let's go see your girl."

"Eddie, I swear on your mother, if you mention leaving Chicago one more time, I will stab you in the eye, and I don't care who hears me threaten it," Lily screams.

Eddie screams back. "Damn it, Lily, you were attacked. In your own fucking home. And I'd ask you if this was the first time he's contacted you, but I know your ass would lie to me."

What did we walk into? This is not at all what I was expecting. The door is wide open; Jordan and Scottie stand right inside, blocking the view of my girl. But boy could I hear her. I don't appreciate the way her friend is yelling at her and am about to push through Jordan and Scottie when Morgan catches my eyes and shakes her head.

"Elijah, how bad is the back of her head? Does she need stitches? Do I need to throw her ass over my shoulder and take her to the ER kicking and screaming?" Eddie asks.

A man answers, whose voice I recognize from the night of the boating accident; it's the EMT, Elijah. "It's not good, Eddie, but I can patch her up here if she'd keep her ass still. And yes, she will need stitches unless she wants an infection, and if that happens, they can shave her head at the hospital," he chuckles.

"I'm going to kill both of you. Jordan," she calls out, "get me a gun, or a really big knife."

"Yeah, I'm not getting involved, darling. I'm going to stay way over here with Scottie, out of striking distance." Jordan put his hands up in surrender.

"Cowards," she grumbles. "Elijah, just hurry up. I need to get cleaned up so I can kick everyone out of my apartment. I want to go to bed, and there are too many people in my apartment right now."

"You are not staying here, Liliana Sterling, and that's final," Eddie bellows.

"See," Bear leaned in close to my ear, "that's how you are *not* going to act."

I nod in agreement. I didn't understand what he meant at first, but seeing how Eddie is talking to her and how she is taking it, Bear is right.

"But how about instead of lurking, we go let her know we are here?" Bear whispers.

"Yeah, yeah, okay." Pushing past Jordan and Scottie, I beeline right for her.

There is something in her eyes when they lock on mine. Relief?

"Alex? What are you doing here?"

Dropping to my knee beside her, I take a second to run my eyes over her body, taking stock of her injuries. "Scottie called me, spitfire, and there's nowhere else I'd be if you need me. What do you need?"

"I... I don't know, Alex."

She sounds defeated. A complete one-eighty from the hellion she was just seconds before. "Hey," I rub my hand on her thigh, "it's okay, talk to me. What do you need?"

"I'm scared he's going to come back."

"Okay, would you like Morgan to pack you a bag, and we can get you somewhere safe tonight? Then tomorrow, after a good night's sleep, you can make a decision on what you want to do next?"

"You won't make me leave Chicago, will you?"

"Baby, no. If you leave, I leave. So how about that overnight bag, and tomorrow we discuss options?"

She nods. "Yes, that sounds good."

"I'm on it," Morgan yells, already moving down the hall.

Jordan steps forward. "She can stay with me, she's already comfortable at my place. She stays there all the time. She practically has her own room."

Eddie shakes his head. "No, I think it would be safer for her to stay with me for now. My neighbor is a cop, and since she won't leave Chicago, she'll be better protected there."

"Are you saying I can't protect her, Eddie?" Jordan takes a step closer to Eddie.

"Cut your shit, Jordan. You know that's not what I'm saying," Eddie grits out.

"What the fuck, Liliana?" Morgan screams from down the hall.

"What did I do now?" Lily groans.

All eyes turn to Lily as Morgan comes barreling down the hall, arms overflowing with boxes.

"Oh, shit. I can explain those," she grimaces.

"It had better be good, because there's more in the closet," Morgan says, dropping the boxes at her feet. Lids open, and the items scatter on the floor.

Everyone but me seems to know exactly what the boxes mean.

"I need a forensics team at Liliana Sterling's apartment. She has been receiving items from her stalker and not telling anyone about it. Maybe the team can get fingerprints, and you guys can finally catch this asshole," Eddie continues to talk to someone on his cellphone as he walks out into the hallway.

"When did this start, Lily?" Jordan asks, arms crossed over his chest, body rigid, but a look of devastation on his face. If Scottie hadn't already explained that Jordan had practically watched Lily grow up and is like a brother to her, protecting her and offering her a place to live to finish high school after her parents were killed by a drunk driver, I'd think he had more than friendly feelings for my girl.

Not that I like the idea of her taking comfort with another man now that I am in her life, but there are certain men I can't make disappear just for having an association with Lily. That would upset her, and that would be unacceptable.

"Lily?" Morgan cries. "When did it start?"

"Fuck, Morgan. The first one showed up on my doorstep just two days after I got back into town. The night you came and took me to the first Yetis game. It was waiting right next to my door when I got home, and they haven't stopped since. Is that what you want to hear? I've been hiding it the entire time?"

She drops to her knees in front of her friend, and next to me still on my knees, unwilling to move. "Why didn't you tell me?"

"Because I just got back, and I didn't want to leave again. You know I was miserable all those years I was gone. Chicago is my home, and I was run out of it over fear. In my delusional head, I thought I could handle him myself and not involve any of you. I wasn't just hiding away all those years I was gone. I took any self-defense course I could get my hands on. But then again, nothing prepared me for him to come out of the shadows and blindside me. I'm so stupid."

Anger sears through me. "No, Lily. You can't think like that. Even someone my size, being blindsided, would be unprepared."

She scoffs.

"Lily," it's Bear that speaks next. "Alex is right. From what Scottie said Morgan heard on the phone, even if you sprinted out of here the second you noticed the door unsecure, he had the element of surprise on his side. You never expected him in your home. Give yourself some grace, and let those that care about you protect you. We don't want you to leave Chicago either, but more importantly, we don't want you to lose your life."

"Thank you, Bear," Lily whispers. "Fine." Grasping my hand, she lifts her head to look into my eyes. "Alex, are you sure it wouldn't be an inconvenience to stay with you for a few days? I don't want to impose."

Scottie howls, and Morgan giggles. "I can guarantee it will be no inconvenience, Lily. Though I'm sure you'll find his guest room is under construction, so you might need to share his bed," Scottie chuckles, and Lily's cheeks turn the most beautiful shade of scarlet.

I will do whatever it takes to protect the woman who has my heart. Including sharing my bed with her.

Chapter Twenty-Five
Lily

It took Morgan all of five minutes to pack my bags and kick me out of my own apartment. She said the energy was now tainted, and we needed to remove ourselves as soon as possible.

"You're quiet over there."

How long was I staring out the window, lost in thought? "Sorry, just a lot on my mind right now." I offer a forced smile.

Reaching over the center console, he grasps my knee and gives it a squeeze. Why does that small action send heat directly between my legs?

"I'm glad you took me up on my offer to come stay with me for a bit. I want you to feel as comfortable as possible, while your safety is top priority. Think of my apartment as yours."

"I'll try to make it so you don't even know I'm here, Alex. I don't want to interrupt your life more than having me here already will."

"Oh, cut that shit out, Lily. You're mine, right? And the idea of having you in my home—well, I couldn't think of anything I want more."

The intensity in his voice gives me chills. But the best kind of chills. "Thank you, Alex. And yes, I'm yours," I whisper.

We ride in silence for another ten minutes before we are pulling into an underground garage. "We are home, Lily."

Home. That's such a wondrous idea. I can only dream of living in a place like this one day.

Alex grabs my bags and we make our way to the elevator. "Tomorrow I'll introduce you to Roger. His title is the head doorman of the building, but in reality, he's the one who runs everything. He's going to be enamored by you."

I chuckle. "Enamored? That's a little far-fetched, don't you think?"

"Oh no, you should see the way he talks to the ladies. He's a smooth talker, just a warning. But he makes sure the building is safe. In all the years I've lived here, neither myself nor my teammates have had any issues with paparazzi or puck bunnies being about to sneak into the building and disturbing us at home. He runs a tight ship, and we all appreciate him."

"He sounds great. Maybe if my building had one of those, tonight never would've happened."

"Now you don't have to worry about that here, spitfire. No one will breach this building, so I just want you to focus on healing and resting."

"That sounds refreshing—not having to worry about unwanted things being left on my doorstep."

"Yeah, about that. I got the impression Morgan still wants answers about those, but I fought her off for now. But it's probably only a delay in the inevitable. Just be aware."

"You fought off Morgan. Sorry, Mr. Big Bad Hockey Player, but I think if she wanted a battle, you'd be on the losing end. It sounds like she conceded for now, which, from past experience, won't last long."

The topic ends as the elevator stops on the top floor. "Here we are," he says, as he unlocks the door and steps aside for me to walk in first.

If I could describe his apartment in one word, it would be homey. It's not at all what I imagined a single, professional hockey player's apartment to look like. Right next to the front door is a row of family photos. Candid shots of Alex and Julie, his younger sister. He comes from a close, loving family, and it shows. It makes me miss my parents even more.

The kitchen and living room are one big connected space. I'm in love with the open concept. And the windows that line the walls are a dream. The view draws me in, and I'm pulled across the room, wanting to experience the Chicago nightlife from thirty stories high.

"Alex, your home is gorgeous."

"You say that like you didn't expect it."

"I didn't. I expected you to live like a bachelor. There's no keg in the corner, or gaming systems everywhere."

"Well, the gaming systems, and there are a few, are in the home theater, but I have them stored away when not in use. Julie likes to try to beat me in Mario Kart when she comes over."

Turning to face him. "Who are you?" I chuckle.

"Come on." He walks over and grabs my hand. "It's been a long night, let me show you the guest room so you can get some rest."

The guest room is, in fact, not under construction. Not that I would've minded sharing a bed with Alex.

Walking past the kitchen, there aren't dirty dishes everywhere, and every surface looks clean. He came from dinner with his family, right after the hockey game. So he didn't have time to come home and clean before coming to my apartment, so this isn't for show. Maybe he has someone come in and clean for him. Most professional athletes do. I know Scottie has someone come three times a week because Morgan is always giving him crap for not being able to clean up after himself.

"Damn, Alex. Your kitchen is amazing. Do you think you'd let me cook in it sometime?"

Spinning me and pushing my back against the wall, he leans in until we are nose to nose. "Baby, you can have the kitchen if you want it. Hell, you can have the entire apartment. Anything you want, it's yours."

I gulp, not sure if he is joking or not. "Alex, you can't say things like that?"

"Why not, spitfire? We already determined you're mine and I'm yours. That includes everything I own." He flashes his panty dropping, charming ass grin.

"You're ridiculous."

"Only for you, baby." Leaning in, he kisses the tip of my nose before moving back, grabbing my hand, and continuing down the hall.

"Do you want a tour?" he asks, watching my eyes dart around.

"Actually, can we do that tomorrow? I think I'd just like a shower and to go to bed. Tonight is starting to catch up to me."

"Anything you need. But what about a bath instead? Your EMT friend said you can't get the stitches on your head wet tonight even though he covered them with liquid bandage."

"Yeah, a bath sounds lovely. But it will need to be a quick one so I don't fall asleep."

Picking me up, I wrap my legs around his waist. "Alex, what are you doing?"

"Just go with it, Lily."

He turns around, and we walk in the opposite direction down the hall. As he opens the door, I immediately know it's his bedroom. It's very masculine. The walls are painted a light gray, the same color as the entryway. The bed in the middle of the room is massive to fit his large athletic frame. What surprises me is how spotless everything is . But after seeing the parts of the apartment that I have, it shouldn't. The best part—it smells like him.

We don't stop in his bedroom but continue to an open door on the far wall. It is his ensuite bathroom. When I say his tub is what dreams are made of, I mean my dreams, or every girl's dreams. It could easily fit four people, or at least two of Alex.

I gasp. "Oh, wow."

"I'm guessing you aren't talking about me." He chuckles as he sets me on the sink, then walks over to turn the water on.

"Sir. Do you know what that tub does to me?"

"I'm hoping to find out someday soon, but not tonight."

"You won't get in with me?" I bite my lip.

His brows furrow slightly. "I'd love nothing more, but not tonight. I can be a gentleman. Not often, but when it's needed. Tonight, you need to relax, do a quick wash, then get a good night's sleep."

"But what if I don't want you to be a gentleman, Alex? What if I need you to want more?"

"Lily," he growls. "You're killing me. I'm trying to do the right thing tonight. Ask me tomorrow, and I'll show you how ungentlemanly I can be."

A shiver runs down my spine. "Promise?"

He shuts off the water, stands, and stalks towards me. "Promise, promise."

Helping me off the counter, he sets me on my feet. "Now why don't you get in the tub, I'll get you some of my clothes, and I'll be back to check on you."

"I have my own clothes, Alex. Morgan packed my bag."

"I know." A deep chuckle escapes him as he turns to leave.

"Can you help me?" My request comes out barely above a whisper.

"What's wrong, spitfire?" His brows furrow with worry.

"I'm sorry, Alex. But can you just help me pull my shirt off? I don't want it to hit the back of my head."

"Anything for you, love."

Alex smiles reassuringly as he tugs on the bottom of my shirt. "Arms up. I won't let it touch your head."

I obey, and he does as he promises.

"Hmm," he coughs out, pointing to the door, "I'm going to..."

He rushes out the door before he can finish his sentence. Once the door shuts behind him, I allow a small chuckle to slip out.

Climbing into the tub is heaven. The water is hot enough to ease my tense muscles. I'll just lean back and close my eyes for a few minutes and enjoy the temperature before I start to wash.

I use his soap to wash, I love that I now smell like him. In a weird way it is comforting. Just as I pull the plug, Alex returns with an armful of clothes and a fluffy white towel.

"Up you go," he says, helping me to my feet and pulling me from the tub, trying to keep his gaze averted from my naked body. Thankfully he isn't looking at my body as he wraps me in a towel. The scar down my leg would definitely be a turn off, and I'm not ready to see his response to it.

After I'm dried off, I look at the clothes in his hands. "Um, Alex. Where are my clothes? I told you I had my own."

"I thought with your head, it would be easier for you to wear one of my button-ups, and then I just grabbed you a pair of my sweatpants. If you saw what Morgan packed you, you might agree with me. You'd practically be naked. I think she had an agenda when she packed that bag, and it was to get Lily laid."

"Oh, Morgan," I laugh.

"Oh, I fully agree with her if that was her plan, but not tonight." After I have his clothes on, he wraps me in his arms and carries me, unfortunately, to the guest room.

"You know, I might be more comfortable in your bed." I look at him with what I hope are puppy dog eyes.

"I'm sure you would be, but I still wouldn't be in there with you, you siren. So stop trying to get my dick." Laying me gently on the bed, he covers me up to my chin before saying, "No means no, Lily."

I let out a giggle. "Fuck you, Alex."

"You have no idea how much I want you too, spitfire. Now go to sleep, your eyes are closing as you argue with me. I'll come check on you before I go to bed." Leaning over, he seals his mouth to mine, stealing my breath.

He's right, tonight has been hell, and every ounce of energy I thought I had disappeared the moment my body hit the bed.

"Good night, sweetheart. Call out if you need anything."

"Night, Alex. Thank you for coming when you found out what happened."

"You never should've doubted, Lily. If you let me, I'll never leave your side again."

I think he left the room, but I'm not sure. The pull of sleep is too strong.

Alex

After tossing and turning for over an hour, I know sleep isn't coming anytime soon. Climbing out of bed, I pull on a pair of sweatpants and a Yeti hoodie and head towards the kitchen to grab a beer. Maybe that will help calm my nerves.

The events of the night keep running through my head. Lily could've died. She's been hiding that the kidnapper is back in her life since she came back to Chicago. How is it that those closest to her didn't even know? Because Lily didn't want them to know. That's how.

But now I am here, and tomorrow I'll be calling my father, and he can help me with whatever tech I need. Will he ask questions? Hell yes. Will he still give it to me? Also, hell yes. This is Lily, the girl that saved my life. Like myself, my father would do anything to keep her safe, even skirt the law.

First thing we need to do is figure out the identity of the person targeting Lily. Why haven't the police been able to do it in all these years? Easy, they don't have the personal stake in it like I do. But now he pissed off the wrong person; he touched the wrong woman. I won't stop until he isn't breathing the same air as Lily. I won't stop until she's safe.

I'm pulled from my thoughts by the sound of a whimper. Was it a whimper? My heart pounds as I move down the hall when I hear it again. It is coming from Lily's room. Not bothering to knock, I rush inside and to the side of the bed she's asleep on. The covers are thrown off, and sweat glistens all over her skin. The sight of the bandage covering half of her head almost sends me back into another rage, but the tears running down her cheeks tamp down my anger.

Without thinking, I drop onto the bed next to her and pull her into my arms. "I'm here, Lily. It's Alex, and you're safe now. No one's going to touch you again. You're safe. I'll protect you, baby. Sleep, I got you."

"Alex. Safe," she murmurs, burrowing into my chest.

When she calms down enough that she stops moving, I reluctantly pull back and off the bed. She is sweat-covered, but I know that her body temperature will drop soon and she'll start shivering if I don't get her covered up. I justify going to my room and taking the comforter off my bed with it being warmer than the one in the guest room. But me being me, the truth is I want her covered in my scent.

I want nothing more than to crawl back into bed with her and hold her all night. But after the hell she went through tonight, I don't want her waking up not knowing how a man got into her bed and freaking out. She'd probably figure out quickly that it was me, but for a split second when she's coming out of her dream state, she may not, and I don't want her to feel fear.

But I just can't bring myself to leave her. Even though she wanted nothing more than to be in my bed, I don't want to wonder in the morning if our first time having sex was just a side effect of the trauma of the night.

Leaving the room one more time, I grab my pillows off my bed and another extra blanket. I'm going to sleep on the floor next to her bed in case she has any more nightmares. This way I'll be right here to wake her up.

Chapter Twenty-Six
Lily

I slowly wake up, and it takes me a second to realize that something is different. The mattress below me feels like a cloud, not the cheap, firm one that I was able to afford when I moved into my apartment. Then there is the smell; I am surrounded by citrus and mint. I'm surrounded by Alex.

Memories of yesterday come rushing back. The game—Alex and his teammates being all scary and territorial with those frat boys, but then fear. My ghost had found me. Not only did he find me, he invaded my home and laid hands on me. He made me feel the need to run and hide.

My secrets are out in the open now. There is no more hiding that I am being targeted again. But then I remember Alex's calming presence. Him arguing with Eddie, Jordan, and Scottie about me staying with him. Not really arguing, just stating a fact, really. That he would and will protect me.

That's where I am, and why I feel Alex all around me. I'm in Alex's apartment, in his guest room. For the first time in a long time, I feel completely safe. How long has it been since I felt this? The night before the accident over four years ago—that's how long.

Looking around me, I don't see my phone nor a clock. Having no idea what time it is and not hearing any other noise, I wonder how long I slept and if Alex had an early morning practice and left me alone.

Why am I suddenly filled with panic at the idea of being alone? No, he would've told me if he was leaving, right? He wouldn't have left me alone in his apartment. I'll just go find him.

Swinging my legs over the side of the bed, I go to stand up, but instead find myself falling face first towards the hardwood floor. Holding my breath, I brace for an impact that never comes. Instead, I find myself wrapped in warm but hard arms and staring into eyes that I'd know anywhere.

"Morning, spitfire."

"Alex?" I squeak. "What are you doing on the floor?"

He smirks. "Waiting to catch you?"

"Smart ass. I'm serious."

"Sorry." He shifts me in his arms. "Here," he says, sitting up, but keeps me on his lap. "I heard you cry out in your sleep last night, so I came in here to check on you. Once you settled down, I wanted to be close in case you needed me, so I kinda laid down on the floor." He nuzzles into the side of my neck, avoiding my eyes.

He what? "Why didn't you wake me up? Or at least lie on the bed with me?"

"Well... after what happened yesterday, I didn't want you to wake up and think a stranger was in your bed. But I still wanted to be close, so the floor was the furthest I was willing to go."

I can feel the tears rolling down my cheeks. "How are you real?" He is silent but pulls me tight. "How am I so lucky that you want me, mess and all?"

"Messy Lily might just be my favorite," he teases. "I wouldn't change a single thing about you."

"Thank you, Alex. For everything," I whisper, pulling back enough so I can lean up and kiss his cheek.

My stomach decides to ruin the moment and growl so loud I'm sure the neighbors can hear.

"Why don't you do whatever your morning routine is, and I'll go make us some breakfast? Does that sound good?"

"That sounds amazing. I'll only be a few minutes."

"No rush. I'll be in the kitchen when you're ready. I put your bag in the closet." He points to a door.

Pulling me to my feet, he kisses me on the top of the head. It's one of the sweetest gestures I've ever felt. My heart races, and I wonder if he can feel it as he pulls me in for one last hug.

Less than ten minutes later, I'm all refreshed. The smell of coffee reaches the bedroom, and I have to stop myself from sprinting down the hall for a cup of liquid gold.

Standing at the stove, Alex is in grey sweatpants and a tight-fitting black t-shirt. Taking my middle finger, I run it around my mouth to make sure I'm not drooling.

"Hey, would you like some coffee?" he calls out, now standing by the coffee machine. Wasn't he just at the stove? Hm. That makes me wonder how long I was staring at him and if he is going to say anything because, from the smirk on his face, he definitely noticed.

"Coffee would be great, thank you. And is that French toast?"

"Yes, ma'am, my specialty. Well, not really a specialty, but my favorite breakfast food, so the one that I'm least likely to burn. And the one I make the most, so I added my own twist to it."

"It's my favorite too, and it smells amazing." Looking around the kitchen, it looks like everything is almost ready. "What can I help with?"

"Nothing at all. We can sit at the table if you want. Or we can sit at the island."

Over in the open space, the table looks like it's never really been used. "Where do you normally eat, Alex?"

"Ummm, the island. But it's just easier when it's just me. I only really use the table when my parents come for dinner."

"Then let's eat here, and we can sit next to each other."

His crooked smile sends shivers to my core.

He sets a plate of perfectly golden French toast in front of me, and I have to stop myself from digging in. Next comes coffee, a ceramic cup of sugar, and a small container of milk. Lastly, a glass of orange juice.

"Alex, is this fresh squeezed orange juice?"

His cheeks redden. "Well, yeah. Julie likes it, so I got used to only having fresh in the house."

"You are the best big brother, Alex. She's lucky to have you." Silence hangs in the air.

Reaching over, he grabs my hand and brings my palm to his mouth and gives it a quick kiss. It's another thing he does that makes my heart melt that much more.

"Do you have practice today?" I ask right before taking a bite of his French toast. Once the bread hits my tongue, I let out a moan.

Expecting Alex to answer me, when I don't hear a response, I lift my head and see his hands clenched so tight his knuckles are turning white and his eyes are on my mouth.

Grabbing the napkin and running it along my mouth, I'm paranoid I have food on my face.

Pushing his plate aside, he clears his throat and gets to his feet. Smirking down at me, I see the hunger in his eyes.

"No, Alex. I'm hungry, and this French toast is heaven."

"Guess what, spitfire?"

"Hmm?" Crossing my arms over my chest, I have a feeling breakfast is over.

"It's tomorrow, and I'm hungry too, but not for French toast."

Bringing my hand up and covering his mouth, he pulls back just enough so he can nip at the pad of my fingertip.

Grinning, he grabs my hand, leading me around the side of the island, and just as I go to continue into the living room, he spins me to face him, pulling me against his chest.

"We're going to play a game, Lily. And a warning—I play to win."

Raising my brow, I'm intrigued. "What kind of game?"

"Hide and seek."

"You have the advantage here; it's not really fair."

He shrugs. He fucking shrugs.

"You have thirty seconds to hide from me. Starting now."

"What happens when you find me?"

"Twenty-five."

"Alex?"

"Twenty."

"Shit," I squeal as I run down the hall. Where the fuck am I supposed to hide? I go to dive under the guest bed when I find it's a platform. "Well, crap."

"Ready or not, here I come."

Sprinting down a few doors, I dive into Alex's closet and wiggle behind some garment bags against the back wall. As time passes, I think I might have outsmarted him. Until a hand clasps down onto my foot, and with one strong tug, I'm launched into his strong, waiting arms.

"Found you. Now I get my prize."

Chapter Twenty-Seven
Alex

Staring into her enchanting green eyes, I feel like a damn virgin. I haven't been one of those since I was fifteen years old, fuck.

Pulling her from the closet and to her feet, she instinctively wraps her legs around my waist.

"Hmm, someone else came out to play," she chuckles, grinding against me, driving me wild.

"Is that what you want, spitfire?" Digging my fingers into her ass, she lets out a moan.

"Cut the shit, Alex. You knew exactly what you were doing when you decided to play your little game. Now you said you wanted your prize. So either collect, or I will go home and take care of it myself."

"The fuck you will," I growl. Turning and walking towards the bed, I set her on her feet. "As much as I like seeing you in my clothes, I need them off. Now."

Keeping her eyes locked on mine, her hands find the hem of her shirt. Pulling it up over her head, I can't take my eyes off her perfect nipples. All I'd have to do is lean forward, and I could have one in my mouth, but no, I need her naked.

Clearing my throat, I notice she's watching me, watching her.

Painfully slowly, she grasps the rolled waist of her sweatpants, bending slightly, she works them down her legs. Never losing my eye contact. Standing before me, she's only in a pair of black boy shorts.

She must have put them on this morning, because she wasn't wearing them after her bath last night. I would've felt them when I held her close before falling asleep on the floor.

"Everything, spitfire."

Her lips curl into a little smile and she turns around and crawls up the bed. Once she reaches the middle, she turns around and kneels facing me. She's playing a dangerous game. My control is hanging on by a thread, and I don't want to scare her if it snaps.

Still fully clothed, I crawl on my hands and knees up the bed to her. I'm not scared to show her how much she should be worshiped.

When we are face-to-face, I can't take it anymore and surge forward, sealing our lips. How it's possible? I don't know. But more blood rushes south, making my cock painfully hard.

Gripping Lily by the hips, I flip her onto her back.

She lets out a gasp, and I check on her for one second before my hands find the band of her panties, and I'm pushing them down her legs.

From the first time I touched her, tasted her, hell, looked into her eyes, I've needed this moment almost as much as I need hockey in my life.

Her fingers run through my hair. The moment I lean in and suck one of her nipples into my mouth, she flexes and pulls hard enough that the roots sting. I love it.

My lips caress her stomach and slowly work their way down. Gripping the inside of her thighs, I spread them wide.

Something in her demeanor changes the second I touch her legs, she stiffens, no longer wiggling against my mouth. "Lily, do you want me to stop?"

There are tears in her eyes. Fucking tears. "Baby, I'm stopping, but please tell me what I did."

Pulling at my shoulders, she pulls me up her body. "You did nothing, Alex. It's me—my leg."

Pushing away from her, I kneel next to her. Reaching across her body, I grab her leg and pull her to her side. "You mean this leg, Lily?"

Tears flow down both cheeks now. This was not how I wanted this moment to go.

"Do you know what I think when I see this scar?"

"That it's unsightly?"

Wack. "What was that for, Alex?"

Wack. I smack her ass again. "Any time I hear you talking negatively about yourself, you will be spanked. Now, listen and listen well. This scar shows your bravery and selflessness. So do all the little scars on your hands that I've noticed without saying anything about. You got those scars saving my life, and it kills me to think of yet another thing linked to me that causes you never-ending pain. Never be ashamed of this scar or any other mark on your body.

They are your battle scars. I will end anyone that makes you feel less than because of them. Do I make myself clear?"

She smirks. "Yes, sir."

"Now, we are going to push aside all negative thoughts and get back to pleasure. Okay?"

"Okay."

Leaning down, I kiss her strong and deep. When she releases control and melts back into the bed, I slowly move down her body, kissing everywhere. Back at her legs, I lift my gaze and make sure we lock eyes as I slowly spread her thighs wide.

"Alex," she moans.

Knowing what she needs, I flatten my tongue and lick her from her core all the way up. This is what I've been waiting for. What happened between us in Sticks was just a tease compared to this.

She squirms and moans below me, knowing she needs more. I add a finger, smiling against her pussy as she gasps.

"Alex, I want you."

Only lifting my face, but adding another finger, I meet her eyes. "You have me. Lily. But if you want something else, I need your words."

"Your dick, Alex. I want your dick," she screams.

Chuckling, I give her another lick before answering her. "Oh, and you will have it, darling. But I need you to shake around my tongue first, then you'll get my dick. Okay?"

I suck her clit between my lips, waiting for her to answer.

"Y-y-y-es."

"Good girl."

Her back arches off the bed, and she's gripping the comforter on both sides of her thighs.

Her legs tremble, and she clenches around my fingers.

"Let go, baby."

"Shit, shit, shit," she screams, and she grinds against my face.

I suck her slit and curl my fingers inside her one last time, and it pushes her over the edge. Watching her come almost has me making a mess in my pants. I haven't done that since freshman year in college, and I sure as shit don't want to do that today.

I slowly move my way up her body, placing small kisses as I go, watching her face as she comes down from her orgasm.

Once I'm hovering over her, she pushes up and takes my mouth, dipping her tongue inside, not even bothered that she's tasting herself. *Hottest fucking shit ever.* As we pull apart, I kiss her quickly on the forehead.

Reaching over her to the nightstand, I pull out a condom.

Lily's reaching over me and pulls my t-shirt over my head as I'm pushing my sweatpants and boxers down my legs. Lily watches my hands, and I roll the condom down my length, a smile lighting her face.

"Are you still okay?"

"Fuck me already, Alex," she begs in a breathless, raspy voice that has me lost.

"Yes, ma'am."

I trace her opening with the head of my cock, notching it at the entrance. Leaning down, I gently take her lips as I slowly sink into her until she's filled with every inch of me.

I haven't even moved yet, but I need a moment to catch my breath. Being seated inside her is different from anyone else I've ever been with. Not to diminish those women, but they were to satisfy a need, and they knew that.

Lily, well, she's home. She's my endgame. This is what I suspect forever is supposed to feel like.

Trying not to lose all control and come before I've even moved, I'm caught off guard when Lily leans up, scraping her teeth along my jaw before nipping at the point of my chin. Fuuuucck.

"There's no way I'm going to last very long, spitfire. Your pussy is strangling my cock, and if I move, I'm going to explode."

"If you don't move, I'll finish myself."

"The fuck you will. Okay, pretty girl."

Clenching my teeth, I give her what she wants—what I need. Pulling back slightly until everything but the tip is out, I watch her eyes light up with pleasure.

"More, Alex."

Propelling back inside, I don't stop as her moans escalate, and the steady rhythm has her legs shaking. "I'm close, Alex."

"Get there, pretty girl."

Less than ten more strokes, and the second her scream leaves her lips, I'm falling right with her. Giving one last shudder, I fall to the side of her, not wanting to crush her.

Burying my face into her neck, I pepper her throat with kisses.

My eyes grow heavy, and before I can fall asleep, I pull out of her warmth and stand up.

"Alex, where are you going?"

"Just to take care of the condom. I'll be right back." Walking into the bathroom, I deposit the condom in the trash and grab a fresh washcloth.

Walking back into the room, Lily's still on her side, watching me move.

"Open up, darling. Let me clean you up a bit."

Red rushes to her cheeks. It's adorable.

Now we're both cleaned up and relaxed. I pull the covers back on the bed. "Let's cuddle, spitfire. A few minutes in your arms, then we'll finish breakfast and have a day of being lazy. How does that sound?"

"Amazing," she whispers.

A few minutes pass before she sits up on her elbows and stares at my chest.

"Alex?" Her eyes are locked on the date tattooed over my heart. The one I got four years ago.

"Is that…?" A small sob pulls from her throat, as she's unable to finish the sentence.

"That's the date you saved my life, spitfire. The day I met the most amazing woman; the day my life truly began."

"Oh, Alex." She cries as I wipe the tears away on her cheeks.

"Sleep, Lily. Now is not a time for tears."

Pulling her into my arms, she's sleeping before I get all the covers tucked around her.

This is perfect. This is how it should be. I'll make sure Lily feels this loved and this safe every day for the rest of her life.

Chapter Twenty-Eight
Lily

The morning sun is streaming through the blinds, reminding me I'm in my room with the blackout curtains. The last thing I remember is Alex pulling me tight against his chest after the fifth round of sex. It was everything I'd dreamed it would be.

I slept through the night, without nightmares.

That hasn't happened in over four years.

That's a welcomed first.

The only thing that changed was that I was in Alex's arms all night and not in a cold bed by myself. Well, that, and the night of orgasm after orgasm.

"Good morning, spitfire," he purrs, walking out of the connecting bathroom with nothing but a towel around his waist.

"Nope," I groan, burrowing deep within the covers. "Don't you 'Morning, spitfire' me, Alexander Bensen."

The covers are ripped away, and standing at the bottom of the bed with the comforter in hand is a smirking Alex. "What's wrong with saying good morning to my girl?"

"It's the way you said it, you ass. You know how sexy you are, but my vagina needs a break. She hurts."

Dropping the towel and crawling up the bed, he says in a gravelly voice, "We don't want a sore pussy. I can make her feel so much better."

He kisses up my stomach until he's leaning over me. "Hmmm."

"I'll go get you an ice pack from the kitchen. That should make her feel better." He jumps off the bed and strides into his walk-in closet.

"I hate you, Alex."

He doesn't emerge, but I hear him laughing. "That's not what you were screaming last night, darling. But your body does need a rest, at least until tonight. So get out of bed and let me feed you."

"No," I grumble. Curling into a ball in the center of the bed since he pulled the covers off and out of reach.

"I'll make French toast." He's leaning against the closet door frame, arms crossed, looking too fucking delicious.

"Fine. Coffee and food." Having no idea where my clothes are, I stalk out of the room, completely naked, and head to the guest room where my bag is. He's such a tease.

Right after breakfast, he needed to head to the rink for practice.

"I could call Coach and explain the situation, and I'm sure he'd be okay with me staying here."

"Get out of here. I'll be fine, I swear." Looking around the living room, I nod. "I'll lie on the couch and watch some TV. Okay? Now get to practice before you're late."

He stands in the entryway staring at me. "I'm going to call Roger on my way to practice and revoke everyone's access to the apartment for the time being. Everyone wanting access will need to call me first. So that means you should not be expecting anyone to knock while I'm gone. No food deliveries or housekeepers, or anyone. I'll leave if you promise to stay here, not answer the door, and rest."

"Goodness, you're cute when you get all protective. Yes, yes, I promise to do all of that. Now will you go?"

"Reluctantly, yes. I'll bring dinner home with me." Dragging his feet like an upset child, he walks back over to me, pulls me into his arms, and kisses me quick and hard.

"Have fun playing with your stick," I call out as the door closes. I know he heard me from the grumbling response.

Messing with him lightens the mood and takes my mind off everything. It helps to make me feel like everything is normal and that I don't have a crazy, obsessive stalker out there. I could get used to this. A normal life with Alex.

The pizza he brought home was to die for. And living in Chicago, I consider myself a pizza snob. "This needs to be a regular meal, please."

Grabbing my plate from the counter, Alex loads it in the dishwasher. "I usually stop at Mollies once a week, so that won't be a problem."

"Thank you for dinner, Alex."

Rounding the island, he picks me up into his arms. Locking my legs around his waist, he carries us into the living room and sits down, holding me tight, onto the couch.

The minutes tick by as I sit in his lap, his arms around me. Pulling the tie from his hair, I run my fingers through his silky brown hair, loving that even after all these years, he still hasn't cut it off. It may seem odd to some, but I love his man bun, and seeing his hair flow around his shoulders reminds me of how we met. Not the sad part of our meeting, but that he's here—and alive.

He grabs my attention from his hair as he pulls me close. "Can I ask you something?"

"Anything." Sitting straight up in his lap, I scan his face.

"Will you tell me what your years were like after you had to leave Chicago?"

There's something in his eyes. Worry? Fear?

"They weren't bad years, if that's what you're worried about. Boring, yes. But it's not like I was looking over my shoulder every day like I would've been if I stayed in Chicago. Not like I have been since I came back."

"Every time I've thought about you over the years, I worried if you were safe and happy."

"Well, I'd say more safe than happy, but that was my fault, really."

"How so?" He's playing with my hair, something I love when he does.

"I didn't give the place I was at an actual chance. It was always the place standing between me and home. Between me and returning to Chicago."

Picking at my nails, I take a few deep breaths.

"When I first arrived in Michigan, I hated it. The home I was staying in was right on the lake in Saint Joseph. On clear days, you could see the Chicago skyline. It made me miss home. I think it would've been easier to live on the other side of the country."

"Didn't living only on the other side of the lake make it easier for Morgan to come visit?"

I couldn't keep the tears away. "No, because I didn't see anyone except on video calls the entire time I was gone."

"What the fuck? Why not? They are your best friends."

"Because both Eddie and Jordan were worried the kidnapper would follow them to me. Morgan wanted to quit nursing school and go with me, but I wouldn't let her do that. As much as I missed her, I knew I'd be back one day and didn't want her putting her life on hold for me. Yes, she could've found another school, but she was on scholarship, so she would've lost it."

Pulling me in tight, he nuzzles the side of my neck. "I'm so sorry, Lily."

"I don't want your pity, Alex. I don't want to see that when I look into your eyes. Bad shit happened, but can we agree to please let what happened in the past stay in the past?"

"Except where it brought us together."

"Well, duh," I chuckle. "That's the best part of everything that's happened."

"We need to continue this night," he beams. "Bath and then bed." Picking me up, we make our way towards his bedroom.

"The bath sounds amazing, but I'm not tired yet, Alex. I still want to talk."

"I said nothing about sleeping, Lily. I said bed."

Oh, oooohhhh. I kiss his neck, then give it a little nibble. "Yes, sir. Bath, then bed, sounds amazing."

Chapter Twenty-Nine
Alex

Beep. Beep.
Why is someone calling me this early in the morning?
Beep. Beep.

Slapping my hand onto my nightstand, I silence my phone before it can wake up Lily. Carefully pulling my arm out from under her head so I don't jar her, I wrap the blankets around her, grab my sweatpants and sweatshirt from the floor and my phone from the table, and walk out to the kitchen.

Pressing Roger's contact, it doesn't even ring once before he answers. "Roger, do you know what time it is?"

"Mr. Bensen, can you please come to the lobby, alone?"

"What happened, Roger? Are you in trouble?" Grabbing my keys, I'm at the front door pulling my sneakers on before he can answer.

"There was a package delivered sometime last night for Ms. Sterling. The company was Speedy Mailers. It's a jet black box, with a red ribbon tied around it, and there seems to be blood dripping from the corner. I was about to call the police but remembered what you told me about your guest being attacked and her working for the city. I wanted to let you know first in case you had someone you wanted to notify first."

He was here, in my fucking apartment building. "Don't touch it again, Roger. I'm coming down."

The lobby is empty at four in the morning. Roger, pale and shaken up, motions me to the mailroom off behind the security desk. Right there on one of the package tables is the same box I saw days earlier in Lily's apartment. Pulling out my phone, I dial Eddie first.

"Alex?" Having been woken up, he obviously sounds worried.

"Eddie, a package was delivered to my building last night for Lily. It's the same as from her stalker. I didn't open it, but I need to see what's inside. There looks to be blood dripping from the corner. Can you get here?"

"Don't touch anything. I'll bring gloves and can put it in an official report. I'll make sure we look inside and see what he sent before they take it. I'll also give Officer Burke a call. He's the one that's been on this case from the beginning. Does Lily know?"

Running my hand through my hair, I take a calming breath. "No, she's still sleeping. If she doesn't need to know, I'd rather she doesn't."

"She'll find out eventually, Alex," he warns.

"I know. But she's still not sleeping very well, and I'm about to head out on my first away game since her attack. I don't need this added to her stress. Can we agree to keep it from her for now?"

"Okay, I'll agree unless whatever's in that box is something she needs to be told about."

"Agreed. Eddie, I'm going to call Jordan and Scottie and give them a heads up. I think those around her need to be made aware."

"Yeah, and they won't tell Morgan unless it's needed either. I just got to my car, I'll be there in ten minutes."

"I'll be in the lobby."

Roger stands behind the desk, fidgeting, as I pace back and forth near the door. Jordan and Scottie are also on their way.

Ten minutes later, carrying a black bag, Eddie strides through the front door, looking like he's aged ten years. "Roger, this is Captain Eddie Carlson with the CPD search and rescue team, Lily's boss, and more importantly, her friend. He's going to take a look in the box and contact the police to come get it. Jordan and Scottie are on their way over. Can you yell out when they get here?"

"Yes, sir," he replies, finally taking a seat.

Once inside the mailroom, Eddie closes the door behind us. Opening his bag, he pulls out a pair of latex gloves and glasses like you'd see in a chemistry lab. "He's never sent anything dangerous, but just in case, please just stay by the door."

Carefully lifting the lid from the box, he sets it to the side. "Fucking hell."

Right as I pick up my foot to move, there is a knock at the door to my back. "Alex let us in." It's Scottie. Opening the door, Jordan and Scottie stand there, irate. Behind them, in uniform, is Officer Burke speaking to Roger.

"Quick, come in, Eddie just opened the box."

The three of us move next to Eddie, who shakes his head and steps back. Looking inside, I recognize the item immediately. It's a Yetis jersey. My Yetis jersey. It's shredded and covered in blood. This isn't a message for Lily, it is a message for me, just like what he whispered into her ear before fleeing when he attacked her and Morgan heard every word. He wants me to stay away from her, but like hell is that going to happen.

"He won't touch her," I announce to everyone in the room. "I'll kill him first."

Fury courses through every fiber of my body. "Why can't he just leave her the fuck alone?" Screaming, I punch the wall, putting my fist through the plaster.

Officer Burke and Roger come rushing into the room. "Sorry Roger, just have maintenance send me the bill for the repair. I'm going back to my apartment; I don't want Lily to wake up alone. Officer Burke, thank you for coming over. If you have any questions, any of these guys have my number. Jordan and Scott, I'll message you guys later."

Not waiting for anyone to respond, I just need to get upstairs and lay eyes on my girl.

Nothing will be okay, and she won't be safe until this guy is no longer breathing.

Lily

Today, from the moment I walked into the kitchen, I could tell something was bothering Alex. He's standing at the island, flipping French toast, sipping on his coffee, and he hasn't noticed me yet.

When he stretches his arms over his head, his abs are on full display. Yum.

I must make a noise because his gaze whips to me, his eyes roaming my body. Hopefully it worked him up that I'm wearing one of his favorite team t-shirts.

Heat courses through my body as his breathing quickens. "Morning, beautiful. I was about to bring you breakfast in bed."

"I woke up and you were gone again. I think we need to make a rule where when you get out of bed before me, you wake me up."

Crossing the kitchen, he pulls me against his chest. "Sorry, love. You were sleeping so peacefully, I didn't have the heart to wake you."

"I'll forgive you this time. But don't let it happen again."

"Sassy pants." He chuckles and slaps my ass.

Setting two plates of French toast on the counter, he moves to the coffee pot.

"Hey Alex, can I ask you a question?"

"Anything, you know that."

"When I walked into the kitchen, you didn't notice me right away, so I stood in the doorway, watching you cook. And not in a creepy way, it's just sexy watching you move. Just don't get an inflated ego over it."

He brushes a loose strand of hair behind my ear as he moves around me to sit down.

"When I was watching you, you looked... sad. Or worried about something. You'd tell me if something was bothering you, right?"

Tilting his head, he studies me for a moment. "Damn, I'll need to watch myself around you. Maybe you should work for the FBI and not search and rescue."

"Come on, Alex, way to deflect the question."

"Yeah, okay. I am worried about something, and I'm just not sure how to broach the topic without overstepping." Reaching over and grabbing his hand, I pull his knuckles to my lips. "Just tell me, Alex. I want to help you if I can."

"Fine, but remember, I didn't want to bring it up, but you won't drop it. I'm worried about leaving for my away game and leaving you here, alone. Even with the top-of-the-line security my penthouse has, I'm worried you won't be safe. The guy that attacked you is still out there, and I feel like my heart is going to pound out of my chest at the idea of you being states away from me."

Blinking a few times, it takes me a second to process the word vomit he just spilled. What? He's anxious because he's leaving and is worried about me? That's actually really sweet.

"Okay, so what would make you feel better in this situation? What options do we have?"

"I could tell the coach I'm not going to the game."

"Get real, Alex. Absolutely not. Try again."

Turning towards me and pulling me from my chair, he has me straddling his lap. "Well, I can buy you a plane ticket, and you can join me on my road trip. You would be out of Chicago, and I would have you close." Burying his face into my hair, he inhales. "That would be the best option."

"Sir, I can buy my own plane ticket, thank you very much."

"Yes, I know. Independent woman and all. But, Lily. I want to do things for you. Let me do things for you. Please? It's just a ticket. It's not like I'm asking to buy you an entire plane."

Tilting his head, he bites the left side of his bottom lip. He is thinking something, and I know I'm not going to like it.

"But, if I did buy a plane, then you could come to all the away games, no problem. And Morgan could even come along any time she wanted."

It's reflexes, or at least that's what I'm blaming it on when my right arm comes out and punches him in the shoulder.

"What was that for? It was a reasonable thought." "Reasonable? Reasonable? The hell it was. A reasonable thought is not whether to purchase a plane just to cart your girlfriend and her friend to your away games. No, absolutely the fuck not."

Grasping his chest over his heart, "You wound me, spitfire."

"I will wound you if you keep up with your crazy ideas."

"Fine. I'll table the idea... for now."

Shaking my head, I know there is no arguing with him.

"So if I agree to go to the game, would it make you feel better?"

I know the answer before he speaks by the smile that spreads across his face.

"Baby, it would make me so happy. You can stay with me at the hotel, and as long as you're okay with it, being at the arena early? If you are a good girl, I can link you up with Rogue, and he can show you to your seat."

"Yep. I'll go. You said the magic word."

"I swear if you say Rogue sealed the deal, I may murder him," he spits out.

"Okay, I won't admit anything."

Yep. Fucking with Alex is definitely fun and becoming one of my favorite things to do.

Chapter Thirty
Lily

Not only was it over the top that Jordan picked me up from Alex's apartment and hand delivered me to airport security, but I don't know what strings he pulled, but Alex had two Yetis employees waiting for me the second I stepped foot off the plane in Washington.

"Ms. Sterling, Mr. Bensen asked that we meet you and make sure you make it to the hotel okay. He, unfortunately, had to ride the team bus, or he'd be here to greet you himself."

"I'm so sorry you both got roped into this, Mr. Bensen is a tad overprotective and worries way too much. But I do appreciate you taking time out of your busy day to help me. I've never been to this beautiful state."

All I have is a carry-on, so gliding past baggage claim, the employees lead me to a town car waiting curbside. "This is us. Here, let me take your bag and put it in the trunk," the driver says with his hand out.

"Thank you." Seated inside, I pull out my phone.

Me: You are ridiculous. I'm not helpless.

Alex: I take it you are in the car on the way to the hotel?

Me: No, I'm heading back to Chicago.

Alex: Lily…

Me: Growl at me and I'll have them turn around.

Alex: Don't make me call them, because I will.

Alex: I just wanted to make sure you were safe.

Me: I will see you at the hotel. If I don't get to meet Rogue, I'm staying with Morgan when I return.

Alex: I don't like ultimatums, Lily. Especially when they involve other men.

Me: Then stop acting like a caveman.

Alex: Where your safety is concerned—never.

> **Me:** We will talk later.

> **Alex:** I'll be waiting, spitfire.

Two can play at this game. I know someone that likes to play pranks just as much as I do.

"Hey, darling. Are you here yet? Alex has been a grump since we took off."

"Scottie. I don't have much time. But I need your help."

There is a pause on the other line. "Are you okay, Lily?"

"Yeah, yeah. What's with you all thinking I can't take care of myself?"

"It's only because we care."

"Fine, well, I think we are close to the hotel, so I don't have much time. I want to do something, but since we are away, I don't know if it will be possible."

He chuckles. "Will it piss Alex off?"

"Oh, definitely. He will be out for blood."

"I'm so in. I might even be able to pull in some of the guys. Tell me what you need."

Hanging up the phone I dare a glance at the guy seated next to me. "Girl, you are poking a bear. But I'm here for it. Can I catch it on video?"

Alex may never forgive me, but I nod.

"I'm not sure if you remember me, but I'm Archie, I run the Yetis social media. The fans will love this. I might even be able to help make it happen."

"You are a god, Archie. Thank you."

"I hope you know what you're doing, doll. Bensen is a grumpy one for sure."

As we pull up to the hotel, Alex is standing outside waiting for us. "He is grumpy, but he's my grump, and I can handle him."

"Famous last words," Archie whispers when Alex opens the door and holds out his hand for me.

"How was the flight, spitfire?"

"Oh, you know?"

"Oh, do I?"

"Yeah, I had this one guy talk to me the entire time, and it was just an enjoyable flight. I usually don't like flying, but this one wasn't so bad."

He bites his bottom lip and chuckles. "You really like being a brat, don't you?"

"Only for you."

"Well, we'll see about that. We have two hours before dinner down here with the team, which I'd really like you to join us for. But until then, I'm going to take you upstairs and show you what happens to brats."

"Promises, promises, Mr. Bensen."

The suite door closes behind us with a definitive click. Not feeling his hands on my lower back, I turn to find him leaning against the door, his gorgeous eyes locked on mine as he slowly unbuttons his shirt.

I bite down on my lip as heat floods my core.

His shirt hangs open, untucked from his pants. Stalking towards me, he doesn't break stride as he lifts me into his arms and moves into the bedroom, depositing me on my feet next to the bed.

Stripping out of the rest of his clothes, he stands before me as I fight to control my breathing.

While I'm still gawking at his nakedness, he makes quick work of removing my sweater. "Fuck, you're beautiful." Pushing me back onto the bed, he removes my shoes, keeping his eyes locked on mine.

"I told you before, spitfire, but you've apparently forgotten, so I want to make something perfectly clear..." He removes my leggings and panties in one quick tug, leaving me lying there in just my bra. "I'm a very jealous man. So when you were talking about meeting another man on the plane and talking to him the entire trip here, it brought out my jealous side."

He runs a hand down each of my legs before placing them both over his shoulders. I'm shaking, and he has barely touched me. "The moment you told me you were mine, that meant every part of you is mine. Do you agree?"

"Yes," I moan.

"So these legs are mine." He peppers each leg with kisses.

"This stomach is mine." He reaches his right hand up, rubbing up and down my stomach.

I can't contain the moan that escapes me. "Alex."

"This pussy is mine." He flattens his tongue, passing lazily through my folds.

"Please," I beg.

"Please what, Lily?"

"Stop teasing me. I'm sorry I joked about another man. There's only you. There will only ever be you. Now fuck me. Please!" I yell.

"Your wish is my command, spitfire."

He sucks hard on my clit while inserting two fingers inside me. He knows exactly where to touch, because seconds later my legs are shaking.

Pulling back, he has the audacity to say, "Not yet, baby."

"Noo, I was so close."

"I know. But you were still a brat, and brats get punished."

"I'll do it myself." Writhing underneath him, I try to move any way to get friction where I need it most, but he's over me, holding my legs still. Not fair.

Unintentional tears run down my cheeks.

"No, baby. Oh, no." Kissing me hard, he reaches off the bed and grabs his pants. Pulling out a condom, I stop his hand. "What if I told you that you didn't have to use it? That I'm on the pill and I trust you." Lowering my eyes, I don't want to see his response. I don't want to be embarrassed if he thinks I'm insane for saying that.

He won't let me hide, though. "Say that again, spitfire." His eyes are filled with lust.

Clearing my throat, "Well, um, I'm on birth control and clean. So if you don't want to use a condom, I'd love to feel every inch of you inside me."

He grabs my chin and lifts my face to look him in the eyes. "Why are you acting all shy and proper, spitfire? Do you know how many times I wanted to fuck you bare? Do you know what the thought of my cum dripping down your legs long after we're done does to me? To be able to smell myself on you?"

"Alex," I moan. Then do it, fuck me bare. Mark me, claim me, make me yours."

His eyes shoot to mine. "Are you sure, Lily? Because that's not one hundred percent, and if we do this, I really won't give you up."

"You wouldn't have given me up anyway, Alex."

He smirks. "True. Okay, love."

Leaning over me, he kisses me so tenderly before lining himself up and slipping just the tip into my core. "Fuck, this feels a little too good. I've never gone without a condom before."

"Neither have I. I can feel all of you, Alex, and I need more." Lifting my hips, I try to pull him in.

Taking a deep breath, he pushes all the way to the hilt in one shot.

"Mine. Tell me you're mine, spitfire."

Gritting my teeth, I shake my head, fighting against the building pressure. "Yes, only yours. Now move."

Rearing back, he slams forward.

I let out a scream that I'm sure can be heard in the lobby.

"That's it, pretty girl, let everyone know how good you feel."

He pumps into me desperately, his eyes hungry and intense. "I'm not going to last much longer. You're squeezing my dick too tight. Such a good fucking girl."

Reaching between us, he squeezes my clit. "Give me one more, Lily. I need you to come with me."

Already on the edge, the extra pressure to my clit sends me over again. Feeling me clench him tight, he spills inside me, filling me with so much cum, I can feel it leaking onto the sheets.

I've never felt that sensation before, of being filled, but by him, I could become addicted.

He doesn't pull out right away but gathers me close and rolls onto his back, bringing me to lie on top.

Overcome with emotions, I bury my face in the crook of his neck so he won't see the tears streaming down my face. Is what I'm feeling love? I know I care for him, but do I love him? I've never told another person that I loved them. At least not one that was more family than lover.

Running his hand up and down my spine, I feel cherished. Closing my eyes, I focus on the beat of his heart.

Dinner was long forgotten. When I open my eyes, the room is dark, and Alex is still beneath me. Shifting my weight, I lift to get off the bed when his strong arms wrap tight around me.

"Where are you going, baby?"

"I need to pee, Alex."

Releasing his arms, he chuckles. "Sorry. Man, I didn't mean to fall asleep. Are you hungry, I'm sure the guys are done downstairs, but we can order room service."

"Yeah, something light sounds good."

Alex

Last night was perfect. This morning is perfect. Having Lily with me is perfect.

Sitting in the visitors locker room, all I can think about is the shower blowjob she gave me before we headed here to the arena. I joked with her after the last one she gave me and the win we had that I'll need one for every game, and she didn't forget. I was only partially joking.

I wish she could've ridden the bus with us, but that's against the rules. So Archie will meet her down in the lobby this afternoon and ride with her to the arena. I have a surprise set up for her when she gets here that I know will make her happy; I just wish I could see her reaction. Archie said he'd record it for me.

> **Lily:** We are pulling up now. If I don't see you before the game, good luck, baby!

> **Me:** Just having you in the stands will give me the motivation I need, spitfire.

> **Me:** Stay with Archie, he will show you to your seat and set you up with snacks.

> **Lily:** Kiss!

"Why are you looking all googley-eyed at your phone? Is it Lily? Did she send you a picture?" Hawkins comes up behind me, trying to look over my shoulder.

"Back off, fucker. Before I lay you out," I warn.

"Now, boys. There will be none of that," Bear chides. "But, dude, you did have a stupid look on your face looking at your phone."

"Leave Bensen alone, he's a man in looooove," Caddel chimes in.

"I hate all of you."

The door to the locker room swings open and all three coaches walk in. "Alright, boys, listen up," Coach Reyes barks. "Go out and get a good warm up, then come back in here and get your game faces on. Last time we played this team, it was close the entire time. I don't want to see that shit this time. Don't play stupid. Let's kick some ass and play good hockey. Got it?"

"Yes, coach," everyone yells.

"Let's go," Bear shouts.

We all line the hall, waiting to be called out for warm-ups.

Coach motions for us to take the ice. Knight, like always, is the first one out. Taking one lap, I make it back to the bench and look for Lily. She's right where she's supposed to be, right behind where we will be sitting. But... what the fuck?

Scottie skates up to me, hands on his knees, laughing like a loon. That attracts the attention of a few other guys, and soon I'm surrounded. Me, I'm still trying to process what I'm seeing.

Stepping onto our bench and pounding on the glass, Lily's eyes drop to mine. "What the fuck are you wearing?"

Rogue, who's sitting next to her, tosses one of his stupid snowballs over the glass and it lands next to me.

"Lily?" I slam on the glass again. "Turn around."

"Bensen, what the fuck are you doing? Get your ass on the ice," Coach screams from down the bench.

"Coach, I'm going to kill our mascot."

"No, you won't." Coach Reyes walks down towards me, but my eyes are locked on Lily. "What did Rogue do to deserve your ire?"

Throwing both of my hands out, Coach looks to where our mascot stands.

Rogue leans over, grabs Lily's hand to help her stand, and then spins her around.

"Okay, Rogue deserves whatever you do to him." Coach laughs and walks away.

"See, Bensen, I told you he'd steal your girl," Knight yells from behind me.

Turning, half the team is behind me, laughing at my pain.

Lily, my girlfriend, was wearing not my jersey, but Rogue's. How the fuck did they even make that happen?

"You. Are. A. Brat," I grit out, pointing to Lily. "And you," I scowl, pointing to Rogue, "better hide, buddy."

The crowd laughs. They fucking laugh. It doesn't help my disposition that this is the away crowd.

"Let's go, Alex. Deal with it after the game," jests Bear. "I'll help you come up with a proper payback if you get your ass on the ice now."

"This isn't over, spitfire."

She blows me a kiss and sits down. Rogue sits right down next to her. I'm sure she's loving this. Me, it just makes me want to annihilate the other team that much more.

The puck drops, and every time someone comes close to our goal, I picture them as Rogue and knock their ass away. Knight is having a good old time laughing at my expense.

"Don't hurt them too badly. It's not their fault your girl's obsessed with the mascot," Knight chirps.

"Fuck you, Knight. Maybe I'll let you have the next one."

"No, you won't. You're too on edge."

"Incoming," Hawkins yells.

A stray puck heads our way. No opposition in sight, I take off up the ice. Our wingers are keeping the other team occupied as Hawkins and I pass the puck back and forth up the ice unopposed. Maneuvering around their defender, it's just me against their goalie. With a flick of my wrist, I send it back over to Hawkins, who hits it into the five hole.

The goal light goes off, and Hawkins is on top of me. "That was fire, Bensen. Let's gooo," he screams. Skating past the home bench, tapping fists with our team, I slow as I pass Lily. Her eyes never leave mine as she blows me a kiss. "Brat," I grumble under my breath.

Pointing to her in the stands, fans around her look between the two of us. Yes, we are the visiting team, but my actions will still make people talk. I want the world to know this girl is mine. And after what that fucker left at my apartment, I want him to know that he didn't scare me. So I hope people are filming.

Chapter Thirty-One
Alex

Me: We listen, and we don't judge, right?

Hawkins: Don't know where you got that shit. We judge hard.

Caddel: Seconded.

Bear: What did you do?

Me: Nothing... yet.

Knight: Lies.

Scottie: Fess up.

Me: Just a question, really.

Bear: Do I need to get bail money ready?

Knight: Hit us.

Hawkins: And then we judge.

Caddel: Hard.

Me: Any of you know how to safely sedate someone?

Scottie: I'm going to kill you.

Scottie: Cap, I'm gonna kill him.

I can literally picture Scottie calling Jordan and them planning my murder. Would my teammates protect me? Maybe Knight. But Hawkins and Caddel would find it too entertaining.

Caddel: Can you just hit them?

He's just stirring the pot.

Knight: No, fucker, he's talking about needing it for the girl. He's not going to hit the girl.

Caddel: Noooo, don't hit the redheaded hottie.

Scottie: I'm going to be at your apartment in fifteen minutes. You better answer the door.

Bear: Scottie, don't kill Alex. I don't need to explain to Coach why we need to find a new defenseman.

Scottie: No promises.

Me: Thanks so much for the support, everyone.

Hawkins: Can I come over and bring popcorn?

Caddel: Pick me up on the way.

I huff and throw my phone on the counter. Lily is still sleeping in the other room, and knowing Scottie, he'll be here to check on her in the fifteen minutes he threatened.

Picking my phone back up to make sure the volume is down for when the desk calls when my visitors begin showing up, it rings in my hand.

Bear is calling.

"Hey Cap. I'm not going to fight Scottie, so don't worry."

"Are you really trying to drug Lily, you dumbass?"

"I wouldn't call it drugging, per se, but yeah."

"Why?"

"It's not really to drug her more to make her relax. That asshole that attacked her is out there. Hell, the lacerations on her head are still healing. She has nightmares every night. I just want something that will... take the edge off. But she's a first responder, so I need to be careful with what I give her. When she's ready to go back to work, if they happen to drug test her, I don't want her to lose her job because of me. But it is tearing me apart watching her walk around like a zombie from lack of sleep."

He snorts. "It's called sex, you oaf. Multiple orgasms cause sleepiness."

"Oh, believe me, I have that area covered. It's like her anxiety doesn't care that her body is exhausted."

There is a long, uncomfortable silence. "Fine. Let me make a call, and I'll have something sent over. Follow the instructions that come with it exactly. Don't make me regret this."

He hangs up before I can ask any questions, like how the hell is Bear going to get drugs to knock someone out? I don't have time to analyze the conversation further, because Roger is calling my cellphone.

"Good morning, Roger."

"Mr. Bensen. Mr. Kasper is downstairs and in a mood this morning. I know he used to be on the approved visitors list, but you asked that all visitors be called for approval since Ms. Sterling came to visit. Is it okay to send Mr. Kasper up? If you say no, he may just try to scale the building."

"Send his ass up, but tell him to be quiet, Ms. Sterling is still sleeping."

He chuckles. "Will do, sir."

Three minutes later, I lean against the doorframe and the elevator opens and produces a threatening looking Scottie.

"Damn, why can't you bring that aggression to our games and take that out on the other team?" I say with a straight face.

"Fuck you, dude. I had my dick threatened by Morgan that if you hurt Lily in any way, she'd castrate me. All because I talked you up and told her you are a good guy and would never hurt her. Now, you go to our fucking group chat trying to find a way to sedate her. Dude?" He shoves past me and moves into my kitchen.

"She's sleeping, and don't you wake her. The nightmares keep her up until all hours, so when she finally falls asleep, I don't want her disturbed."

Wringing his hands, I can see the tension in his shoulders. We've been teammates and friends for years, and part of being a defender is reading body language. Scottie's body language is telling me he is close to snapping. "Do you think we should make her leave Chicago?"

"Make her?" I scoff. "We are talking about the same woman, right? I don't think anyone *makes* Lily do anything she doesn't want to do. What is this really about, Kasper?"

Looking at me, he shakes his head. "Four years ago, your accident almost destroyed her. She blamed herself for saving you first and not taking your sister out at the same time. She blamed herself for enjoying a few drinks with Morgan, then jumping into the river to save you guys. No matter how many times she was told neither of you would've survived without her, it took her years to believe it. Then, being the target of that madman, she was forced to leave her home. She changed being away from Chicago for four years. Every time we spoke, it was like another piece of her was gone. No longer was she her happy, carefree self. She withdrew into herself, and for good reason. Now, come to find out, the moment she steps back into the city, she's a target again. He was with her, and he didn't take her. Why?"

"I don't know, Scottie, but now that she's here with me, I won't let anything happen to her. From the moment she pulled me out of the water, I've had this overwhelming feeling that I had to meet her, and when I did, do you know what I felt?"

"What?"

"*Mine*, Scottie. That if Lily would have me, she would be mine. I can't explain the emotions I feel when I'm near her, but all I want to do is protect her. By any means necessary. Do you understand?"

"Yeah, I think I finally do." Standing up, he stretches his arms above his head. "By any means necessary, Alex. Just don't hurt her, or Jordan and I will make it so your body is never found."

"Scottie, if you wanted to hit that point home, you should've threatened me with Morgan coming after me. She scares the shit out of me."

He snorts. "I said we'd only come after you if you hurt her, the jury's out on what Morgan will do to you just for breathing in her direction wrong. Lily and Morgan are a package deal. Besides the years Lily was in hiding, they've been inseparable since middle school. Don't piss her off, you won't like the outcome. Play nice, and Morgan won't be an enemy. You've already earned one gold star by bringing Lily here to heal and the promise of protection."

"I won't," I promise. "Now get out of here. I want to make Lily a nice breakfast, and you aren't invited."

"What the fuck, dude? Your French toast is fire, why can't I stay?" He punches my arm as he moves towards the door.

"Just go, and I'll call you later so we can discuss security for when I'm at practice and away games. I wish we weren't in the middle of a season. I don't like the idea of leaving her here, and since she can't travel on the plane with us, she'd need to travel alone. That wouldn't be the safest option right now either. The last game she went to was fine, but how many times can she do that before she's on that guy's radar again?"

"Yeah, okay. I'll talk to Jordan, and we can come up with a plan."

Once the door is closed and locked behind him, I go back to the kitchen to start on breakfast. Scottie is right, I'm making her my French toast. No one can resist my French toast.

Chapter Thirty-Two
Lily

It's game night, and as much as I'd love nothing more than to be there, in person, cheering on the Yetis, I woke up with a migraine from hell. Groaning and tugging the covers over my head, Alex's large arm tugs me closer as he burrows his nose deep into my hair.

"Morning, spitfire."

"Mmmm. Too loud. Shhh," I groan before grabbing one of the extra pillows and placing it over my head, trying to block as much light as possible.

"Lily, what's wrong?" he whispers, trying to keep his voice as low as possible.

"Head. Dying."

"Do you need me to call a doctor? Get medicine?"

"My medicine is in my bag. Morgan would've packed it. It's prescription. Sumatriptan."

Jumping out of bed, I hear him in the bathroom, rummaging through my toiletry bag. A moment later, the sink turns on and off, and the bed is dipping. Warm arms are behind my back, bringing me to a sitting position. "Here, baby."

Cracking my eyes open, I see my two small pills in his hand. Once I take them, he reaches over to the nightstand and grabs the water cup. Bringing the glass to my lips, I take a small sip.

"Thank you, Alex."

Helping me to lie back down, he leaves the bed again and is in his closet searching for something, only to return with a Yetis brand sleeping mask.

"Here, Lily, this might help. I've never used it, but a lot of the guys wear them every time we travel. I've never had a problem falling asleep anywhere, so I never bothered with it." Carefully pulling my hair back so it doesn't snag on the strap, he helps pull it down over my eyes.

"Oh yes, this is amazing," I hum.

I hear him let out a quiet chuckle. "I'm glad it works. I'll grab a few more for you. They keep them in the locker room for us."

"You are too good to me."

"Not possible. Now try to go back to sleep. I'll lay with you and get my snuggle on."

"Sounds perfect." Feeling the heat from his body helps to relax me enough to give in to the exhaustion pulling me back under. Right before sleep takes me, I feel his lips on my head, then hear his whispering.

"Sleep now, precious girl. I'm here. I'll always be here. Forever."

Umm. Forever. I like the sound of that.

Chapter Thirty-Three
Alex

Tonight's a home game, so the arena is packed. With a sold out game and all eighteen thousand seats filled, not having Lily in one of them makes it feel less meaningful. Especially knowing she's at home not feeling well. That stubborn woman wouldn't let me miss the game on threat of withholding sex.

Her words, and I quote, "You are a professional; this is just a fucking headache. You will not disappoint your fans because your little girlfriend needs to sit in the dark for a little while. So get your sexy hockey ass to that arena and score me a goal."

She wasn't even out of bed before I needed to leave for the arena, and it took her threatening to call Bear for me to finally walk out the door. Before I left, I brought her five different types of drinks and snacks, and set the TV to the channel that would play our game but kept it on mute in case she fell back asleep.

"Alright boys," Coach addresses us from the center of the locker room. "Your fans are hungry for a win tonight, so go out there and show that other team whose house they are in."

Sticks start slamming on the ground, hyping each other up.

"This is the Yetis's house. So go out there and show them no mercy."

"Let's fucking go," Bear yells. "Yetis on three. One, two, three."

"Yetis," we all scream. Loud enough for our fans to hear us down the tunnel.

As we skate onto the ice, I think again how it sucks to know Lily isn't here to be cheering me on tonight. Jordan and Morgan are in his season ticket seats tonight, and to make myself feel better, I skate up to Scottie and tap his shoulder. "Yo, did you go say hey to your girl?"

"Not my girl, asshole," he mumbles and turns to skate into position.

"Are you sure?" I chirp back before moving back to the goal and into position for puck drop. Yeah, I feel a little better now that I've riled up Scottie for the night.

The referee takes his position, and at the sound of the buzzer, the puck is dropped and the game begins.

"Let's go, assholes," Knight yells from his crease. Hawkins looks at me and nods, and that's all we need to be good to go.

Bear wins the face-off and passes the puck to Scottie, who takes off down the ice like a bat out of hell. Looks like my chirping helped, because not thirty seconds into the game, Scottie scores. Fucking-a-right.

Watching him skate past Morgan, she's jumping up and down, pounding on the glass. He smirks until he notices me watching him, then I see him mumble what looks like 'jackass.' I deserve it.

The game continues to grow more intense with every passing minute. Neither team is willing to let off the gas.

Not having to split my attention with the ice and the stands, the time flies by. The last minutes count down, and we are up by three. When the final buzzer rings out, the fans are in chaos.

"First round is on me at Sticks," Bear calls out.

"I'm out, Cap. I'm going to shower and head home."

"Everything good with Lily?" he questions, eyeing me with concern.

"Yeah, she was going to come tonight, but she woke up with a migraine, so she stayed home. I'm just going to pick up dinner and have a nice quiet night in."

"Let me know if you need anything once you're home. I can always run it over."

"You're the best, Bear. Thanks, man." Smacking him on the back, I rush through a shower so I can hopefully skip the press line.

Lily

Ding.

Lifting my phone off the counter, I see it is the message I've been waiting for. Roger is letting me know Alex has arrived in the parking garage and is on the way up. It's crazy what a little food delivery to the doorman can get you.

Jumping up to my spot on the counter, all the lights are off; now I'll sit here and wait for Alex to find me. Knowing him, it won't take long.

Listening intently, I hear the elevator ding, then the key in the door. When Alex pushes inside and notices the lights are off, he's quiet as he drops his hockey bag by the door and removes his shoes.

"Lily," he calls out, but I don't respond. I bite the inside of my cheeks to hold in a giggle. He seems to like games, so I hope he likes mine.

It's hard to follow his shadow as he moves around the dark apartment looking for me and calling out my name. He hasn't turned on any lights, probably because I had a migraine when he left me earlier today.

"Lily, where are you?" he calls out a little more frantically from the direction of his bedroom. Lights are not coming on as he's moving throughout the apartment.

"Lily?" He's near manic; I feel bad and am about to jump off when the kitchen light blares on and I'm bathed in fluorescent lights. Lifting my gaze, I lock eyes with a pissed off, shirtless Alex.

"What the fuck, spitfire? I was about to call Eddie. I thought that psycho somehow got past security and found you."

"I—I—I'm so sorry, Alex. I just wanted to play a little joke." Tears spring to my eyes, and I can't stop them from flowing down my face.

He takes a step toward me, and I involuntarily flinch.

"Baby?" The regret on his face is evident. I didn't mean to flinch; it was just a reaction.

"Lily, you know I'm not actually mad, right? I was just scared," he whispers, hands by his sides where I can see them.

"I didn't mean to flinch, Alex. I'm sorry. I don't know why I did that," I cry out, arms wrapping around myself.

"Can I come to you?"

All I can do is nod. He's next to me in three steps, stepping between my open legs.

"Baby, look at me." He tilts my chin up. "I didn't mean to raise my voice. Please, I'm sorry, baby. I was just so scared when I couldn't find you. As long as the guy that hurt you is free, please don't do that again. Okay?"

I bury my face into his chest.

His arms go around me, and he moves in as close as he can.

"I'm scared too, Alex. So I won't do anything like that again," I mumble against him, not willing to pull back to look at him.

"You're allowed to be scared, be cautious, but not in here, not with me. Because, Lily, I'll take care of you, protect you. With my last breath. I promise."

There's a change in the room as the energy shifts around us.

He pushes off the counter and takes a single step back so he can look into my eyes.

My tongue slides across my lips, and as much as I try, my breaths quicken. He's still riding high on the adrenaline of their game win, and I like seeing Alex carefree.

His brown eyes are glassy from desire.

He wants this as badly as I do. As he closes the distance between us, he never breaks eye contact.

With one hand on my waist, he uses the other to pull the scrunchie that holds my hair in a loose, messy bun on the top of my head free.

"You should wear your hair down more often. My spitfire," he murmurs while sliding his fingers through my long, wavy hair. Twisting one curl around his finger, he gives it a tug.

A gasp slips through my parted lips.

"Oh, Lily," he growls as he buries his face in my hair.

"Do you know what seeing you in my jersey, with no pants on, does to me?"

"That was the plan," I chuckle.

My laugh is cut short as his mouth slams against mine. Fisting the sides of the jersey, he's pulling me as close as our bodies will allow.

Kissing him is like coming home. It's hard to explain, but not only does it make me hot as hell, it brings a sense of calm to my anxiety-filled life. Unable to hold in a moan, the sound breaks the spell we are under.

"Fuck, Lily." His palms drop to my bare thighs, sliding them up and down my legs before pushing them wide.

With a half smile on his face, he drops to his knees in front of me. He leans in and places a kiss on my calf, working his way up my legs.

"Lily?"

"Hmmm." That's all I can get out.

"Do you have any attachment to these panties?"

"What?"

"Never mind," he says a second before both hands are on the black lace, and using his chest to keep me from flying off the counter, he gives one quick tug and the sides snap.

"Alex," I gasp out. "What the fuck?"

Chuckling against my sensitive skin, he says playfully, "They were in the way, and now they're not."

Before I can get a word out, I feel the first graze of his tongue, and the argument leaves my mouth. Gladly falling back onto my elbows, my eyes roll back as his head buries deeper between my legs.

"As much as I love your tongue, Alex, tonight I want more."

Using my foot, I hook it in the front of his sweatpants and push them down his legs, huffing when my toes aren't able to push his boxers down with them. Lifting from my elbow, I sit straight, rubbing my chin along his manicured beard, and I run my hands down his chest. Stopping my hands just above his boxers, he lifts his eyes to meet mine.

I slip my hand inside his black boxers, giving his hard cock a squeeze.

"Spitfire, if you keep doing that, I'm going to embarrass myself."

Licking the seam of his lips, he growls, pulling back slightly.

"We don't want that, big man, now do we?"

His hand snakes up my back, leaving goosebumps everywhere he touches. Lacing his fingers through my hair, he grabs a fistful, and jerks my head to the side. "Tell me what you want, baby. What does your body need?"

"You. I need you."

"I need you too, spitfire. I need you so fucking much. You're going to hold onto me, because I'm going to take you fast," he orders.

"Damn, Morgan was right. Your adrenaline after a game leads to great sexy time."

"Fuck yeah, it does." Reaching into the drawer next to us, he pulls out a condom.

I look at him in shock. "Do you have them just hidden around the house?"

"Well, yeah. When you moved in here, I may have stashed a few here and there." He shrugs like it's nothing.

"You don't need to wear one if you don't want to. It's not like we haven't already done it without one."

Bringing both hands up to caress my cheeks, he looks into my eyes. "I didn't want to assume, Lily. But if you are giving me the green light to take you bare every time, I will warn you now, I'll be taking you every chance I can get. In the shower, on the couch, in the car... anyplace will be fair game."

Biting my lower lip to stop from grinning, I nod my head. "I want to feel all of you, Alex, with no barrier."

With a growl, he takes my mouth, delivering a bruising kiss.

Lining himself up at my entrance, he holds my eyes as he drives into me with a single thrust. Letting out a scream, my pussy clenches down on his cock.

"Fuuuuck, you feel too good, Lily."

He's moving, pounding into me. "Oh—Alex—" I cry out, holding onto his shoulders like my life depends on it.

"Gonna own you, spitfire. You want me to fill you up with my cum so you can watch it drip out of you?" he groans.

"Yes, Alex. Please," I whimper.

"Get there, Lily. I need you with me," he pants, not slowing down.

I'm a shaking, mewling mess as he pounds into me from this angle. My legs are shaking, and I'm so close. He can tell. Reaching a hand up under the jersey, he pinches my sensitive nipples, and it hurdles me over the edge.

Slamming home once more, we cry out our release together.

Still buried inside me, we stay in each other's arms until our breathing levels out. My head rests on his shoulder, and he's placing small kisses on my neck and exposed shoulder.

"Shower?" he questions.

"Shower," I lazily agree.

His grip on my thighs softens as he steps back and slips out of me. The feel of his warm release between my legs brings me a feeling I'm not used to. Being claimed? Loved?

He turns to the side and slips an arm under my legs and keeps one on my back. Lifting me from the counter, I curl into his chest, enjoying the warmth.

Setting me on the counter in the bathroom, he turns the shower on before turning back to me.

"Ready for round two, spitfire?"

Chapter Thirty-Four
Lily

Why did I agree to this? I'm going to be sick. Maybe I can sneak out and leave him a note before he makes it back from practice and the grocery store.

Pulling out my phone, I hit the video call.

Less than ten seconds later, my bestie's face fills the screen. "Ho, what's up?"

"I need help?" Sinking down to the floor, I feel like my chest is constricting and my lungs won't take in air.

"Lily. Talk to me. What's happening? Where's Alex? Do I need to call him or 9-1-1?"

Shaking my head violently, I try to force the words from my mouth. "I agreed to dinner with his parents and sister, Morgan."

"Lily, damn it. You're having a panic attack. You need someone there with you. I'm leaving the hospital, but I'm calling Scottie because I don't have your boy toy's number, which you really should give me, and if he doesn't answer, I'm calling Jordan. You need to breathe for me, Lily, before you black out. Everything will be okay. I'm going to call them and call you right back."

She doesn't wait for me to answer before she disconnects. Two minutes later the video request rings out. Hitting the accept, Morgan's voice fills the room.

"Lily, Jordan is right around the corner. He was in a business meeting, but you come first. He probably isn't on the approved visitor list, so that will be a problem with sweet-pants Roger, but Jordan won't let that stop him from getting to you. I left a voicemail and text for Scottie. They must still be on the ice. I'm going to stay on the line until my brother gets there."

Tears stream down my face, and I focus on breathing, even though it feels like my entire body is trying to shut down. Time stands still, so I'm not sure how long it takes someone to get to Alex's penthouse. One minute the apartment is silent except for Morgan telling me to "breathe in, breathe out," then the next second, right outside the door is filled with arguing.

"I don't care who you say you are, sir. Until I can verify with Ms. Sterling, you don't step foot inside Mr. Bensen's home. Don't make me call the police."

"Call the fucking police. Make sure you spell my name correctly. Neither you, nor them will stop me from getting inside to check on my friend. Now open the damn door."

"You are not going in there without me."

"Fine."

I hear the door open and Morgan yelling for Jordan. "I'm here, Morgan. Try to call Scottie again."

"Okay, take care of Lily."

I'm scooped up into strong, familiar arms. "Lily girl, look at me."

"Is Ms. Sterling okay?"

I hear Roger and the concern in his voice.

"She's having a panic attack, but she will be fine. You can head back down to the door. Alex said you keep the building safe, and I appreciate that. Lily, here's a special girl, and her safety means the world to me. Thank you for your help today."

"I can't leave without Ms. Sterling telling me it's okay."

"It's...okay...Roger..." I'm able to gasp out.

Roger and Jordan exchange a few words, but I tune them out.

Hearing the door shut, Jordan carries me through the kitchen, already knowing he is grabbing me an ice pack, and we move to the living room. As he sits on the sofa, he keeps me on his lap, pulling me close. Placing the ice pack on the back of my neck, it's something I've done for years as a way to ground me. Once my breathing starts to even out, he pulls the ice pack off my neck, keeping me on his lap but reaching behind us to pull the blanket down and wrap it around us.

"Are you ready to talk about what happened?" Jordan questions, worry in his voice.

"I'm sorry for all the bother," I say in a whisper. "As soon as I thought about dinner with Alex's parents, I had flashbacks of the accident. But now I'm worried Alex will think I don't want to meet his parents."

"He's going to have a right to be worried, Lily. I'm sure Morgan's messages made it sound like you were dying, and you know Scottie can't relay information for shit."

"What if he doesn't understand?" Tears well in my eyes again.

"He will, Lily. He's crazy about you. Anyone with eyes can see it."

"Are you sure?"

"He's sure, spitfire," Alex announces as he makes his way across the room. "Oh, baby. Are you okay? Roger had me so worried. I thought a maniac was trying to break into our apartment to get to you."

Jordan and I both looked at him. "Roger? Not Scottie?"

"Oh, Scottie, too. But I always check my phone as soon as I get off the ice, and I have so many missed messages from Roger. Scottie was in the shower, and I made him get out and check his phone. That's when we put two and two together, and I rushed straight home."

Sitting down next to Jordan, Alex reaches over and pulls me into his lap.

"What happened, baby?"

Tears roll down my cheeks. "It's so stupid. I'm sorry to cause such a fuss."

"No, no, no. Nothing you do is stupid, Lily. I just want to be able to help you as much as possible."

Jordan, rising from the couch, says, "I'm going to head out so you both can talk. Call me if either of you needs anything. I'll call my sister as I leave so she's not storming over here."

Reaching up to shake his hand, Alex says, "Thank you for everything, man. I can't thank you enough for being here for my girl."

"No thanks needed. I'm always here for either of you." He walks out the door, leaving us alone.

"Now, spitfire, do you want to talk about it?" Looking deep into my eyes, I see no judgement, only worry.

Letting out a deep breath, I decide to just spit it all out. "Fine. I'm worried about the dinner tonight with your family. I know you've told me about them, but I won't be able to handle seeing any animosity in their eyes. Are you sure they don't hold any ill feelings towards me?" Letting out a sob, I bury my face into his chest. Inhaling deeply, his scent calms me as he squeezes me tighter.

"Oh, baby. That's what has you worried? I've had to stop my mother from storming over here no less than a dozen times because she can't wait to meet you. If you are still uncomfortable, I will have no problem calling them and postponing. When you are feeling anxious, just remember this: you fucking saved my life. My sister's life. My parents feel indebted to you. They are going to love you."

"I will always save you, Alex. You are important to me."

"Hell, Lily, you are my everything. Just remember that when you are nervous."

"Thank you, Alex. I will try to remember those words. And no postponing. This needs to happen sometime, and I will choose to believe everything you've just said. Now that you are home, I am okay. You are my calm, Alex. My happy place, because I feel safe with you."

"I'll always keep you safe, Lily. Against anything and everything."

We sit together, holding each other tight, for a while. It's only when Alex's phone beeps, that we are pulled out of our bubble.

Looking at his phone, he tilts it so I can see. It's a message from his mother.

> **Mom:** I don't think I can wait until dinner. Can I come now? What if I bring dessert?
>
> **Alex:** One hour, and we are going to order in. Bring something chocolate.
>
> **Mom:** I will bring all the chocolate. See you both in one hour.

"How about we make tonight easy and order in? I know you and I were going to cook together, but my parents would be happy with sandwiches if that's what we served."

"Yeah, that sounds good. And they can come over whenever. I just need time to shower." Standing from his lap, I move down the hall.

"I hope you don't think you're showering alone, love." He's hopping down the hall, pulling off clothes as he goes. Giggles escape me, and I run fast towards his room.

Not even making it to the bathroom door, strong arms lift me from behind. Yes, a shower with Alex is just what I need to relax and get out of my head.

One hour on the dot, pounding resounds throughout the apartment.

Arms wrap around my waist, and Alex leans down to kiss the top of my head. "You ready, spitfire?"

"As I'll ever be."

"Alex, If you don't open this door, Mom's going to use her key," Julie yells through the door.

"Let's just stand here and see how long it takes her to give in," Alex whispers. "I bet thirty more seconds and she's bursting through the door."

He was wrong. She didn't last another ten seconds. As she walks through the door, her eyes are covered. Alex's dad and Julie, arms full of bags, stand in the doorway.

"Alexander Bensen, you better be decently dressed," she yells, not knowing we are only a few feet in front of her.

"If you are worried about my state of dress, you shouldn't have barged into my apartment."

Removing her hands from her eyes, her face lights up when she sees us. Alex steps forward to give his mom a hug but is shocked silent when she pushes him aside and barrels towards me. "Oh, my darling girl. It's about time my selfish son allowed me to come meet you. The girl that kept my family together."

Not having a choice, I'm pulled into the warmest hug I've felt since my parents passed away.

"It's nice to meet you, Mrs. Bensen."

"Oh, none of that bullshit. It's Jade. We don't do formal things in our family, unless it's at work."

Julie and his dad stand back and give Jade time to get to meet me out of her system. There are tears and hugs. "Julie darling, come meet Lily."

I should've expected the hug, but I wasn't expecting her to slam into me so hard that I almost fall and take us both down. Julie's arms wrap around my waist, and she holds tight. Tears catch in my throat as I try to keep my emotions in check.

Running my hand down her beautiful, brown hair that matches her brother's, I say, "It's great to see you again, Julie."

It's Alex's dad's turn next. Alex just leans against the kitchen wall, watching the interactions. Being pulled into another giant hug, Alex's dad whispers to me, "It's great to finally meet you, my girl."

"Um, Dad, that's my girl," states Alex, which brings laughter all around.

"Of course, of course, Alex. But don't get jealous; I think you may lose her to your mother and sister anyways." He smirks.

"I didn't say I wouldn't share, but she's still *my* girl."

I love seeing the free side of him. I've caused him so much worry and stress lately, it is nice to see him joking with the people he loves."

Looking at his phone, he announces, "Dinner's on its way up. We don't need to eat right away, but I wanted it here in case people were ready."

"We brought eight different chocolate desserts. We couldn't decide what to bring, so Dad told them a little of everything," Julie excitedly explains.

Grabbing the bag from the floor, Alex takes it to the table and starts removing containers. "Damn, Dad, you did good. I'm tempted to skip dinner and go straight for dessert." Alex looks at me and wags his eyebrows. His father sees and just laughs. They aren't embarrassed to be open in front of each other. I miss the feeling of being part of a family, so I'll enjoy this time together.

After promising Julie no less than a dozen times that she can spend the night soon, Alex and I are finally alone. I let my mind wander and picture what it might look like to someday be a part of the Bensen family. Then I internally chide myself for thinking I belong with them.

Walking over to the dishwasher, I place my wineglass inside and set it to run. Thinking about going back over to the couch and watching the city below move about, I'm stopped when two muscular arms wrap around my waist.

"Was tonight what you expected?" He kisses the side of my neck before nuzzling his nose into my hair.

"Tonight was everything, Alex. You don't know the weight that has been lifted off my chest after meeting everyone. Thank you." Leaning back into him, I allow myself to take in his warmth.

"How about we make it an early night, and you can thank me in the bedroom?"

Turning in his arms, I dramatically gasp at his comment. "Are you ever not horny?"

"Not when you are in my arms, spitfire."

My cheeks heat because my body wants him too. Fake yawning, I move out of his arms. "I think going to bed sounds nice. I am suddenly tired, so a good night's sleep is just what I need."

Alex picks me up in his arms and moves towards the bedroom. "Oh, darling, the last thing you'll get tonight is a good night's sleep. I plan to keep you awake for hours," *kiss*, "and hours," *kiss*, "and hours."

"You're mighty confident in your stamina, aren't you, Mr. Ego?"

"Girl, you have no idea the stamina I have, but I will take pleasure in proving it to you."

"Looking forward to it, big guy."

Chapter Thirty-Five
Lily

I feel like a prisoner, and no one will help me. Eddie tells me just to enjoy the time off, Morgan tells me to relax and catch up on some reading, and Jordan is conveniently ignoring my calls and only texting me back things like, "haha it can't be that bad." I want to strangle them all.

Well, I've had enough. Alex can't keep me trapped in this apartment no matter how much he tries. Last night, when I told him I needed to get out for a little bit, he gave me puppy dog eyes, then proceeded to toss me on the bed and give me so many orgasms I don't even remember falling asleep. That bastard can just shove his sex manipulation up his ass; I'm out of here.

They have a game tomorrow night, so he only has practice today, but not until this afternoon. Right now, he's in the shower, and by the sounds of his low singing, he's enjoying himself, so right now might be my open window. My only window. He never takes his eyes off me when he's around; it's like he's afraid I'm going to disappear into thin air or have a mental breakdown. Unfortunately, disappearing is what I'm about to do, but I'll leave a note and hope that he can forgive me.

> *Dear Jailer,*
>
> *I just needed some air, and I will be back soon. I know you're going to freak out when you realize I'm gone, so jump back in the shower and get yourself off again and relieve some of that tension, or don't stress so much. You're too young for a heart attack. If you're at practice when I get back, I'll send you a text as soon as I walk in the door. I promise I'm not running. Well, technically I am, that's where I went—for a run. But I will be back.*
>
> *Try to understand this from my perspective. I'm sorry, and I'll see you soon.*
>
> *- Lily*

The water in the shower just shut off; I have to move it. Rushing to the front door, I grab my running shoes, not taking the time to put them on. I'll do that in the elevator. As quietly as possible, I shut the door behind me, thankful that Alex has an automatic electric lock.

Running to the stairs, I go down one flight before cutting over for the elevator just in case he notices I am gone and comes out into the hallway in a towel. Because yes, Alex would chase me down in a towel. I have zero doubt of that.

Making it to the lobby, Roger, the very personable doorman, is waiting for me, arms crossed, tapping his right foot.

"Ms. Lily, Mr. Bensen just called down in a panic looking for you."

Whipping my head around like he is going to pop out from around the corner, I jump. "Sorry, Roger, I can't talk right now. Just going for a run and don't want to waste the daylight."

He is yelling behind me as I put my headphones on and push through the doors. He is no doubt jumping onto a call with Alex, ratting me out. Snitches get stitches, Roger.

I don't even make it half a block before my smartwatch is vibrating, letting me know I have an incoming call. Well, he will just need to wait. If I answer him now, I know I'd have no self-control and will hear the disappointment in his voice and turn right around.

No, I need to run. I need to breathe fresh air. He can give me this time. We haven't heard anything from that psychopath since they've hidden me away in Alex's penthouse, so the chance that he is out on the street this very minute is unlikely.

Alex

Pulling out my phone, I have two calls to make. The first one, I dread more.

It only rings once before he picks up. "Bensen, what's going on, man? Practice starts soon, where are you at?" my captain asks.

"Bear, I'm about to lose my shit."

He chuckles. The fucker actually fucking chuckled at me. "What did the fiery redhead do now?"

"She broke out of the apartment while I was in the shower, left me a bullshit note about needing air, and then when I tried to get the doorman to stop her, she brushed him off and pushed past him," I grumble.

"Always take her in the shower with you. Rookie move leaving her alone, dude. So I'm guessing you won't be at practice; I'll get that covered with the coach. Do you think Lily's in danger? Do you need us to help look for her? You know your guys' safety comes first."

"No, I'm good for now. If I need anything, I'll call or text you. If she's not back within the next hour, I'll let Morgan know. I don't think Lily will ignore her, I think she'd be too scared. At least I would be. That chick scares the shit out of even me."

"Isn't that the truth? I think the only person that's not scared of her is Scottie. He riles her up on purpose. I think it turns him on. It's gross. But I'm gonna hit the ice early; keep me updated."

"Will do. Thanks, Bear."

As soon as he disconnects, I make my last call. I have a few things to get ready before Lily comes back, so I'll need to make this one quick.

I almost think I'll need to leave a voicemail before the call finally connects. "Alex, how's my favorite son doing?"

"Only son, Dad. Hey, I only have a minute, but I need a favor."

"Hmmm. A favor, huh? Well, before you ask, just know that your mother is already trying to find an excuse to come back over to your place. That girl of yours made quite the impression on her last night. And your sister hasn't shut up about her, not that we'd ever tell her to stop. There's nothing we'd ever be able to do for her to repay her for keeping our family together."

"Well, my favor may be a little awkward. Just don't tell Mom, okay?" I chuckle.

"You know I don't keep anything from your mother."

"It involves Lily, but I swear to you, it is for her own safety."

There's a few seconds of silence. "For her safety, huh?"

"One hundred percent."

"Okay, ask away."

Lily

The second the door closes behind me, I know I made the wrong decision to leave the apartment without talking to Alex first. Every step of my run, I second guessed my decision. Taking my shoes off, I turn to head for the shower; that's when I see him.

Leaning against the kitchen island, arms crossed over his chest, shirtless with his chest heaving and a look on his face that has my brain screaming at me to turn around and run.

"Hey, spitfire, did you have a good run?" His voice is low but not threatening.

"Um, yeah. But shouldn't you be at practice?" I try to sound casual, but at the same time, I'm sure the apartment below us can hear the pounding of my heart.

He chuckles, pushing off the counter, and slowly walks towards me. "Practice? While you're out running the streets with someone out there trying to kill you? Hardly, spitfire. I don't think I'd even be able to hit the puck right now, and I don't think Coach Reyes would be too amused."

He speaks casually, but the way he is moving towards me looks more like stalking.

Can I make it to the bedroom and lock the door before he catches me? Give him time to cool down? Absolutely not. There was no chance at all. So I stopped trying to run.

"Where are you trying to go, Lily?"

He slides up behind me, wrapping his arms around my waist. Maybe he isn't as upset with me as it first appeared.

Alex

With a false sense of security, she never saw the betrayal coming. Running my hands up her body, Lily lets out a little moan. Sagging against me, I feel like a bastard because she is getting turned on. As my left hand stays on her stomach, my right hand moves to the right side of her neck. "I'm sorry, Lily," I say seconds before I give her a quick tap to her carotid sinus, and she collapses into my arms.

During our confrontation, my phone rings, but of course I don't stop to check it. The package from my father is set to deliver in the next five minutes. That will be perfect, because I don't know how long Lily will stay out, and I need the medication that will be inside the package.

I already had the guest bed prepared in case a few drops of blood spilled, so I place her gently on it. Our bed in the master is ready for after I'm done with the next steps of my plan.

By the time Lily is situated on the bed, the package should be waiting on my doorstep. Not knowing how much time I have before she wakes up, I rush to the front door, only it isn't the package waiting for me, but my father.

"I don't have time for explanations, Dad. I'll call you later." I grab the bag out of his hand and try pushing him out of my apartment, but he won't budge.

"If you think I don't know what you're doing, you're an idiot, and I didn't raise an idiot for a son. I just want to make sure you do this right, okay? Do you want my help or not?"

Do I want him involved? No. Could I use his help? Absolutely. The last thing I want to do is hurt Lily. "Fine. Let's go."

Turning on my heels, I lead the way to the guest room.

Dropping to my knees beside the bed, I feel a hand on my shoulder. "I never thought I'd see that day that my son was so in love that he'd commit so many felonies."

"Shut the fuck up, Dad, and help me," I huff.

Grabbing the bag from my hands, Dad dumps it out at the foot of the bed. He holds up the vial of midazolam, which he seems to know the correct dose Lily will need for what we are about to do. Knowing he'd never hurt the woman I'm obsessed with, I trust him completely.

As he brings the needle closer to her arm, my jaw clenches tighter. "Dad?"

"She'll be okay, Alex, this won't hurt her. But if you are second guessing this, you need to tell me now. Once we start the next steps, it will be harder to stop, and if we finish this, you'll need to be prepared to accept the consequences for when she finds out. Because she will find out eventually."

"I know, and I'll handle it when it comes to that. If this protects her from the psychopath that attacked her—the same one that hurt Julie—any repercussions will be worth it. And wouldn't you do the same thing if Mom was in danger?"

He nods his understanding. "How do you know your mother doesn't already have one? Enough talking, let's begin."

Instead of fumbling my way through what is next, I put aside my hesitation of letting another man touch Lily and let my dad do all the work. I hold her hand while she sleeps through my father making an incision in the healing lacerations on the back of her head from her recent attack and places a tracker that is smaller than my pinky nail.

Looking over his shoulder, I watch my father apply skin glue to Lily's head so there won't be any stitches to alert her to the new incision.

"There, it's all set. While she's sleeping, let's clean up and set up the app on your phone." He grabs the paper bag and starts throwing all his medical waste inside, not wanting to leave anything behind that Lily could find.

"I'm going to move her to the other room, so I'll meet you in the living room."

Carefully lifting her to avoid her head, I move towards our bedroom. Dad, standing in the doorway, is shaking his head. "Son?"

Looking into the room, I see the handcuffs I attached to the side of the bed are visible.

"Alexander?"

"She ran from me. Why do you think I wanted the tracker?"

"I hope you know what you're doing. You've only allowed me to meet her once, but I don't know any woman that would appreciate waking up handcuffed to a bed without her permission."

"Noted. Let's just set up the app so you can go home to Mom."

He chuckles. "Yeah, you better hope your mother never finds out about this."

"You better not tell her." I glare at him.

"Me? Hell no. She'll bury me in the backyard just for helping you in this crazy plan of yours. My lips are sealed. As long as you forget my comment about your mother already having one."

"Agreed. And thanks, Dad, for never judging me."

"Oh, Alex, maybe one day I'll tell you about the time in college your mother thought we needed a break. The only thing I'll say about it is she got her break at our lake house. That's where she learned she liked to be chased through the woods."

"Ugh, Dad, too much."

His laughter booms through the living room. "You started it. Now let's finish this before Lily wakes up, then you can figure out how you will survive her when she tries to kill you."

Chapter Thirty-Six
Lily

What the hell is wrong with my head? Did I go out with Morgan and drink too much? Why am I having a hard time remembering what I did before I fell asleep? Ugh. Whatever I was doing, I need a shower; my body felt sticky.

As I try to sit up, my left arm won't move. Using my right hand, I throw back the cover and see there is a handcuff on my wrist, and it is attached to the side of the bed. Bile rises in my throat, and I look for anywhere to vomit. Not seeing anywhere, I just lean over the side of the bed, but nothing comes out.

Pulling at my arm, the metal digs into my skin, sending pain down my arm and into my chest. "Alex," I bellow. Fear creeps into my chest. I'm in Alex's bedroom, so my stalker hasn't found me, but why the fuck am I chained to the bed?

The door cautiously opens, and Alex stands there, leaning against the frame, watching me but not saying a word.

"Unlock these now, Alex." I stare straight into his eyes and I tug on the handcuff. Pain, once again, shooting up my arm.

"Stop fighting them, spitfire. You're hurting yourself."

"Don't call me your fucking spitfire, you psychotic asshole. Get these off me, NOW!"

"I can't do that, Lily."

"Why, Alex?" Tears stream down my face, and I refuse to wipe them away. I am not crying because I'm sad; I'm crying because I want to murder this man standing in front of me, and I can't reach him.

"Because you left, and I didn't know if you were safe."

This is all because I left the apartment without his permission? "That's no excuse to chain me to your bed. You're no better than the kidnapper."

"You don't mean that," he whispers, looking devastated.

"I do, Alex. I mean every word," I hiss. "How am I supposed to trust you after this?"

"If you need to hate me for now, I'll live with it. Why? Because I know you're safe. When I got out of the shower and saw your note, all I could think about was all the ways he could take you, hurt you, and I'd never see you again. Your pain is not something I'm willing to compromise on, Lily. I would destroy the entire city to find you. Can't you understand at all why I had to do this?"

"No, Alex. I can't. Do you not understand what having my choice taken away does to me?" I sob. "I was given no choice when I had to leave my home years ago over my safety, and it almost killed me to be away. Now the person I thought I could trust above anyone else has taken away my freedom and chained me to their bed. No, Alex, I don't understand."

His hand flies to his chest and rubs over his heart. "For four years I searched everywhere for you, Lily. You know this because I've told you. What I haven't told you is that I dream about what would happen if that psychopath got his hands on you. I dreamt about how he would torture you, destroy your body, your spirit, before taking your life. That has been the nightmare I've lived with the past four years, and that was before I even *knew* you. Before I fell in love with you. Yes, I love you, Lily. When I got the call that he found you, touched you, hurt you, before I knew you were okay, it felt like I was dying with you. So yes, I went a little crazy, but I'd do it again if it meant keeping you safe. Your life means more to me than anything, my love, and I hope one day you can forgive me. Because if you think this is crazy, you don't want to see the level I'd go to if he comes near you again."

We stare at each other, no more words spoken. The tears stop falling down my face, and his chest stops heaving.

Finally, he shakes his head. "I'm going to make you breakfast, if you need me, call out."

"You're not going to uncuff me?" I cry out.

"When you promise not to leave, I will. Lily, I can't have you risk your life."

"It's my life to risk."

"It's our life, Lily. Because if anything happens to you, you'll take me with you, because I won't live if you are gone. If you don't exist anymore, I don't exist. If something happens to you, they may as well give you an extra-large coffin, because I'd be crawling right in there with you." He sighs. "Rest, I'll be back soon."

My body is betraying me. I was going to freeze him out, go on a hunger strike, but the moment the smell of coffee and French toast wafted into the bedroom, I knew I'd have to find another way to show him how destroyed I am by his betrayal.

The door opens a few minutes after the smells hit me, and Alex walks in with a tray covered in all my favorites and sits down on the edge of the bed. Not looking him in the eyes, I cover my body and move as far across the bed as my confines will allow.

He reached out to touch my knee but stops as I flinch and pull away.

"Lily, you need to eat."

"I'm not hungry," I whisper, even though it is a lie.

"Fine, but I'm going to leave this here. I have a game tonight, so I'll be gone for a few hours."

Darting my eyes to his, "Can you release me first? Please, Alex."

"Will you run?"

When I don't respond, he stands and moves towards the door.

"I love you, Lily. We will talk when I get back," he grits out.

Just as the door is closing, I call out. "Did you mean what you said?"

"I don't know what words you mean, Lily. But I never lied to you. So if it came out of my mouth, it was the truth."

"When you said you won't live if I'm gone."

"Every. Fucking. Word." He turns and walks out the door.

Listening to the sounds around me, I make sure he is out of the apartment before giving in and reaching for the orange juice. The taste is a little off, maybe it is a different brand. Who knows?

His words play over and over in my head. He loves me? I haven't said it back to him, but I've been feeling the same way for a while, but can he love me and still do what he did? He said he has nightmares about me, and if I'm honest with myself, I've been having the same nightmares for years, and they scare the shit out of me. Then there is him saying that if something happened to me, he wouldn't be able to live. That's crazy, right?

Or is it crazy that I want to give in to him and let him take care of me? I've lived every day for the last four years thinking it might be my last, never letting anyone but Morgan, Jordan, and Eddie get too close. What if I want to be selfish and let someone else take care of me? What if I want someone to care for me enough to be crazy obsessed, but in the best way?

When Alex comes back, I'll talk to him about it. Right now, I have this need to sleep.

Chapter Thirty-Seven
Alex

Her pulse has evened out; it looks like she fell asleep. Maybe she drank the orange juice. If that's the case, she should be out for the next couple of hours.

"Put your phone away and get on the ice before Coach flips his shit," Bear calls out from the doorway. "Didn't you hear me yell the first two times?"

"No, sorry. I'm coming now."

"What has your attention on your phone?"

"Uh, nothing." Tossing my phone into my locker, I turn to head to the ice.

Bear, unnaturally quiet, is reaching into my locker. "You're hiding something. Tsk tsk tsk."

"It's none of your..."

"God damn it, Alex."

Bear has my phone open. I guess I didn't lock the screen, shit.

"Should I prepare bail money? Is this what I think it is?"

"Probably? It's something my dad was working on. Originally created for livestock so farmers can track them from the comfort of their homes and see if any are in distress, it works on humans too."

"I don't know if you're a psychopath or a genius."

"I guess it will depend if Lily kills me if she finds out I put a tracker in her, and that won't even matter if she doesn't forgive me for handcuffing her to my bed this morning," I tell him with a shrug.

Wack. I don't even see Bear's fist before it connects with the side of my face.

"I don't know what the fuck you two are doing in here, but if you are ready to earn the money we pay you, get your asses on the ice before I bench you both," Coach Reyes screams.

"This isn't over," Bear threatens, poking his finger into my chest.

Am I a coward? Normally, no. But the second the game is over, I rush out of the locker room without showering while the coach is talking to Bear and before he is able to stop me.

On the way home, I stop and pick up a variety of pastries and a bouquet of flowers. Not that either would be enough of an *I'm sorry* for Lily to forgive my actions, but I'm going to try.

The apartment is quiet; Lily is still sleeping. In the bedroom, the food is still untouched, but as I expected, the orange juice is gone.

After a quick shower, I dress in only my boxers, lift the comforter, and crawl into the bed. I'm resigned to stay on my side of the bed until she mumbles in her sleep. The medication I slipped into her juice won't allow me to wake her up yet, so I pull her into my arms, hoping that will comfort her at least a little.

The heat from her body penetrates deeply into mine. Soon, I am struggling against my body to stay awake. I want to savor the feel of her against my skin, knowing as soon as she wakes, the fight will be back. A fight I deserve. But a fight I won't back down from, because everything I do, I do to protect her, even if she can't see it.

I feel it the moment she wakes up. She is no longer melding into my arms, but now she's stiff as a board. Her breaths hasten, and I can feel her pulse race.

"It's just me, baby," I whisper into her hair.

"Remove your arms from around me, Alex," she hisses, trying to roll out of my grasp.

"I don't think so, spitfire. We are going to talk and get everything out in the open now. I'm not going to have you turning away from me."

"You don't have a choice, Alex. I want my phone, and I want to leave. You handcuffed me, you fucking psycho."

"Would you believe me when I tell you I did it because I love you?"

"No. Because that's not love, Alex." Her eyes glisten with unshed tears.

Grabbing her shoulders, I force her to look at me.

"Yes, Lily. Love. All-consuming, boundless, unwavering, obsessing love. You will find out that what I feel for you may not be conventional because I don't care about what is considered conventional love. I know what I feel for you and how you invade every fiber of my being. You are in every breath I take, every beat of my heart, every move I make. From the moment we met, you've owned every part of me. If you are taken from me, I am nothing. Will be—nothing. Because you are the other half of me. We are endgame, we are everything."

"Fuck you, Alex," she screams, shaking and crying.

"Tell me what you're thinking, Lily?" I'll do anything to have her trust me again—anything but let her go.

"Why do your words penetrate my heart when I told myself to harden it against you and your psychotic ways? Why does what you say make it feel like your actions are justified? Why… why does it feel like I want to accept your crazy when that will make me just as crazy?" She whimpers and pulls her arms into herself.

"It's because you can tell how deeply I love you and only want you to be safe. How I wasn't lying when I said that without you, there's no me. Even if your brain hasn't caught up yet, your heart has. That's why you are having an internal struggle, and I'll give you all the time you need, as long as you talk to me and don't leave me."

My lips crash to hers. It was a calculated risk I was willing to take. She can push me away and yell that she hates me, but her body doesn't lie.

Feeling her reach up and grab my hair, she pulls it free from the tie. Not able to control a shudder that racks my body, I look deep into her eyes.

"Don't ever do anything like this to me again, Alex. Or it won't be endgame, it will be game over. Now take these fucking cuffs off my hand so you can make it up to me properly."

"So you're not leaving?"

"Don't handcuff me again without my permission. And sure as shit don't ever drug me again. I can't stand not being in control of my body, even if I trust you with every cell of it."

"I can agree to those terms. I love you, Lily. With my entire heart."

Chapter Thirty-Eight
Alex

Scottie: Alex, where's Lily?

Me: She's sleeping. Why?

Scottie: Morgan said she's not answering her calls or texts, and that's not like her.

Me: She's just sleeping, leave her alone.

Scottie: No way. One of the guys said they saw Bear sock you in the face yesterday. Why did he do that?

Me: I called him old.

Scottie: Don't make me move this to the team chat. I'm sure I'd get more answers.

Me: Dude, fuck off, she's fine. I'll have her call Morgan when she wakes up.

Scottie: Are you sure you didn't lock her in a dungeon or something?

Me: I'm blocking you.

Scottie: If Morgan doesn't get proof of life by tomorrow, I'll drive her over there myself. This is your only warning.

Me: Message received.

Chapter Thirty-Nine
Lily

Me: Game tonight? Alex said he got us tickets.

Morgan: Girl, I was about to castrate your lover boy if I didn't hear from you today.

Me: Sorry, I've been sleeping a lot lately. These nightmares are a bitch.

Morgan: Nightmares I understand, ho. Tonight drinks are on me.

Me: Nope, tonight drinks are on Alex!!!!!! He said something about them being club seats, so we have in-seat service, and everything is on him.

> **Morgan:** Daaaammmnnn. Okay. Okay. I can get behind this. I can rub it in Jordan's face that we are in club seats.

> **Me:** That's the spirit.

> **Morgan:** Should I pick you up?

> **Me:** No, I'm going to head to the stadium early with Alex. It makes him feel better that I'm not here alone, even though he's finally agreed to let me go back to work. It wasn't so much that he agreed as that I told him I was doing it and he couldn't stop me. But me going in a few hours early will make him happy, so…

> **Morgan:** Barf. But I understand. I'd do it too, if someone asked me to.

I was hesitant to come to the stadium early, but it's peaceful. Sitting here enjoying the smell of the ice, the chill reaching my bones, it brings back memories of when I was a child and my father would take me skating.

Alex: Are you sure you don't need anything else? I can have someone run it out to you guys.

Me: Leave those people alone. They work hard enough and don't need to cater to overpaid hockey players any more than they already do.

Alex: That's what they're here for.

Me: The fuck it is. I bet you anything that's not what their job titles are.

Alex: Anything?

Me: I swear, you need help. I wouldn't put it past you to make them change their job title.

Alex: Hmmm. Good idea.

Me: Fuck off, Alex. Head in the game.

Me: You could send Rogue up to keep me company.

> **Alex:** Not funny, spitfire.

> **Me:** KISS! Now get ready for the game, I don't need Bear blaming me if you play like shit.

> **Alex:** I'll tell him Scottie did something, and he could blame him.

> **Me:** How about you just don't play like shit. Come on, sexy hockey man. Focus.

> **Alex:** Oh, I'm focusing all right. Focusing on how I'm going to get you naked when we get home.

> **Me:** I'm going to get a drink. No more texting.

> **Alex:** Rude.

Twenty minutes and two drinks later, Morgan comes bouncing down the stairs.

"Damn, I think we need to keep these seats. Jordan can have his back; I was told before I walked down here that all food and drinks are included. And—we have our own bathroom for club members. Hells yes!" she squeaks.

"They are amazing, aren't they? I love being next to the ice, and we are only three rows up, and we can see more of the ice. I think I like these seats a bit more."

Morgan nods her agreement while sipping on her cocktail. "Warm-ups don't start for a half hour, should we see how many drinks we can finish before they take the ice?"

Before I even answer, I'm grabbing her hand and pulling her back up the aisle. They said we'd get seat-side service, but I don't have time to wait. "Yes. I need all the alcohol. I have to tell you something, and I need liquid courage to do it."

Stopping and jerking my arm back, she glares at me. "Am I going to need an alibi? Because Jordan will give me one. And do I need to go into that locker room? What happened?"

"Chill, girl. Drinks first. Lots and lots of drinks. Then and only then will I spill."

"Fine," she resumes walking. "But I will demand all the details."

"Always," I giggle. I expect nothing less from my best friend.

We didn't make it back to our seats for warm-ups, and knowing Alex, I'll hear about it later. I purposely left my phone at my seat so I wouldn't need to answer any messages. Plying Morgan with five shots, I told her everything Alex had done to me recently.

I see literal fire in her eyes. "I'm gonna kill him. And if I can't kill him, Jordan will.

"Cut the shit, Morgan. I told you because I needed to tell someone, and we keep each other's secrets. So no telling Scottie or your brother.""Fine. But let's go back to our seats, I don't want to miss puck drop."

This wasn't the end of it; I know her too well. But I still don't regret telling her, we tell each other everything.

We make it back to our seats as the announcer is calling out the starting lineup. Even with the darkness and flashing lights, we see Alex staring in our direction. Morgan locks eyes with him, giving him the two finger 'I'm watching you,' sign and even goes as far as to make a cutting motion across her throat."

If I wasn't paying close attention, I would've missed the change in his expression.

"He's going to be in his head, Morgan. You could've at least waited until after the game."

She shakes her head. "No fucking way. He had to be put on notice."

"I love you." Pulling her in for a quick hug, she never takes her eyes off him.

Oh, I'm going to hear it later.

Well, they won, no thanks to Alex. He got yelled at by the coach and Bear so much, I stopped counting how many times. He kept looking our way and looked nervous. I hope he doesn't think I was upset or going to leave. We spoke about this the other night, and I told him I was okay after everything.

The final buzzer rings, and they win 4-3. It was close.

"Ms. Sterling and Ms. Hawthorne, will you follow me, please?"

"Archie! Why are you being so proper?" Giving him a hug, he stands perfectly still, but I catch a smirk.

"Mr. Bensen is in a rare mood tonight and watching us right now. I don't need him to yell at me for giving you both a hug. But I was ordered to bring you both downstairs the back way so you are out of the crowd."

Morgan and I look at each other and nod. At the same time, we throw our arms around Archie and hug him tight.

"Y'all are trying to get me killed, aren't you?" he whispers as he glances to the players' bench and to where Alex is still watching.

"I'll protect you, big man," Morgan says cheekily while giving Alex the middle finger.

"Let's go, killer," I laugh.

We don't have to wait long for the men to start emerging from the locker room. Hawkins is first.

"Gorgeous, gorgeous, ladies. I don't know what you did to our friend, but you might want to run," he snickers.

"They aren't going anywhere."

I love Alex's growly voice. It sends shivers to my core.

"Hey babe. Great game," I call out, knowing he is standing right behind me.

"Great game, my ass. Morgan, Scottie will be right out. I'm going to take my girlfriend here so we can talk before we meet you guys at Sticks."

"I have my eye on you, Bensen," Morgan warns.

"Of that, I have no doubt, Morgan."

Picking me up and tossing me over his shoulder, he goes out a back door to the parking lot.

"So why was Morgan threatening me tonight, spitfire?"

"I have no idea what you're talking about, sweetheart." I bite my lower lip to keep from laughing.

"I'll get it out of you, one way or another," he grumbles, setting me on my feet next to the car door.

"I'm sure you will, big guy. I'm sure you will." Patting his cheek causes him to grind his teeth.

"Fuck the bar, we're going home."

"Hmmm. I can get behind that idea."

Leaning over, he buckles me in. I don't make it very far before my eyes feel heavy. That's what happens when Morgan hears free drinks; we don't stop.

Oh well, I'm sure I'll hear Alex's lecture tomorrow, but for tonight, I'm going to let the dreams take me.

Chapter Forty
Lily

> **Morgan:** Wake up, bitch. I'm on my way over with mimosas and baked shit. We need to talk about the bomb you spilled yesterday and how I'm going to torture Alex with the information.

> **Me:** Is there any use trying to deter you?

> **Morgan:** None, unless you want me to call my brother and tell him what your psycho boy toy did to you.

> **Me:** Don't you dare. Fine. See you soon.

Less than ten minutes later, there's a knock at the door.

I don't even bother to do my hair, just throw it up in a messy bun. Wearing Alex's Yeti hoodie and a pair of pajama pants, I can't put off the inevitable any longer and open the door.

"Let me see your eyes," she says, dropping the bags in the hallway, being her normal dramatic self, grabbing my face, and peering into my eyes.

"What the hell, Morgan?"

"I'm seeing if you're drugged and if I need to get my medical bag from my car."

"I'm not fucking drugged. Now get your ass inside before I shut the door and lock it."

Huffing, she pushes past me. I can see why she'd be suspicious, I'd kill someone if they did that to her.

Making herself at home, she sets the champagne and OJ on the counter and spreads bag after bag of pastries from her favorite shop across the counter.

"I hope it's okay that I have store bought OJ, I don't trust the OJ in your fridge not to be drugged."

"Let it go, Morgan. He wouldn't do it to anyone else."

Spinning on her heels to face me, there is fire in her eyes. "But it's okay for him to lock you up and drug you? How long has it been going on, Lily?"

"Not long, Morgan. Believe me, please, that I would tell you if I needed your help. Hell, you know I'd send up an SOS flare if I needed you. I... love him, and he did it because he was worried that the kidnapper would get his hands on me again. And he didn't do it until I snuck out of the apartment while he was in the shower, and I wouldn't answer my phone. He was just the right amount of crazy that I understood where he was coming from. Does that make sense?"

"I may be just as crazy as you, but yes, it does. But that doesn't negate that he drugged you, Lily. He could've just fucked you into submission, but no, he drugged you and handcuffed you to the bed. And not in a kinky kinda way. So let me have my moment and threaten to cut his balls off."

"Even if I like those balls?"

"Ho, of course, even if you like them. Because he needs to know that he needs to tone down the crazy, or at least run it by me first, or it just won't fly in this relationship."

"Oh, are you in this relationship with us now?"

She snorts. "Of course I am. I've been here since day one. We are a package deal. Right?"

"Yes, bitch. I just like when you get all needy and shit. I feel loved. Now let's drop this for now and get these mimosas flowing. I don't know when Alex will be back from his morning skate."

Alex

"Mr. Bensen," Roger calls out to me, looking a little nervous.

"What's up, Roger."

"Sir. Ms. Hawthorne is upstairs. I just wanted to warn you."

"Warn me?" I stop walking and look at the elevator. "What kind of mood was Ms. Hawthorne in when she arrived, Roger?"

"Well, if it would've been possible for fire to come out of her eyes, I guarantee the building would be ash by now."

"Roger, then why did you let her upstairs?"

"Because she's on the approved list, sir. And with all due respect, she scares me more than you do."

Breathing out a sigh, I know I can't put off going upstairs. Or can I? I'm sure one of the guys needs help doing… something today.

No. Man the hell up, Alex. Pressing the button for the elevator, Roger calls out another warning.

"Oh yeah, she also had a few bags in her hands, and they were clear, so I saw the champagne bottles."

Great. Hopefully I'm not walking into two weepy, emotional women. Tears are my kryptonite.

The second I open the door, I realize how wrong I was in my assumption. They aren't weepy at all, they are murderous. And by the sounds of the song they are singing, I am their target.

Pulling out my phone, I shoot off a text to Scottie.

> **Me:** Might need backup. Came home to a drunk Lily and Morgan. If you don't hear from me in an hour, they murdered me.

> **Scottie:** Heading your way now. Morgan doesn't need to be taking a rideshare home drunk.

> **Me:** Thanks, man, I'll leave the door unlocked. Tell Roger you're here as my reinforcements; he was worried.

> **Scottie:** I'll bring him an airplane shot bottle. He's the man.

> **Me:** Hurry… I just made eye contact, and it isn't good.

> **Scottie:** Rookie mistake.

Morgan sees me first, and instead of telling Lily, she just turns up the music and joins Lily in dancing around the kitchen, banging my pots together. What the fuck. They were singing their own rendition of *'The Chicks - Goodbye Earl'* but changed the lyrics to *'Goodbye Alex.'* I'm officially terrified.

Slowly, I walk through the entryway and into the kitchen, scanning for weapons within grabbing distance as I move. Nothing except the pans they are banging together. I'm in the clear. Lily spins, still singing, and catches my eyes.

Gasping, she drops her pans, stops singing, and for a count of five, she's silent. That's when the uncontrollable laughter starts. First Lily, then Morgan joins in. At this point, it hasn't reached the manic laughter you hear in horror movies right before someone jumps out and loses a head, but it might be moving in that direction.

"Alex, when did you get home?" Lily wheezes.

"When did you decide you wanted me dead, Lily?" I challenge.

Morgan starts jumping up and down with her hand raised. "I know this answer. It was when you drugged my best friend and handcuffed her to the bed."

It's at that moment that not only Scottie, but also Jordan walk through the door.

"Repeat what you just said, Morgan," Jordan bellows.

Lily—the ever peacekeeper—slaps Morgan on the ass as she runs past her, past me, and, to my annoyance, jumps into Jordan's arms to give him a hug.

"Jordan, one of my longest friends," she says, kissing him on the cheek, "remember you don't look good in orange, and you love me."

"Lily, what did Morgan mean when she said you were drugged and handcuffed?" Turning his head in my direction, I can feel the judging from across the room.

Biting her lower lip and giving him a shy look, she playfully says, "I don't think you want to know, Jordan. Just ignore your sister, we've had way too much to drink."

Stalking back over to her friend, she leans up and whispers into her ear. I can't imagine what she said, but Morgan scrunches her nose. "Fine," she concedes.

"Let's go, bro. Lily wants to fuck her man on the kitchen counter, and I really don't want to be here for that."

All three of us men groan, and Lily gasps but doesn't deny it. Interesting.

As she passes me, she gives me a hug, pulling me tight to whisper in my ear. "You be good to her, or I will cut your balls off, put them in the blender, put a tube down your throat, and feed them to you."

"Yes, ma'am. I only ever have her happiness and safety in mind."

"I believe that, and that's the only reason you are still standing, or breathing." Pulling from my arms, she turns to Lily. "Love you, ho. I'll message you later to check in."

The door clicks shut, and the apartment is silent. Walking up behind Lily, I snake my arms around her stomach, pulling her against me. "So, what was that about you wanting me to fuck you on the kitchen counter?"

Chapter Forty-One
Alex

Alex adds Scottie to chat
Alex adds Bear to chat

Scottie: What's up, Alex? Why the secret chat?

Bear: Did you do something stupid?

Me: Why do I have to do something stupid to talk to my two closest friends?

Scottie: Yeah, he did something stupid.

Bear: Should we be talking about this over chat?

Probably not, but what the hell.

Me: It's fine, I'm just freaking out and need to be talked down before I DO do something stupid.

Scottie: Where's Lily?

Me: She's getting ready for work tomorrow. THAT'S why I need to be talked down. I know I can't keep her handcuffed in the apartment. I learned my lesson. But that psycho is still on the loose.

Scottie: ???

Bear: ???

Me: That's neither here nor there. She's finnnnne. But tomorrow she'll be out there, and I won't be able to protect her.

Bear: Won't she be with Eddie?

Me: Yeah, but…

Scottie: I get it, dude. I do. But you can't hold her hostage.

Me: I can't? Why not?

Scottie: For fuck's sake.

Me: What if it was Morgan?

Scottie: …

Me: Yeah, see. You'd want to lock her away and keep her hidden.

Bear: He has you there, Scottie.

I wonder how pissed she'd be if I broke out the handcuffs again? Her trust in me would be gone, that's for sure. But if it meant keeping her safe?

Scottie: You can't, Alex.

Bear: Have you told her your fears?

Me: Yeah, and she understands. She's scared too. But she also doesn't want to let him rule her life. He's been doing it for the past four and a half years.

Bear: Have you met any of the other people she works with?

Me: Not really. She hasn't been back to work since her attack, and before that, we weren't officially a couple. Though...

Scottie: Though... what?

Me: My dad did a background check on the entire search and rescue department for me, and they all checked out.

Bear: Of fucking course he did.

Scottie: That's handy.

Me: Yeah. And it was my mom's idea.

Me: Do you think Coach would be okay if I skipped practice tomorrow so I could watch out for her?

Bear: No.

Scottie: You are just asking for your balls to be cut off, aren't you? If she finds out you're following her, she will kill you.

Bear: He's right.

Scottie: Say it again, Captain.

Bear: Fuck off, Scottie.

Me: Okay, okay. I got it. I'll see you dickheads tomorrow.

Bear: Don't do anything stupid, and you better be at practice.

Scottie: Don't make me show this chat to Morgan.

Me: Screw both of you.

Fine, I won't follow her, per se. But at least she still has the tracker I inserted, so I can watch her movement without the threat of my balls being removed from my body. One day at a time, but I won't be able to breathe until the CPD finally catches that psychopath.

Chapter Forty-Two
Lily

Two more hours until Morgan will be here to pick me up and we head over to Bear's house for game night. Why in the ever loving world did I agree to this? I've been staying with Alex for weeks now, and things are going very well, maybe too well.

Every day, Alex makes me feel more loved than I've ever believed I'd be. And it's all the little things that he does to me and for me. The amount of love I feel just when he walks past me and runs his fingertips down my arms is unmeasurable.

Alarms start blaring, and equipment starts clattering. Eddie's running towards me, "Lily, missing child at Navy Pier. CPD called for assistance."

Navy Pier calls are a nightmare, especially when they involve a child. The water is right there, and you'd think with how crowded the area is that people would see when a child goes over the side, but that's not always the case. Jumping to my feet and following him to the rig, all my gear is still prepped in the back, and I'd change into my dry suit on the way. Hopefully I won't need to get into the water, but I don't mind searching in full gear if it means being ready in the worst case scenario.

CPD has the pier mostly evacuated, and search parties are already in progress. We've been on a few calls where kids hide in one of the games because they don't want to go home or they are mad at their parents. "Two person teams spread out," Eddie yells.

I link up with one of the CPD officers, Officer Walden; we try to do this to spread out resources. "Hey, I'm Lily, search and rescue. Do you know if they've started checking along the water?"

The officer tilts his head and just looks at me. I'm not sure what it is, but I'm not getting a warm and fuzzy feeling from him. He looks familiar, but I'm not sure from where.

"No, not yet," he finally speaks.

"Okay," I say, taking charge of the situation. Maybe he is just new to the force or not used to situations like this. Unfortunately, this isn't my first time with a lost child down by the water. Dropping my bag and pulling out two spotlights, I hand one to the officer. "Here, let's start right here and move in that direction towards the vehicles." Pulling out my radio, I relay my plan to Eddie and the rest of the team so they can mirror my actions.

Almost to the parking lot, the water meets the retaining wall. Shining my light down the wall, there is no sign of the missing child. "Let's turn around here and go over to the other side," I tell the officer.

"No," he hisses.

"Excuse me?" I ask. Unsure if I heard him correctly.

"We aren't going to keep searching, Liliana." He steps closer to me.

I take two steps back. My shoe reaches the edge of the dock, so I have to stop. No one's called me Liliana in years, except for Eddie when he's mad, but never in front of any of the CPD officers. "Who are you? I'm guessing you aren't Officer Walden."

Looking down at his uniform, he chuckles. "I absolutely am Officer Walden. And you're Liliana Sterling, but I'm also known by a different name. Or a few different names."

Pulling the gun from his belt, he points it at my chest. "Scream and I shoot you, then I'll go pay a visit to your best friend Morgan Hawthorne, her brother Jordan, and then that douche that couldn't keep his fucking hands to himself, Alexander Bensen."

Realization dawns on me too late. "It was you."

He looks at me like I'm stupid. "Of course it was me. It's always been me. How have you liked my gifts? I've been waiting for you, Liliana."

"You're... But you're a cop. Now I remember you. You came to my apartment with Officer Burke." I can't breathe. Head whipping around, I try to catch sight of one of my teammates. Where is everyone? Alex. I need Alex.

"I've always been there, in the shadows. I was hiding in plain sight, stupid people." Taking the three steps that separate us, he latches onto my arm, shoving the gun into my side. "Now, we are going to walk quickly to the parking lot, and you aren't going to yell. If you do, I will not hesitate to shoot you. I have many identities and can disappear easily. You are disposable. The only question is, do I only take you, or you and everyone you love?"

Even though I know never to go to a secondary location with a psychopath, the gun he is holding and the threat to those I love most make all my logical decision making skills go right out the window. Alex once told me he couldn't exist without me; well, the same goes for me. But all I can hope for is that after I was gone, his family would keep him breathing.

We aren't stopped once on the way to the parking lot. I mean, why would we be? It's frustrating how few people even look in our direction. I was hoping I'd at least be able to have the chance to signal someone, but there is nothing.

My mistake is focusing so much on trying to find help that I don't notice Officer Walden take a plastic bag out of his pocket, nor do I see him open it before he's placing the rag that is inside over my nose and mouth. As soon as my brain registers the pungent smell, I know I have no chance to fight back. Ether is quick acting, and I was fucked. Alex's face fills my mind as everything goes black.

As my brain fog is lifting, I become aware I am being lifted out of a trunk. My hands are bound with the same red silk rope that has adorned my "gifts" for the past four years. The same red rope that was tied around the girl they found in the vehicle that hit Alex and Julie years ago.

Opening my mouth to scream, nothing comes out.

"Ah, she's awake. I was hoping I didn't give you too much. It would've been such a waste if I accidentally killed you too soon."

Tossing me over his shoulder, he moves into a house from an attached garage. I try to focus on the little details, but my head is pounding, I am upside down, and my vision is blurry.

"Where are we?" I mumble.

"Oh, don't worry your pretty redhead where we are. We won't be here long. Your lack of presence was noticed at the pier, so we'll need to lay low here for now until it is safe to move you. I'm thinking less than twenty-four hours, and I'll be able to get you out of the city. Then it'll be just you and me for the rest of your life. Then I'll find someone else to focus on. Maybe your friend Morgan would like an admirer. I'll have to see how long you can keep my attention."

We come to a door at the end of a long hall that, and from the sound of it, has a bunch of locks on the outside of the door. Well shit. He opens the door to the dark room and drops me inside. "I'll come check on you later. You can scream all you want, no one will hear you here. There's no one around for miles."

I need to stay calm, but how? I know how. Alex would know something terrible happened the moment Morgan let him know I wasn't with her. He'd find me, he told me over and over again that I was his and he was mine. Yes, he wouldn't stop until he found me.

Alex

"No, fuck you, Charlie. We aren't playing strip twister just because girls are coming to game night. Bear, I swear we're going to be down a player at our next game if you don't control your guys."

"Charlie, stop chirping your own teammates. Save that for the ice." He hands me a beer. "And Alex, stop acting like a little bitch and take a joke."

Scottie and Knight don't even stop the video game they are playing but join in on the teasing. "Oooooo, Cap called Alex a bitch," Knight laughs.

"I didn't call him a bitch. I told him to stop acting like a bitch," Bear throws back.

Scotties pauses the game when his phone rings. "What's up, Morgan? You ladies on your way? Pizza will be here soon." He stands up and looks around the room. "No, Lily isn't here. I thought she was coming with you." His brow furrows in confusion. "I'm going to call Eddie, and you call Jordan. I'll call you right back."

What about Lily? Standing right next to Scottie, he can see the worry on my face. Pulling out my phone, I pull up the tracking app I had on her phone; it shows her at Navy Pier. The rest of the team has moved in close, needing to know what is going on.

"Scottie?"

"Lily never called Morgan to pick her up from work and bring her over, so Morgan went to her building. They said there was a missing child call at the Navy Pier, but it was found out to be a prank call, so everyone was recalled. Lily never returned. They are trying to find her now. That's all they would tell Morgan because Eddie wasn't there because he was still out looking for her. I'm calling him now."

Scrolling through his contacts, he pulls up Eddie's number. I don't know why he has Lily's boss in his phone, but I'm glad he does. "Hey Eddie, it's Scottie. Morgan said Lily is missing. What's going on?"

Scottie paces as he listens, grunting "uh huh" every once in a while. "Okay, let us know what you find out. I'm heading to her place now, and I'll call Morgan and Jordan."

"Round up," Bear yells, without even having all the information. Whatever it is, he knows the team is here to help. "Tell us, Scottie."

Placing a hand on my shoulder, he squeezes as he calls Morgan, placing her on speaker so everyone could hear.

"Scottie." Her voice squeaks with fear. "I'm at Jordan's, and he hasn't heard from her. I'm scared. Did Eddie say anything?"

"Put me on speaker, Morgan, I wanna talk to Jordan too."

"Okay, you have us both," she says, her voice shaking.

"The teams here too. I called Eddie. He could get in trouble for telling me some of the stuff he did, but he doesn't care. He said they were called to the Navy Pier tonight, about two hours before the end of their shift, for a suspected missing kid. It was later found out to be a prank call. When everyone was recalled, neither Lily nor an Officer Rod Walden checked in. Lily's gear bag was found on the Pier, and her cell phone was found in the parking lot.

"When Eddie looked into Officer Walden a little more, it looked like he was a transfer to CPD four and a half years ago and has had a bunch of behavior issues. No one wants to work with him, and his superiors consider him a recluse and withdrawn. Nothing that is considered a fireable offense, unfortunately.

"At the search, Lily was paired with Officer Walden. But it's suspicious that neither has been seen or heard from since. Officer Walden's vehicle is also missing from the parking lot. Eddie is at the Pier right now with his team and CPD. They are treating this right now as a missing persons case of both of them, but he's worried Walden may be connected to Lily's stalker."

Some of the teammates look confused. As much as Lily has been around lately, not everyone knows anything other than she and I are involved.

"Alex," Morgan's voice comes through the phone, "if it's him, do you think he'll hurt her?"

Darting my eyes to Scottie, I can see the pain in his.

"We'll find her, Morgan. Hey, can I talk to your brother?"

"Why can't you talk to him on speaker, Alex?" she asks accusingly.

"It's called plausible deniability, Morgan. And there are some things I'm not willing to involve you in, even if it involves your best friend."

"Fine. But you bring her home, Alexander Bensen, at any cost. If something happens, I'll call in any favor I have throughout this entire fucking town. You hear me?"

"Loud and clear, Morgan. Loud and clear."

"Alex, I'm here," Jordan states.

"Meet at my place in thirty minutes. I need my computer to access something, and that's how long it will take me to get there with traffic."

"Got it." Jordan hangs up, no other questions asked.

Turning to my teammates, I take a deep breath. "Here's the Cliff Notes version of what's going on to fill in some of the blanks for you guys. You are my brothers, my family. My girl, the love of my life, is missing. She may have been taken by the man that almost killed me and my baby sister four years ago. He's also the kidnapper the CPD has been searching for for over four years, and since Lily is the one that saved me and my sister that night four years ago, she's been his target all this time, and now he might finally have her.

"I've done some not-so-legal things to keep her safe up until now. And I need to get home to get information that will help me find her. I will not allow any of you to be involved from here on out, because I wouldn't be able to live with myself if something happened to any one of you.

"Bear, can you please just call my dad and let him know what's going on? He will know what to do."

My captain shakes his head.

"What do you mean no?"

"You call him on the way to your apartment, but to say we're out of it, you're out of your mind. Like you said, we're family, and family sticks together. I won't speak for anyone else, but I'm in this with you, so let's go."

"Me too," Knight yells. "I've been needing a reason to break some bones since the refs won't let me fight like you guys can."

"Because no one touches our goalie, you Viking twat. And Alex, you know you aren't leaving me out. Lily is like my sister," Scottie says from next to the door.

"Us too, boss." Hawkins and Caddel are making their way to the door.

The entire team wants to go. Bear had to put a stop to it. "Okay, okay. If we could go rolling through Chicago twenty-three deep, we would. How about the rest of you stay here and wait for word? If we need backup, I'll call and you come running."

That satisfies the team. For now.

The six of us pile into my Navigator and head to my apartment.

"So, how illegal are we talking here, boss-man? Like mafia level?" Caddel yells from the back seat.

"Yeah, dude," Knight leans between the front seats, smirking. "How illegal are we talking? For research purposes only."

"If you've hurt her..." Scottie starts before catching Bear's glare from the passenger seat.

"Shut the fuck up, Scottie. We all know you'll cut off his balls if he hurts her. You tell him enough," Knight snorts.

"All of you shut up so I can think. You'll find out when we get to my house anyway. But judge me all you want, because I'll be able to do what the police can't; I'll be able to find her."

Bear slowly turns to face me, trying not to laugh since he is the only one that already knows the answer. "And how will you be able to do that, Mr. Bensen?"

"Uh, hell." All eyes are on me. "You fuckers. Fine. I put a tracker under her hairline when she slept. It is in the same vicinity of where she was injured after that psycho attacked her outside her apartment, so she wasn't able to tell there was another tiny incision. Are you happy?"

Seconds pass before the SUV erupts in laughter. "Damn, man, you're fucked up." Knight laughs as he slaps my shoulder. "I love it."

"Where the hell would you even get something like that?" Scottie asks.

"His dad's company," Bear says. "You may as well tell them how fucked up you really are."

"Yeah, my parent's company makes more than just computer parts, they just don't announce it," I say, having the weight off my chest now that my closest friends know and aren't judging me. They are actually supporting me.

As we pull up to my apartment, I park in front of the building. "Hey, Roger, sorry about the car. It's an emergency. We'll be right back down, promise."

Being the amazing doorman that he is, he doesn't miss a beat. "No problem, Mr. Bensen. I will keep an eye on it until you return."

Waiting for the elevator is torture. Seconds seem like minutes, and in this case, every second counts. I need to get to my computer like I need air to breathe. I need to see the red dot on my screen and see where Lily is.

Six large ass hockey players in a tiny elevator would've been amusing if this were any other time. I'm surprised we don't exceed the weight limit, but finally we arrive at my penthouse.

My laptop is still on the kitchen island where I left it that morning. Pulling up the tracking app, it is pinging East Grand. They are right next to Navy Pier.

Scottie is over my shoulder and relaying the information to Eddie. Eddie's on the phone with the CPD; they are sending patrols to their location, but we are closer, and I'm not waiting. As he hangs up with Eddie, he calls Jordan, who got stuck in traffic and isn't here yet.

"I'm not waiting for the CPD boys, you can wait here, or you can come with me. But make the decision now." I grab my laptop; using my phone's hotspot, I will be able to keep an eye on Lily's tracker. As I walk out the door, I know every single one of my brothers is right behind me.

Chapter Forty-Three
Lily

The door to the closet I'm in is thrown open, and my eyes can't adjust to the bright light.

"Well, looks like it's time to go. Somehow they are onto where we are, so we are moving now. I wanted to wait until dark, but plans have a way of changing."

Putting the gun to my temple and wrapping his hands around my hair, he guides me back through the house and out to the garage. "Back into the trunk, bitch. And before you think about trying to escape, I removed the trunk latch and reinforced the taillights so you can't kick them out. So don't even try."

I wish I was able to get a sense of if we are still in Chicago or not. Either way, I am outgunned—literally. At least if I play along with his delusion, he'll hopefully keep his promise and stay away from my people. If I play along, hopefully I'll get my chance to escape or strike against him. Even if it takes me weeks or months of playing along with his delusional game.

My brain isn't foggy anymore, and now all my training is kicking it. As part of search and rescue, we have to know the ins and outs of all different places we could possibly, though unlikely, get trapped.

At the time, I thought Eddie just wanted to torture me, but he and one of the other guys grabbed me up and tossed me into a trunk and told me to get out. I thought, easy, all trunks have the glow-in-the-dark latch. Wrong. They don't. But what some, not all, of them have is a latch to be able to get from the trunk to the back seat. This is an older model vehicle, so hopefully this one has it, if he didn't remove that also. Feeling around, I find the latch towards the front of the trunk; tears spring to my eyes. How did he miss these?

As my fingers coil around it, the car takes a hard left. I lose my grip and slam against the other side. That won't deter me; I'll keep trying. I have everything to lose.

Alex

"Where the hell is he going?" Bear questions from the passenger seat. "They're on Park Drive heading towards the Pier. Do you think he has a boat docked?"

My heart plummets. "If he does and they reach it, we'll never catch him. Scottie, call Eddie back and tell him. He's the only one with a boat that could get to her in time."

Lily

We are slowing down, I have one shot at this. If I can surprise him at all, I'll have the advantage. If he gets me out of the truck, with him having the gun, he could do anything with me, and I'd either need to give up or give in. Neither is an option I want to consider.

My hands are still tied in the rope, and no matter how hard I try to tear at them with my teeth, they aren't budging, so I'd have to work around them. At least he didn't tie my feet.

"You got this. You got this. Think of Alex. Think of Morgan, Jordan, Scottie, and Eddie. You are doing this to protect them." After a few deep breaths, I am ready to go. I'd need to move quickly once I pulled the lever. I had the plan in my head; now to time it. The car slows more, then takes a hard right. It doesn't quickly accelerate, so maybe we are coming up on traffic or our destination. So I need to move.

Pulling the latch, the seat in front of me clicks but doesn't move. I'll need to move it myself, thankfully. Pushing the left seat down as quietly as possible, I try not to attract his attention. Glancing out the window, I see the cranes. Are we down by the water?

Wiggling out of the trunk, I crouch behind the driver's side, watching as Officer Walden searches intently for something out the front window. That's when I hear the sirens, and so does he. The sirens cause him to look in the rearview mirror, and we lock eyes. Whipping his head around, he starts to shout but is cut off when I jump up and throw my arms up over the headrest and pull the red rope tight against his throat.

Putting my feet flat against the driver's seat, I pull back with all my strength. He lets go of the steering wheel but doesn't take his foot off the gas pedal, all while trying to get his hand between the rope and his throat. His car is old enough that his seats are manually adjusted, so even as he tries to push back against me, I am in the position of power and keep my feet planted. I'm running out of strength and need his air to run out. Now.

My luck wouldn't extend that far, and because he still has his foot on the gas, and apparently we are on the dock, we go right over into the water. This is where my training would be on my side. He only has seconds left of air, and I can hold my breath for minutes. One of us isn't leaving this car, and I have the better chance.

As the car hits the water, the more he flails. "If you would've just left Chicago, you wouldn't be in this situation. But no, you couldn't leave me the hell alone. You have no one to blame but yourself, you bastard. You will burn in hell." With one more attempt to claw my hands away, his body finally goes limp. Relief surges through me at the idea of being able to save the people I love. Holding tight for a few more seconds, just to make sure, I let go when the water hits the bottom of my chin.

I've already been in the water too long. Today before our call, the lake was reading thirty-six degrees. I'm already losing hand and finger coordination, so I need to move fast. Soon, I have the possibility of losing consciousness, and if I do that while still in this car, this bastard wins, and that I won't allow.

The vehicle is sinking faster than I hoped, and I need to get out of here before I am sitting at the bottom of the river. Looking around me for something to break the glass, I can't find anything. "Shit." I could wait until the car is submerged, then roll down the manual windows, but that will expend a lot of energy. If it's my only option, I'll do it. Now if only my damn hands weren't tied.

Looking at the ropes closely again, I notice he never removed my bracelet. "Fucking idiot." This is my way out. Once I hit the window, the water will rush in, but I'd make it to the surface, this is my job.

Pulling back the band on my bracelet, I'm not able to get as much of an angle as I could if my hands weren't tied, but I'll make due. I release. It doesn't break the first time, but it cracks. "Damn it. Again." Pulling it back again... success.

Water floods the vehicle, and I'm plunged into darkness and more freezing water. My lungs are seizing, and I know my normal three minute breath hold is drastically reduced. Taking one second to orient myself and climb out the window, my time is running out. Dusk is upon us, so the surface light is barely visible. I have one shot to determine up from down, and if I choose wrong, I am dead. Making a break for it, I kick as hard as I can. As my vision blurs, I know my air will run out before I make it to the surface, and I hope that my momentum will propel me to the surface for a chance at someone spotting me.

I love you, Alex. I love you, Alex. That's what I repeat over and over to myself as I kick with everything I have until I have nothing left.

Alex

"What the fuck?" I scream, slamming my hands on the steering wheel. "It says she's right here."

"Put that computer away," Knight yells from behind us. "Cops."

"I've got Eddie on the phone, he's with them. He says to tell them you followed the car but lost sight," Scottie says as he is getting out of the SUV.

Four cop cars slide into the lot next to us. The next few seconds are chaos. Guns drawn and screaming, until Eddie runs up with another office. "Put them away you fools," Eddie chastises, arms in the air.

"Don't you recognize them? They are the starting line for the Chicago Yetis, and that one there," he practically yells, pointing to me, "is Liliana's boyfriend. So put your weapons away."

Walking up to Scottie, he grabs his shoulder. "Sorry about that, boys, Lily's like their sister. Now, where is she? Scottie said you were following her. Which we will talk about later." He looks pointedly at me, and I just shrug.

Bear walks over. "We followed her here, sir. She should be right here."

"Fuck, no," Eddie moans, looking over at the water. "Get my gear!" he screams, and officers go scrambling as Eddie runs to the edge.

That's when we see what he saw. Bubbles. She is here, and we fucking missed it.

Someone is running up to us with some kind of suit and a tank when I see a flash of red. Lily? It is her, but she isn't moving. She is floating below the water, and her hair is billowing with the waves.

Rage tears through me, and before anyone can stop me—and I did feel Bear grasping for my arms, but he was too late—I run the few steps to the edge of the pier and dive over the edge. The second my body hits the water, it is like being stabbed by a million tiny knives. I'll never complain about being on the ice ever again.

Eddie is cursing me out from the dock but also giving me directions. Fighting against the waves, I'm not in the best position to see where Lily is. The officers line the dock holding spotlights, guiding me to Lily's location. It feels like I am fighting against the water forever before I feel her in my arms.

Her skin feels like ice, and when I turn her over, her lips are blue and she isn't breathing. "Swim, Alex!" Eddie yells. He's at my side before I even realize he's jumped over the edge to help me. "Let's get our girl out of here so we can help her, yeah?"

Hands are all around us as we pull her lifeless body to the edge of the dock. A backboard is lowered into the water, and even though I don't remember hearing any of his words, I see my hands doing what Eddie needs them to do.

Once Lily is secured, she is pulled up onto land, and we need to swim a little further down to climb a ladder. The second she's out of my sight, it feels like a piece of me is ripped away. I need to see them working on her—I need to see them breathe life back into her. If she doesn't survive this, I won't survive this.

Bear and Knight are at the ladder waiting for me with blankets that I push out of their hands. Hawkins and Caddel are trying to hold Scottie back from getting in the way of the paramedics working on Lily.

I don't realize Bear and Knight are holding my body up until one of the paramedics yells out, "We got a rhythm." At those four words, my legs no longer want to hold my massive body weight. Watching the paramedics shock her heart took years off my life.

"Alex, you need to get out of those wet clothes. Here." Eddie hands me a Chicago Search and Rescue sweat suit. "They are taking her to Chicago General, meet us there."

"I'm going with you," I argue.

"No, Alex. Change in your SUV and meet us there. They are still working on her, and you will get in the way. I'll go with her. I promise we will do everything we can for her. She's strong."

He doesn't give me time to argue before he is running after the paramedic, jumping into the back of the ambulance, and it's taking off down the road.

Why am I still standing here? "Let's go, dude. I'll drive." Knight pulls my arm towards my car. They already have blankets and towels piled in the passenger seat for me to dry off with as I change. Thank goodness for tinted windows, because I am about to get naked going down the highway and don't care who sees me.

Pulling up outside the ER doors, Knight drops me, Bear, and Scottie off, and the rest of them go to park and update the rest of the team. Scottie said Morgan and Jordan are on their way.

"I'm sorry, Mr. Bensen, only family is allowed back at this time. I can't give you any information," the nurse at the intake desk says through the glass.

My roar can be heard through the halls, and apparently I seem scary enough that security comes running. "If you don't let me see my girlfriend right now, I will break down that door and find her myself."

Bear, normally the voice of reason, chuckles behind me. "You might want to listen to him, ma'am, between the three of us, your doors don't stand a chance."

"I'm calling the police. You need to leave this instant. Ruffians," she screeches.

"Fucking hell. I can't leave you alone at all, can I?" Eddie calls from behind us.

"Oh, Captain Carlson, thank goodness you're here. I need your help," the nurse yells.

"No, dear, you need to let them through, all of them. Please and thank you," Eddie says calmly.

The nurse looks like she wants to argue until the two uniformed officers behind him nod their agreement.

Lily

It is so hard to keep my eyes open. Mild hypothermia will do that to you, plus, I guess I technically died for a bit. So the doctor said I'm allowed to be tired. I'll be able to go home tomorrow. The only reason they want to keep me tonight is because they are pumping me full of antibiotics since the water I inhaled isn't the cleanest, and since my heart stopped, they are just being cautious.

It will be a miracle if Eddie lets me near the water in the next few months. Two hospital stays in only a few short weeks—yeah, he is going to be insufferable.

My eyes fight to stay open. I was hoping to see Alex before allowing my body to give in to the exhaustion, but it looks like my body is going to win. Unable to fight it any longer, I allow my eyes to close, bringing on the darkness.

The sound of a chainsaw pulls me from my sleep. Taking a moment to orient myself to my surroundings, I quickly realize it isn't a chainsaw but one of Alex's teammates; I'm just not sure which one. From what I can tell, my hospital room holds at least half the Chicago Yetis hockey team, and they are scattered in what looks to be folding camping chairs like you see at cookouts and tailgates. What the hell?

"Ouch," I mumble as I try to sit up, but my chest is weighed down.

"Baby?" Alex whispers, shuffling next to me, removing his arm from my chest and moving his hand to my cheek. My eyes lock on his and fill with tears. With the little strength I have, I reach up to his head and pull him down to my chest.

"I thought I was going to lose you," he whispers.

"Me too," I admit, inhaling the scent of his clean shirt. Citrus and mint. Me, I probably smell like hell.

Leaning up on his elbows, he brushes the stray hair off my forehead and looks into my eyes. "You are so beautiful, spitfire."

"I look like hell, Alex."

His lips pull up in the corners. "True, but the second I get you home, I'll feed you, put you in the tub, clean every inch of your body, then fuck you until you're all dirty again, and you just fall asleep in my arms. How does that sound?"

"It sounds like you two need a private room, fuckers," Jordan groans from the chair on the other side of the bed where he's been stationed.

"Whoops, sorry, dude. I forgot you were sitting there." Which, of course, from his smirk, is a lie.

"Obviously." He stands, leans down, and gives me a kiss on my forehead. "You gave us a scare, brat. How are you feeling? Should I go get the doctor?"

"It looks like sometime while I was sleeping they took my IV out, so my antibiotics are done. So yeah, if you could get the doctor, maybe he'll let me go home. I don't want to be here a second longer than necessary."

Nodding, Jordan moves for the door and accidentally kicks the leg of his chair. This startles Bear, who jumps to his feet, starting a chain reaction of jumping hockey players. If I wasn't still exhausted, I would've been jumping for my phone to record them.

"Hey, trouble," Knight greets me from the foot of the bed. "Do you need us to get you anything? Maybe another Rogue to snuggle?"

"Oh, Gunnar," I laugh. "I'm good, Alex is still jealous of the other one. A getaway vehicle would be great. I hate hospitals."

"I think I can do that. I still have old-boys car keys, and between Hawkins and Caddel, they can cause a diversion, Bear can carry you on his back, and I'll pull the car around. Yeah, we got this, you just give me the signal and we'll make it happen."

I can't help but laugh; these men that I've come to know, that are Alex's family, have become special to me too.

"Oh, hey, Alex. Before I forget to ask, I know I was out of it, but I heard Eddie tell one of the officers that it was you guys that found me. How did you know where I was?"

Chapter Forty-Four
Alex

I'm not about to tell her about the tracker I inserted into her hairline without her permission, so I"ll have to lie. "Just luck, I guess, love."

Her eyes narrow on mine. Does she know I'm lying? Bear bites the back of his hand to keep from laughing.

I am saved from having to answer any more questions when the door opens and the doctor steps inside. "I heard we have a patient eager to go home?"

My teammates almost have to keep their promise to break Lily out. The doctor wanted to keep her another night, but she threatened to sign an Against Medical Advice form.

Morgan saves the day when she tells the doctor that she won't be leaving Lily's side for the next twenty-four hours and will drag her back by her hair if needed. The doctor wanted to argue until Lily said it was either Morgan or the AMA form, so that's how Morgan ended up in our guest room for the night. Not like I would've told her no anyway. I was Team Doctor and wanted Lily to stay another night after what happened. But my girl is stubborn, and I love that about her.

The elevator ride to our apartment seemed to take forever. I never left her side while she was in the hospital, so I trusted my friends to set up a surprise for me.

With the threat no longer hanging over our heads, I want Lily to feel safe, loved, and most importantly, that she's mine. I thought I lost her... again, and I'm not about to let her out of my sight.

Morgan told me that Lily would love my surprise, and I hope that she's right. If she doesn't, I may need to pull out the handcuffs that found a home in my bedside table.

With a long, settling sigh, I stop us in front of the door.

"Is everything okay, Alex?" A deep crease forms between her brow as her eyes search my face.

"Everything is perfect, spitfire. Welcome home." Scooping her up in my arms, I hold her tight as I open the door.

It takes her several moments of confusion as she looks around just the entryway before letting out a gasp.

"Alex, why is the stuff from my apartment here?"

Setting her on her feet, I guide her through the kitchen and into the living room. Her eyes never stop searching, finding more and more of her stuff.

Sitting on the couch, I pull her onto my lap so she's facing me.

"Lily Sterling, while you were in the hospital, I made an executive decision to keep you. With Morgan's complete approval, of course, because she's the one that rallied the guys and helped me with this surprise. I don't ever want to sleep without you again, or when I need to because I'm on the road, I want to think of you here in our home. And yes, I had your name added to the deed. Morgan moved about three-quarters of your belongings here while you were in the hospital, and hopefully you will allow us to collect everything else. Lily, will you live with me?"

Tears glisten in her eyes. "Yes, Alex. I want to live with you. I want to make this our home. I want to be here for you every night, especially when you have a rough game. I'll be here with you."

"Together," I whisper against the side of her neck.

"Together," she whispers back.

"I'm glad you agreed, love, because I wasn't going to let you go."

"What would you have done if I said no, Alex?" she challenges.

"Oh, you know. I had the handcuffs at the ready." Bringing both hands up, I cup her cheeks before placing a chaste kiss to her lips.

"Handcuffs, you say?" She has a twinkle in her eye.

"Handcuffs, Lily."

Rubbing herself against my lap, she can feel how turned on I am.

"I think I need to see these handcuffs again." Biting her lower lip, I growl.

"Hmmm, what am I going to do with you?" I lean forward and nip her ear.

"Handcuffs. Definitely, handcuffs."

Epilogue
Alex

April - Last game of regular season

"Sid, I swear, don't fuck this up or I'll tie your ass to the damn Zamboni."

"Naked," Caddel yells from behind me.

"Then why should I help you if all you're going to do is threaten me?" Holding the damn Yeti head in his hands, he glares at us.

"Because for some reason—which I don't know why—the woman I love has an obsession with you that I can't get her to give up."

"Oh, yeah." Sidney smirks. "If I knew that, I would've upped my game every time you sent me after her."

"Oh, shit," Hawkins murmurs. "Coach Huxley, you might want to get in here if you want to keep your son alive."

"For fuck's sake, men. We have a game about to start. What the hell is going on?" Coach Reyes bellows as he marches into the locker room, followed by coaches Jameson and Huxley.

"Bensen's trying to tie Lily to him and recruiting Sidney's help. But Lily is obsessed with Rogue, and now Sidney's sassing Bensen, and Bensen's threatening to end Sidney," Scottie explains as he stands on the bench next to us, pretending to eat popcorn as his eyes dart between me and Rogue.

"Fuck all of you. I'm calling this off. It was stupid." Taking my helmet, I whip it into my locker.

"Like hell you are, Bensen. You are going to man up and make this a night Lily will never forget. She deserves this," scolds Bear, standing behind me, arms crossed and leaning against the lockers.

"Sidney will behave himself and play his part. Right, Sid?" Coach Huxley warns.

"Do I have to? Winding up Bensen is so much fun."

"Sidney, do you remember the time you threw a snowball at Scottie's woman, Morgan?" I ask.

"Not my woman," Scottie says under his breath. Hawkins looks like he wants to retort but bites his lower lip to keep quiet.

"Yeah, that was a fun night. I didn't expect her to hit me back," he chuckles.

"Well, if you do anything that will make this night not absolutely perfect, I'll tell Morgan it was your fault her best friend of almost twenty years didn't have the perfect proposal. Is that what you want?" I threaten, and Knight, in full goalie gear, stands next to him, glaring.

I want the man to play his part, not piss his pants.

"Yeah, yeah. I got it, dude. I will keep to the script." Pointing over his shoulder, "I... ah, need to get out there and hype up the crowd."

As he runs out the door, everyone bursts out laughing. Tonight is going to be perfect.

Lily

Tonight is fucking horrible. We are in club seats, so tell me why the frat boys are back.

"I don't think they remember what happened last time, or they're too drunk to care," Morgan leans against me and whispers into my ear.

"I'm not going to sit here all night and be catcalled by a bunch of drunk assholes." I grit my teeth and look around for anyone else I recognize.

"I don't think that will be a problem." Grabbing my head and turning it a few rows away where Jordan and Eddie sit, the guys have their eyes locked on the boys behind us. Jordan is on the phone talking rapidly. When he is done, he notices we are watching him; he gives us a smirk and turns back towards the ice.

"Ladies, ladies, ladies. It's a pleasure." Archie, standing only a few steps behind us with security, looks at us shaking his head before turning to the frat boys.

"Gentlemen, the Yetis would like to extend the invitation to you to enjoy the game from one of our comfortable suites. Food and drinks included, of course."

Whoots and fist bumps happen all around us. "Hell yeah, let's go, boss man," the one that, the last time, told me to smack Morgan's ass shouts. Filing quickly out of their row, Archie gives a little bow. "Enjoy the game, ladies," he smirks.

"Which one do you think did it? Alex or Scottie?" laughs Morgan.

"Protective alpha-holes," I murmur.

"But we love it, we can't deny it," Morgan says as she bounces around.

Looking at her watch, she asks if I want a refill before warm-ups start. "Yeah, that sounds great."

The music changes to the Yetis warm-up song. Standing and cheering, I search the ice for Alex. Where is he? There are a few guys missing from the ice: Alex, Scottie, Bear… my heart is racing with the idea of something being wrong. Looking around for Morgan, she is nowhere in sight. Looking at Jordan in his season seats, his gaze is on the ice.

> **Me:** Is everything okay?

It's not like I expect him to answer. I mean, he should be on the ice. But if something happened, maybe he'll have his phone with him.

I see Archie near the players' bench. Waving my arms, I finally grab his attention. Lifting my arms and shoulders, he can tell I'm questioning him about something.

Did he just smile at me? Yes, Archie has a big smile on. Can't he see I'm freaking out about something?

"This isn't their normal warm-up song," the man sitting behind me comments.

I wasn't paying attention to the music, I just need to lay eyes on Alex. But now that he mentioned it, this is a very odd song for them to warm up to.

You Are the reason, by Calum Scott, is playing through the system.

Wack.

What the hell? Whipping around, Rogue is three aisles up, but instead of a snowball in hand, he has a bouquet of tulips. I grow more confused as he makes his way down to me and holds out a hand.

"Rogue, what's going on?" Confused, I reach my hand out to his waiting one.

Tugging on me, I look around as I follow him to the side door that will lead us behind the stands.

Through the doors, there is Morgan, tears in her eyes. Turning to look at Rogue, I see Jordan and Eddie are right behind us.

"Morgan?"

"Just go with it, babe."

Rogue, still having hold of my hand, leads me through a door that leads to the players' tunnel.

"I really don't think I should be here." Turning to leave, Rogue hands the flowers to Morgan and he picks me up. Dreams do come true, I just won't tell Alex.

Seconds later, we are at the door to the ice, skating has stopped, and all eyes are focused on the group of players in the middle of the ice.

Bear, Knight, Scottie, Hawkins, and Caddel are standing to the side, holding signs that we can't see the words to. Alex is standing in front of them.

No, no, no. My brain knows what is about to happen, but my heart is telling me there is no way.

Alex skates up to the door, and Archie hands him a microphone.

"Hey, spitfire," he grins.

"Alex. What's going on?"

Lifting the mic to his mouth, "Liliana Sterling, from the moment you saved my life four years ago, my life has never been the same. My soul knew it had found its other half. For reasons neither of us could control, we had to spend years apart before fate stepped in and brought us back together. But I never gave up hope. Now that I've found you, I'm never letting you go. I will hold on to you as we walk through this crazy life together. I may not be your first love, but it would be an honor to be your last. So I have a question to ask, with the help of my brothers."

The guys hold up their signs, and Morgan stands behind me squealing.

"I wish more than anything that your parents could be here, but know, I asked Eddie for permission before I did this. So what do you say, Lily, my spitfire? Will you marry me and make my soul complete?"

My heart is going to explode. Literal fireworks are going off in my chest. "Yes, yes, all the yeses."

Still nodding my head, Alex steps off the ice and lifts me into his arms. "I love you, spitfire. Forever and a day."

"I love you too, Alex."

Friends and family surround us, and the crowd is on their feet cheering.

"Now you better go win for me, Mr. Hockey Man."

"There was never a doubt, soon-to-be Mrs. Bensen." He leans in and kisses me hard.

Someone clears their throat next to us, and reluctantly we pull apart.

"I'm so happy for you two, but I need my star defenseman to get his ass back on the ice and warm up. Is that possible, Bensen? Can you disengage yourself for a few hours and play some hockey?"

"Yes, Coach. Sorry, Coach." He smirks and steps backwards onto the ice as the coach slams the door shut.

"Girl, let's go get drunk and watch hot, sweaty men play hockey." Morgan throws her arm around me, and we walk back toward Archie, who leads us back to our seats.

Since there is an empty row behind us, Jordan, Eddie, and Alex's parents and sister join us. The Yetis win 4-1. The perfect start to the rest of our life.

"Now when you get home, you can have hot sex with your fiancé, not just your boyfriend," Morgan giggles, jumping up and down, clapping her hands.

"For fuck's sake, Morgan." Slapping a hand to my face, I don't drop my smile.

My fiancé—yeah, I like the sound of that.

Gunnar

I love watching my friends get their happy ending. I try to tamp down the extreme jealousy that's eating away at my thoughts. Alex and Lily deserve all the happiness in the world. I just can't help thinking about the girl that was taken from me eighteen years ago. The girl that I've hired numerous private detectives to find, but still nothing.

Kinsley. The girl I met on the first day of kindergarten, is my happy ending. I've never loved another woman, and I never will. It's her or nothing for me.

I won't give up looking, ever. I'll find her one day, and when that day comes, I'm never letting her go.

ABOUT NICOLE RAE / NICOLE KEEFER

Nicole is a crime fiction and romantic suspense author who loves to read and write about bad-ass females and over protective alpha males.

She uses her personal military experiences and educational background in Forensic Psychology to bring life to her stories.

When not reading, writing, or watching the Washington Capitals kill it on the ice, she likes to enjoy a quiet life with her family in the mitten state.

You can subscribe to her newsletter at www.nicolekeefer.com

www.ingramcontent.com/pod-product-compliance
Lightning Source LLC
LaVergne TN
LVHW040038080526
838202LV00045B/3390